The Temptation Of Grace

KRISTIN VAYDEN

LYRICAL PRESS
Kensington Publishing Corp.
www.kensingtonbooks.com

LYRICAL BOOKS are published by

Kensington Publishing Corp.
119 West 40th Street
New York, NY 10018

All Kensington titles, imprints, and distributed lines are available at special quantity discounts for bulk purchases for sales promotion, premiums, fund-raising, educational, or institutional use.

Special book excerpts or customized printings can also be created to fit specific needs. For details, write or phone the office of the Kensington Sales Manager: Attn.: Sales Department. Kensington Publishing Corp., 119 West 40th Street, New York, NY 10018. Phone: 1-800-221-2647.

Lyrical and the Lyrical logo Reg. U.S. Pat. & TM Off.

First Printing: May 2019
ISBN-13: 978-1-5161-0572-4
ISBN-10: 1-5161-0572-9

ISBN-13: 978-1-5161-0573-1 (ebook)
ISBN-10: 1-5161-0573-7 (ebook)

10 9 8 7 6 5 4 3 2 1

Printed in the United States of America

Books by Kristin Vayden

From Lyrical Press

The Gentlemen of Temptation series:

FALLING FROM HIS GRACE
ESCAPING HIS GRACE
THE TEMPTATION OF GRACE

From Lyrical Press e-books

Elk Heights Ranch series:

HEART OF A COWBOY
THE COURAGE OF A COWBOY
THE COWGIRL MEETS HER MATCH

For everyone who knows what it's like to experience failure, brokenness, and hopelessness and shame. May you find the truth that Ramsey discovered: You are enough. You always were.

May you rise another day, and like an eagle soar. Because who you were doesn't have to define who you are today.

Prologue

To say that Ramsey Scott never had a childhood would be an understatement. His mother, God rest her soul, passed away shortly after delivering him into the world—a world that gained a sudden chill at the departure of her sweet soul. His ever-scowling father, the Marquess of Sterling, took the small swaddled babe from the midwife and strode into the hall from the birthing room, without a backward glance. There had been little affection between the two parents, and as such, Ramsey's mother had been a means to an end . . . the end being an heir.

His father, now assured that his line would continue, had a single purpose in mind.

Honor.

But not in the way the virtue deserved attention. No, honor in its most depraved form, honor that came from perfection, from abstaining from scandal, honor that came at a dear price.

Because the only other option if not honor, was

shame. And it was indeed something with which the marquess was quite familiar. Shame had followed him his whole life, at the hands of his own father . . . and as stories go, as history goes, it was bound to find repetition within the sterile halls of Glenwood Manor. So, even before Ramsey Scott was an hour old, so started the path of his life.

A path that had but one end.

Ruin.

Because who can achieve perfection?

None.

Yet who can attain shame?

All.

Every last one of us.

Chapter One

Edinburgh, Scotland—for now

Miss Iris Grace Morgan had always hated her name, and with the current schedule of arriving in London in a mere week, she made a decision.

She would come to London not as Iris, the woman who couldn't waltz to save her soul, nor as the lady who was utterly a failure at all things ladylike. No, she would arrive as *Grace*: the woman who personified all things that, well, she was not. It *couldn't* hurt her to have a name that implied what she was not, but she certainly hoped it would indeed *help*. After all, her governess, now her guardian's wife, had taken great pains to pull the lady from within her charge and give her some much needed polish, along with a much-needed friendship.

But as much as she had tried, Iris—Grace, that is—wasn't entirely sure that she had taken on said polish.

Lord Kilpatrick had assured her that she would make a splash, which was very kind of her guardian. But she wasn't concerned about making a splash. She was certain she would.

She just wasn't sure it would be a good splash. It would probably be of the clumsy variety where she'd trip on her own two feet, smash into some cranky dowager, and spray lemonade across the ballroom. It could certainly happen.

It had almost happened last night after dinner, only it wasn't lemonade, it was white wine, and it wasn't her own two feet she'd tripped over. It had been the bloody chair.

Samantha, her guardian's wife and her once governess, had given her a kind smile, and helped her clean the mess before Mrs. Keyes, the housekeeper, clucked over them and shooed them away from it all.

Grace smiled at the memory. She loved it at Kilmarin. All the servants were kind, and they didn't expect her to be anything that she was not. Sothers, the butler, was ever so patient with her, and opened the door extra wide, just in case she misjudged the step, and Mrs. Keyes never complained once when she'd accidentally spill or trip over something or another.

Even Samantha. Grace frowned over how many times she had stepped on her toes when trying to learn how to waltz. It was her utter Achilles heel, that dance. She hoped fervently that she would simply just melt into the woodwork of the London ballroom whenever the first strains of a waltz began.

Because while many young ladies wanted to be in the limelight, and find a suitable match, Grace was utterly content simply *not* to make a scene. But have a season she would, and it wouldn't be long in coming. No. They were planning on leaving Kilmarin in just a few days' time to travel to the viscount's London home, where she could ease herself into society

Dear Lord, this was going to be a disaster.

If they could only just talk to potential suitors, not dance. She could do verbal arabesques with her words! She could speak intelligently on almost any subject, and her parents, God rest their souls, had given her an education that Eton couldn't claim, but they had neglected to teach her the one thing she needed most at the moment.

How to be a lady.

So it was with utter trepidation, more than a few prayers, and several late-night dancing sessions that she allowed Maye to pack her belongings for the trip to London.

It couldn't be that bad . . . could it?

She knew the answer to her own question.

Yes. Yes it could.

First off, London was not as she expected. Having traveled much of the known world with her parents, she could boast about seeing the Sphinx in Egypt, or the marketplaces of India, but London—that was one place she had never had the opportunity to visit. Her father had always called it "dreary ol' London" and her mother hadn't ever corrected him.

To say that Grace's expectations were low would be an accurate statement, but she did anticipate some sort of wonderment surrounding the hub of their beloved England. All throughout the carriage ride to their destination, she had found beauty in various natural aspects of the woods, moors, and a river or two. But as they closed the distance to Town, where all her successes or failures hinged, her chest seized up, much like the thick air perfumed with humanity and smoke. A dreary drizzle smeared the carriage windows, hindering her view as they entered the cobbled streets of London. The air seemed thicker, and she glanced over to Samantha, scrunching up her nose.

"You'll grow accustomed to it." Samantha smiled kindly, if not a little amused.

The viscount glanced to his wife and squeezed her hand. "It's much worse if you go further into Town. 'Tis a pity." He opened his mouth to say something else, then shook his head and glanced to the window.

Grace tipped her chin, curious as to what he was about to say. "Was there something else?" she asked.

He turned to her, his expression conflicted. "You've probably seen something like the slums when you traveled in India. It's a problem here, and the sanitation is horrid, if even existent. It's another reason I prefer the Scottish countryside." He shook his head. "It's a legislative problem that parliament has done little to remedy, and a bit of sore subject with me."

"I see." Grace nodded.

Samantha tipped her head to gaze at her husband, but she did not offer any comment on the subject.

Grace turned back to the window. "Where is your home?"

"Mayfair, of course. It's quite close to Hyde Park, which I have no doubt you'll retreat to often."

"Lovely," Grace breathed, thankful for some aspect of London to find appealing.

"But you'll have to remember to take care. You're

in London now and all proprieties must be observed," Samantha added, arching a brow.

Grace suppressed a groan. "Understood."

"*Understood* doesn't mean you have plans to follow those proprieties," Samantha replied knowingly. Her hazel eyes were wide and observant; her expression also implied that she was awaiting a verbal promise that Grace would abide by the social parameters.

Grace let out a long sigh. As soon as she released the breath, she held up a hand. "I know, no sighing. Drat, this is going to be a disaster. I even breathe wrong."

Samantha reached across the carriage and patted her hand. "You do far more things right than you do wrong. Focus on the ways you succeed, not your failures. We all fall short in one area or another, but when those areas become our focus, we lose ourselves." She spoke with the sage wisdom of someone twice her age as she gently retracted her hand.

Grace twisted her lips. "Must you always be right?"

The viscount chuckled.

Samantha cast him an amused gaze. "I'm not always right. He can most certainly attest to that!"

To his credit, the viscount didn't reply or offer any proof of her statement, and again Grace found herself the focus of the conversation. "I'm still awaiting your promise," Samantha encouraged.

And that was the truth of it. Samantha had the patience of Job and the appearance of an angel. She always encouraged, rather than discouraged. It was impossible to be cross with her, or to be offended by her insistence that Grace abide by any of the rules they had set about. It was irritating at times, and at others as comforting as hot tea on a chilly day.

Today it was of the irritating variety, but that spoke more of Grace's disposition than Samantha's. Regardless, Grace nodded. "I promise. I'll do my best to observe all the proprieties required of a lady of quality."

"Thank you. And I will always be in the wings coaching you through it all; you are not alone." Samantha nodded.

The carriage jostled them a bit as it hit a rut in the road, then turned left down a different street. Grace glanced back out the window, the condensation dripping down and making small rivulets in the glass, distorting the view further. She longed to wipe the moisture away with her glove, but she was afraid to get her gloves dirty—just another confinement of society.

India and Egypt were looking more and more welcoming, even with their suffocating heat. At least there she didn't have to wear gloves.

"We'll arrive shortly," the viscount announced, glancing to the window and dismissing the view as overly familiar.

Sure enough, within a few minutes the carriage paused, rolled forward a few more feet, then came to a stop. The carriage wobbled slightly as the coachman stepped from his perch. A footman opened the carriage door, causing light, mist, and the scent of smoke to swirl into the cab. Grace's eyes strained to absorb all the details of the view. She waited impatiently as Samantha alighted from the carriage, and then eagerly offered her hand to the footman so that she might disembark as well.

The first thing she noticed was the trees. They towered over the walkway, creating a canopy over the houses that lined the street. As her gaze lingered down the road, she noted the boxwoods that lined the front of each residence. It was orderly, it was manicured.

It wasn't natural.

But then again, what had she been expecting? This was a cultured city, and she could take a lesson from the perfectly curated vegetation. She was a wild rose, but she was being planted in London and as such, needed to adapt to her environment. She could do it; she would do it. There wasn't any challenge she had backed down from, and she certainly wasn't about to start now.

"Come." The viscount gestured to the front entrance of his London home, and as they approached the door swung open, revealing a butler younger than any butler she had ever before seen.

He stood stiffly straight, his eyes forward as if soldiering the front door and preparing to meet his commanding officer. Grace studied him. He couldn't be much older than she, but much taller. His shoulders appeared too wide for his lean frame, and she averted her eyes as they approached the door.

"Thank you, John." The viscount nodded, earning a bow that was snapped in place like a salute. "Allow me to introduce my wife and ward." The viscount gestured to Samantha and Grace.

Grace kept her eyes from going wide. Even she knew that it wasn't common to make introductions to the help.

John—she'd never heard a butler with such a normal name—turned his gaze first to Samantha and gave a sharp bow, then turned to Grace, executing the same greeting without a word. His eyes were the color of rich earth, and utterly unreadable.

Grace nodded in greeting, and then followed her guardians into the well-appointed house. The three steps to the door led into a glistening marble foyer. The tall ceilings gave an open feeling that was oddly in contrast to the misty and gloomy outdoors. A person started toward them from the long hallway, and as she grew closer Grace noted the beauty of the woman in housekeeper's clothing. She couldn't have been more than forty and five, but she carried herself with a dignity that was more quality than help. Grace noticed her warm smile, and felt a shiver of curiosity. Never before had she seen such a lovely housekeeper. Granted, she hadn't been around any London residences, but she rather thought of the grander stations of butler and housekeeper as elderly staff members, dignified by the age of the person holding the position.

"Ach, Mrs. Marilla!" The viscount gave a warm greeting to the housekeeper, and Grace stood back to watch the interaction with interest.

"My lord." The housekeeper curtseyed loyally, and her gaze turned to Samantha with delight. "And this is your lovely wife. I must say the entire staff is ever so happy for you! May I offer my personal congratulations, along with those of the staff." She curtsied to Samantha, clearly pleased.

Samantha stepped forward and nodded kindly. "Thank you."

"And this is Miss Iris Grace Morgan, my ward."

Grace stepped forward, nodding her head slowly to try and pretend at possessing more decorum than she actually had, even if it was just to a servant. "If you wouldn't mind, I prefer to be called by my middle name, Grace. And it's lovely to meet you."

Samantha cast her an approving smile. She might not be able to curtsey well, but at least she could nod without ill effect. If only she could nod to the rest of the London ton, but she had a feeling that a well-executed nod would be more offensive than a poorly executed curtsey.

"We are ever so pleased to have you here." Mrs. Marilla replied, then clapped her hands gently. "All is ready, my lord. And I informed cook of your arrival and refreshments will be served whenever you wish. Is there anything else that I may do to serve?"

Grace turned to the viscount, watching as he gave an approving grin. "No, all is in order as usual. Between you and Mrs. Keyes, my life is well organized. We'll take tea in the red parlor in a half hour."

The housekeeper nodded. "Would you care for me to show you to your rooms, Miss Grace?"

Grace cast a quick glance to her guardians, then back to the housekeeper. "Yes, please."

"This way." Mrs. Marilla gestured to the stairs and led the way up to the second floor. Grace cast a glance below to the viscount and his wife, but they were clasping hands as the viscount tugged Samantha into a side room. Grace blushed and turned her gaze away. The viscount and Samantha hadn't been married so long that she was immune to their obvious affection, but she had become less embarrassed by it. Rather, she saw it as a grand example of how love should be. It was clear from their obvious affection that they were very much in love, and it was endearing to behold. Such thoughts made her focus shift to the future ahead of her, because love could be just over the horizon for her as well.

Just as she started to think about it, the housekeeper paused by a large maple door. "These are your rooms. I had Regina prepare them and if you need anything at all, she is your personal maid and will take care of any needful thing. And as always, you may ask me for assistance at any time. We are so happy to have you here, Miss Grace."

Grace thanked her, and then softly turned the brass handle to the room that would begin her adventure.

Yes. She resolved to think of the next step in life as an adventure. It was far less daunting to think of it in such a context. After all, much of her life had been one adventure after another; this was simply a different variety of adventure.

Light spilled onto the polished wood floor from the windows opposite the doorway, and Grace paused a moment to acquaint herself with the room. It was decidedly feminine with the delicate canopy bed and its floral coverlet against one wall. Beside the bed was a side table that held a clear crystal vase of yellow tulips. As her eyes scanned further, she saw an expanse of green just beyond the window, and it called to her. Putting one foot in front of another, she walked to the window and pushed back the sheer curtains obstructing her view. The view was across the street directly in front of the house, overlooking a narrow strip of trees and grass that was the middle ground between another row of houses. A robin flew from a high branch and swooped down to the grass below, and then it was startled by a squirrel that rushed by. The robin took flight into the hazy gray sky.

Grace released a breath, and then turned to survey the rest of her room. Beside the window was a writing desk, and along the same wall was the fireplace with two snug chairs framing the warm flickering flames. A looking glass and vanity completed the room before her gaze returned to the door. It suited her well, as she had every expectation that this room would be the perfect retreat when necessary.

And she was certain that at times, a retreat would be very necessary. Samantha had explained that they would be engaging in several social gatherings upon their arrival, and there was no reason to expect that their social calendar would do anything but continue to fill up. There was one aspect that had them all concerned.

The Duke of Chatterwoood.

In short, the duke was Samantha's father. But, because Grace had had the blessing of a wonderful father, she was disinclined to give the title of father to the man who had sired Samantha and her sister, Lady Liliah Heightfield. The duke was a cruel, tyrannical man whose oppressive nature had sent his daughters into hiding.

But they were returning to London.

Married, and as such, under the protection of their husbands, but none of them trusted the duke.

His pride had been mortally wounded. And Grace had heard on more than one occasion that the viscount didn't expect the duke to allow such a slight to go unpunished.

Grace had tried to use this possibility as justification to stay in Scotland.

But they, the viscount, Samantha, or Lord and Lady Heightfield, would not hear of such a thing.

They thought of it as cowardly, and in truth, they

had nothing to hide. But they would take extra care and be vigilant. So the decision was made . . . and here she found herself.

In London.

She took a seat by the low-burning fire and sighed.

For better or worse, she was going to make a debut.

And she was far more inclined that it would be for worse.

Chapter Two

Ramsey Scott, Marquess of Sterling, watched the floor of Temptations with a watchful eye. Already the evening buzzed with the news of the arrival of the Viscount of Kilpatrick and his new wife, the missing youngest daughter of the Duke of Chatterwood. It was a scandal for sure, and if there was anything Ramsey hated more than scandal, he couldn't name it. Scandal. The very word caused his skin to crawl, his stomach to clench, and his mood to turn foul. Like walking on eggshells, trying to keep from fracturing them, he constantly tiptoed around the word, and the disasters it created.

He pushed his thoughts aside and his gaze flickered toward the door. John was on the other side of the curtain, watching those who came, and those who left, making notes in the registry as each person passed him by. The card tables were full, and the brandy was flowing like the Thames in spring. All in all, it was a quiet night, aside from the gossip mill working overtime.

But that was to be expected in a gambling hell; secrets were traded as currency just as frequently as pounds. Many a man had lost a fortune in the trade of secrets, and there was no reason to expect that truth ever to prove false.

Just another reason to hate scandal. If it didn't break your heart, it could break your bank.

Or both.

Oftentimes both.

He would know.

Again, he pushed his thoughts aside. Tonight they seemed to follow him like the London fog. Pushing off from the rail of the balcony, he walked down the carpeted hall and toward the servant's staircase. The darkness was welcome, and he paused a moment in the cool stone hall of the stairwell. It was far easier to let your secrets be kept by the dark than by people.

People betrayed you.

People had their price.

The darkness, it only repeated the secrets back to you.

And then welcomed them to the grave.

Ramsey continued down the stairs and out into the lower hall. He paused by one of the doors into the main gaming room. Everything was in order; he wasn't needed, so he turned right and headed to his private office. The music faded slowly as he walked away from the people and toward the seclusion he knew and loved. As he reached his office, he unlocked the door, passed through, and closed the heavy wooden door with a soft click, a strong barrier between silence and folly.

He turned to his desk and noted the several ledgers there awaiting his approval. Numbers, now that was a friendly thing if ever there was one. They were constant, true, and easily understood.

After pouring himself a small glass of brandy, he sat behind his desk and opened the first leather-bound book. As he scanned the numbers, his mind did the quick calculations and associated them with the columns to the right. In short work, he finished with one page, turning to another.

When the new entries were complete, he turned to the book of wagers.

This was the book that could make or break a patron. Because sometimes a game of faro wasn't satisfying enough for a gambler's heart, so often the men would offer a wager on something other than a card game.

A marriage.

A boxing match.

The damn weather.

It was insanity, yet he wasn't opposed to taking their money when the wager was lost.

He opened the red leather-bound book and began to read the wagers.

Lord Garlington places a bet of five hundred pounds on Trent Waverly winning the boxing match on 15th May 1817. Lord Farthington accepts the wager and places five hundred pounds on the opposing fighter.

Both men signed their names.

It was a simple process really. Two men would wager each other, and Temptations would take a cut of the winnings.

But if a man wagered against the house—which sometimes happened—then Ramsey would have to put forth the terms and sign.

And most times, the house would win.

He scanned the various wagers, his gaze narrowing upon seeing a familiar name.

Westhouse.

His blood chilled, and his teeth clenched.

He was bloody well sure that Westhouse wasn't a member of the club; in fact, he would bet his life on it. Yet there it was, clear as day.

It was an innocuous bet, something about a horse race next week, but it was the name that sent him into a fit of rage and frustration.

Perhaps the other person initiated the bet. He scanned the page for the name: Lord Wolfston. But it was not common for a patron to wager against a non-member.

He made a mental note to ask John later. If Westhouse had darkened the door of Temptations, John would know. Nothing got past John; that was the reason Heathcliff, the Viscount Kilpatrick, had employed him as butler for his day job. He was the most secure individual one could ask for. A sniper, he was injured in the war against Napoleon and lost his memory. But his injury had an odd side effect. While the poor fellow couldn't remember a thing about his life before the injury, he could remember every single detail since, with perfect clarity. Add in his lethal training and he was a formidable foe, or a great friend.

Thankfully, they all counted him as a great friend.

He would be invaluable at Heathcliff's town home, especially with the duke's wayward daughter returning as Lady Kilpatrick.

Ramsey leaned back in his chair, closing the wager book. He had questioned Heathcliff's plan of returning to London. He had encouraged his friend to wait a few months, hoping the Duke would take time to cool his temper. But Heathcliff had been insistent, saying that his ward needed to debut.

Ramsey couldn't understand what a few months, hell, a few seasons would do to harm the newly gained ward. But it wasn't his business, and he wasn't in any position to care. Rather, he just hoped it didn't affect Temptations. Because certainly then it *would* be his business. Equal partners, Heathcliff, Lucas, and Ramsey himself were all staked in the exclusive club, owning it, sharing it, and using it to hide for various reasons.

Ramsey thought back to almost a decade ago, when in his second year at Eton. What a bloody mess he'd been. He could see it now, but then, at the time, there was no other way to understand how life worked. There were those who succeeded in life, and those who did not.

There was no in-between.

No second chances.

And once a failure, you had no hope of ever rising above it.

Thus was his life, his mantra, his chains.

His father had sent him to Eton as soon as he came of age, and it had been a welcome escape from Glenwood Manor and the iron control of his father's cool calculations and demand for perfection. Eton had represented freedom, a chance to have some sort of privacy. But what he imagined was not what was to be. His father kept close correspondence with several of the professors at the institution.

Ramsey discovered it on his first holiday home, and the reckoning that followed.

He'd never been a particularly bad child; he just hadn't been perfect.

And perfection was the only acceptable trait.

He'd come back to Eton a few days later with a new respect for following each and every rule. He took to memorizing them, much like his Latin biology vocabulary, and like proverbs, he'd speak the rules over situations.

This, needless to say, didn't earn him many friends.

It did, however, earn a lot of ridicule.

It wasn't until he got between Lucas and Heathcliff during a fistfight that he stumbled upon a friendship that was as unlikely as it was ill fated. But even against all odds, the relationship stuck. And Ramsey accredited that friendship to saving his sanity, and even saving his life.

Ramsey took a deep breath and pushed back from his chair, slamming the wager book shut with a final slap of the binding. It was enough reliving of the past.

"I'm not who I once was." He repeated the words to himself quietly, allowing them to wash over him like a cleansing rain. He closed his eyes for a moment, mentally shaking off the chains of his past and leaving them on the table . . . when they whispered enticingly for him to pick them up, to hold on to everything they represented.

Old habits die hard.

Old lies refuse to fade away.

And somewhere deep in his soul the memory of his father whispered: *history will always repeat itself* . . .

And worse than the lies and the habits, that was what chilled him most.

Because the only way to keep from repeating the past is to learn from it. But what does one do when the past is now just a secret buried with the man who owned it?

Ramsey could answer the question. Because it had been the only truth he'd ever been utterly sure of.

What does one do? One fails.

He would fail.

Because deep in his soul, as much as he wished to deny it, he knew that only two options were possible in life.

Perfection and failure.

And he was the second.

And would always be.

Chapter Three

Grace resisted the urge to scratch along the rough collar of the new gown that was being fitted. She tried to distract herself with the various baubles around the edge of the fitting room. When that failed, she turned her attention to the salt and pepper hair of Mrs. Bourne, who was meticulously, and rather slowly, pinning the hem of the new gown. Grace fancied that the woman's coiffure had seen better days, but that could also be attributed to the fact that this was the third gown that Grace was being fit for, and there were certainly other ladies with appointments after her.

It was at this point that Grace decided that she didn't wish to be a bluestocking, as much as she had romanticized the idea. Perhaps just a bluestocking in personality, not in actual labor. Could that be an option? Mrs. Bourne stood and arched her back before evaluating her handiwork.

And Grace held her breath, hoping for the words that meant she was finished.

But alas, Mrs. Bourne's brow puckered, her green eyes narrowed, and she bent down again and set to work.

It was exceedingly difficult to not slouch, or sigh in irritation, but Samantha was just beyond, sitting on a chair and watching with that expression that let Grace know she was expected to behave well.

Not for the first time, Grace imagined herself a young girl just out of leading strings, yet it wasn't too far from the truth. Her attention span was probably comparable to that of a tot.

Samantha had the patience of Job, Grace reminded herself.

For that, Grace decided to be thankful and try her best to act civil.

A few minutes later Mrs. Bourne stood up once more, and evaluated the hem.

Grace tried to keep her expression from looking too hopeful.

Samantha covered her mouth, but her eyes betrayed her amusement.

Grace decided that hiding one's feelings was over-rated.

Mrs. Bourne nodded, gave a bright smile to Grace, and then turned to Samantha. "My lady, I do believe I'm finished with this one. The alterations are minimal so I expect to have this and the other two dresses ready tomorrow afternoon, if that will be satisfactory?"

Grace eyed the floor just below the stool she stood upon, wondering whether, if she stepped without assistance, would that pull out a pin? She wanted to get down and dart to the dressing room, but . . . it wasn't worth the risk, she decided.

"That will be more than satisfactory. Thank you." Samantha stood and walked toward Grace

"Miss Grace?" Mrs. Bourne offered her hand and Grace stepped carefully from the stool and onto solid ground.

"Thank you."

In short work Grace was redressed in her walking dress and she and Samantha quit the modiste and stepped into the not entirely fresh London air.

Several clouds loomed threateningly overhead and Grace gave them an irritated glare. "Does the sun ever appear?"

Samantha chuckled. "When it wishes to, but I'm afraid it doesn't bow to our will as often as I'd like."

Grace arched a brow and continued on their stroll down Bond Street. The carriages and hacks rolled by, the horse's hooves clicking on the cobblestones while the harness jingled like little bells. There was an odd music to the bustle of the city, one that was familiar to Grace. In all of her travels she had come to the conclusion that large cities had a life of their own. The sounds, smells, and culture were just different enough from the surrounding area to give the places their own flavor. It was quite fascinating. In India, the scent of curry was the first memory that hit her. In Egypt, the dry heat and the scent of the Nile when you came close, fishy yet tainted by the desert air. And London, as she breathed in deeply, wondering what identity it would claim. Smoke, humanity, and rain. Not exactly exotic, but relevant most certainly. It could be worse, she supposed.

"What are you thinking so strenuously about?" Samantha asked, her expression kind and curious.

Grace colored. "I was woolgathering."

"Apparently. About?"

"How each city I've visited has had defining features."

"Oh?" Samantha nodded. "One day I will actually learn to predict where your mind takes you."

"I hope not," Grace muttered, feeling heat in her cheeks.

Samantha gave a small laugh. "I probably never will, but it would be fascinating to see what you've seen, and be able to compare it to new things. Tell me, what did London compare with? Anything?"

Grace shook her head. "I'm afraid it defies categorization," she teased. "But I must say that when I think of it, I'll remember smoke"—and before she could continue, a fat raindrop hit her nose, creating a small splash onto her cheek—"and rain," she finished.

Samantha nodded and cast a wary glance to the sky. "Let's return to the coach." They carefully crossed the street and strode a few yards to where the Kilpatrick coach waited.

Bond Street wasn't very far from the viscount's town home, yet even in that short ride the rain had progressed from a few drops to a torrential downpour.

"It sounds like thunder," Grace commented, glancing up at the top of the carriage.

"It won't last long," Samantha replied with the confidence of someone who had lived there her whole life.

"Are you sure?" Grace gave her a dubious look.

"Certain," Samantha returned.

When they pulled up to the house, John walked out with a wide black umbrella and, as a footman helped Samantha and then Grace alight from the carriage, he carried the umbrella over each of them till they made it safely into the foyer.

"It's a bit wet out there," Samantha commented teasingly.

"Indeed, my lady. Is there anything we need to fetch for you from the carriage?"

"No, thank you John," Samantha said.

He bowed his head respectfully and went to shake out the umbrella.

"Well, just the two ladies I was about to search for." The viscount was ambling down the hall, his words meant for both women, but his eyes only on his wife.

Grace glanced away, feeling the intruder.

"Oh? Lucky for you, here we are," Samantha replied teasingly.

"I find I *am* quite lucky." He chuckled, his brogue making the words even lighter in inflection.

"I rather think so, after all, you're married to me," Samantha returned.

The viscount laughed, deep and rich. It was a comforting sound, one that made Grace relax, and feel safe. Though not old enough to be her father, the viscount certainly gave her the security of one, and it was welcome.

"Tonight, Ramsey," he paused and Grace looked up to him. "The Marquess of Sterling, that is, will be arriving and I wanted to introduce you."

"I finally will get to meet the man I've heard so much about," Samantha replied.

"For dinner, I assume?" Grace asked.

"Yes. We have a few business matters to discuss and with Lucas, Lord Heightfield, still in Scotland for the next few weeks, it's just Ramsey and me to keep everything running smoothly."

Grace nodded, biting her lip to keep from smiling at the informal way the viscount addressed his friends. It was understood, yet ironic, because as a lady she would be required to address the gentlemen formally, yet she had only heard of them by their Christian names, and when she thought of them, especially Lord Heightfield—with whom she had grown pretty well acquainted in Scotland—it was always by their Christian names as well. It would take a concerted effort not to make a faux pas, but apparently that was just one mountain she'd have to move, and she'd rather get out all her faux pas in front of friends rather than the London ton.

Though she was sure she had enough bad luck to make mistakes abound in any situation.

Such was life.

Or hers, at least.

"Why the frown?" the viscount asked, and she shot her gaze to his.

"Fretting, mostly."

"Oh? Shocking that. You have nothing to concern yourself with Ramsey . . . blast, that's going to be a pain in the arse." He shook his head.

Samantha swatted his arm, probably for the use of the word "arse" in front of Grace.

Grace bit her lip to keep from smiling, and waited for him to continue. He gave an unrepentant grin to his wife, and then spoke. "You must address him as Lord Sterling, which I know you understand. And I'm not helping matters by using his Christian name. I apologize; it will take some work on my part and I'm not entirely sure I'll succeed. But at least know that I'll try."

"I cannot ask for more, and I'm already sure I'll slip up at least once. As long as he refuses to be scandalized, we shall get along famously I'm sure."

The viscount gave a low chuckle. "Yes, well . . . of the three of us, R—Lord Sterling is the most aware of propriety." He frowned slightly, his brows drawing over his eyes. "Honestly he might be a real asset when we begin your debut. I'll mention it to him." He nodded, as if approving of his own brilliant idea.

Grace was tempted to groan, but in truth, she should accept all the help she could get.

"If he's to arrive shortly, we should take a few moments to change." Samantha stepped forward, kissed her husband on the cheek, and backed away quickly, neatly dodging his outwardly grasping hand.

"You're getting slow in your old age," she teased, retreating toward the staircase.

"You're learning my tricks. I'll have to come up with some new ones," he answered, arching a brow while he gave her a wide, almost predatory grin.

Samantha paused at the bottom of the stairs, and Grace passed her as she ascended to the second floor.

She strode purposefully to her room, not turning back because she was quite certain that while she didn't understand much about love, she knew one thing for certain; it was fun to play hard to get, but it was more fun to get caught.

A giggle echoed softly down the hall just as Grace closed her bedroom door, a smile teasing her lips.

It would be nice to be chased, even nicer to be caught, but only by someone you could trust. She had seen such a relationship in her parents, and again with the viscount and Samantha, but she was certain it was uncommon. She'd heard stories, she'd seen small windows into life on the other side of the equation, and that wasn't what she wished to experience.

She rang for her maid, and once Regina arrived, she changed from her slightly damp walking dress into something more suitable for dinner. Regina freshened up her hair, and Grace dismissed her. She should take leave of her room and go downstairs to the parlor and await their guest, but she was rather inclined to stay in her room a few minutes longer, to absorb the silence and read, even if it was just for a few moments. The temptation was too great and she picked up *A Midsummer Night's Dream* and started where she'd left off. She'd just reached the part where Puck puts the magic love drops on the eyes of Demetrius when a knock sounded on her door, causing her to jump slightly. She tucked a length of lace in the book and set it to the side. Eyes bleary, she stood and walked to the door. As she opened it, she belatedly realized it had been a much longer break than she had intended on taking.

Regina was on the other side of the door. "Pardon miss, but my lord wishes you to join him and Lady Kilpatrick in the parlor downstairs."

"Of course." Grace nodded, feeling abashed at neglecting to be prompt. Regina gave a quick curtsey and walked away. Grace ran her hands down her skirt, smoothing it and taking a deep breath before she started in the opposite direction towards the stairs. A wayward lock tickled the side of her face and she tucked it behind her ear. This was the perfect opportunity to practice all that she'd been taught at Samantha's kind hand . . . and as such, she was profoundly nervous.

True, he was a friend of the family, but Lord Sterling would also be a very good judge of whether she could pass muster for the rest of London society. A test—she had to think of it as a challenge. There, thinking of it that way was helpful. She took the last stair and twisted her lips. She'd much rather rise to the challenge of something she enjoyed, something she was actually good at, and this was not something in which she excelled.

Drat.

There was no way but through it, and she wasn't a wilting flower. No. She was made of something far more durable; she couldn't think of anything as an example at the moment, but that didn't signify. It was still true. She could, she *would* do this!

Shoulders back, she held her head high and walked down the hall toward the parlor, where she knew they all waited. With one deep breath she pretended a grace she didn't possess and walked into the parlor.

Which was immediately discovered to be empty.

"Blast it all," she muttered, her shoulders sagging slightly. She had the urge to stomp her foot for good measure, but she held some sense of decorum and promptly walked over to a chair and took a seat. While she had assumed she was late, she clearly wasn't the latest. She rather thought it was on purpose. Leave it to Samantha to hedge her bets and make sure she arrived on time. Samantha was far too discerning; it was irritating as much as it was helpful.

Grace tapped her toe on the rug, shifted to find a more comfortable position, then blew out a frustrated breath. She was bored already.

The sharp sound of heels clicking on the floor in the hall just beyond had her sitting up straight in her chair, lest the viscount or Samantha walk in and see her slouched and in an impatient position. But the man who rounded the corner was most certainly *not* the viscount.

Good Lord, but the man was tall! She imagined that if she were beside him, he could see clean over her head, and then some. His gaze immediately met hers, and a shiver of . . . something . . . shot through her. It wasn't unpleasant; it was however, foreign, and she took note to evaluate it later. She stood, not knowing what else to do, and watched the way he paused as he entered, appearing slightly unsure. His eyes were a pale blue, framed by dark lashes and brows. His hair was meticulously combed into a classic fashion, one that defied trend but somehow fit him. He tucked his hands behind his back, not smiling, simply . . . watching.

It was all sorts of disconcerting, and, as often happened when Grace felt uncomfortable, she started talking.

The talking wasn't the bad part; it was the inability to stop the talking that usually got her into trouble, but it was too late now. Her mouth had opened and the words started to pour forth.

"Good evening, you must be Lord Sterling." She impressed herself with the pause she gave to at least allow him to nod. "It's a pleasure to meet you. I've heard so much from the viscount, though he never mentioned your being so tall. Though, that may be because he is quite tall himself, but I dare say, you're taller, aren't you?"

She took a breath, forcing herself to stop, but when he didn't answer, she felt compelled to continue. "I rather thought Samantha and the viscount would be down here already, but they get distracted quite easily. It's rather sweet if you ask me. I had my suspicions when the viscount first arrived at Kilmarin House, that it was a match from the start." Her arms tingled, her fingertips were warm and she tried to force herself to stop talking.

If the damn man would just say something, *anything!* What ever happened to chivalry?

He blinked, as if slowly digesting everything she was pouring forth in a rush of language. But he made no reply, which of course, forced her to—

"Ah, I see you've met my ward!" The viscount strode in, saving Grace from her own folly and inability to harness any semblance of self-control. She could have kissed his feet in gratitude for her rescue.

It was horrifically annoying to need to be rescued from oneself. Inconvenient as well.

Lord Sterling gave a tight sigh at the sight of his friend, as if releasing tension from his body. "Yes, indeed. Though I don't think the lady ever mentioned her name." He shot her an expression that appeared almost amused. But she couldn't be sure. He was so very . . . controlled.

"Then allow me to make the formal introductions. "Lord Sterling." He gave a sidelong glance to Grace, as if saying, "See, I remembered." "This is my ward, Miss Iris Grace Morgan, but she goes by the name Grace." He finished with a sweep of his hand.

"A pleasure, Miss Grace." He bowed smartly, the movement oddly graceful for his height.

"A pleasure, Lord Sterling." Grace gave her best curtsey, lowering her body and inclining her head just enough. Her only regret was that Samantha wasn't there to behold it.

"My apologies." Samantha's voice gently floated through the air and Grace looked up to see her arrival. After an approving smile to Grace, Samantha stood beside her husband and faced their guest. "Ah, Lord Sterling." She offered her hand.

He took it, kissing it quickly, and turned to the viscount.

"And this lovely and fascinating creature is my wife."

The viscount grinned proudly as he gazed lovingly down on Samantha.

"A pleasure to meet you. We've long awaited the lady that could tame this beast of a man." He gave a grin that transformed his face.

All the stoic lines of expression melted into an amusement that took years off his face, and the effect was stunning. He was beautiful, handsome but not in the classic way. His eyes smiled as much as his lips, which, now that they had drawn her attention, she could see were full and wide. For the first time, he acted like an old friend versus some barrister coming to discuss someone's estate.

Grace pulled her gaze away, not wanting to be caught staring.

"It wasn't difficult to tame him, though I don't think that is the correct sentiment."

"You can't tame a Scot," the viscount added with a sturdy nod.

"Scot with a very English title," Lord Sterling replied with an arched brow.

"If the English wish to give me land and money, who am I to stop them?" He shrugged.

Lord Sterling gave a slight shake of his head, as if he were used to the viscount's antics but not willing to prolong them.

"Shall we all sit? I'm sure dinner will be announced shortly, but I wish to hear any news that you're willing to share." Samantha gave a meaningful glance to the viscount, and Grace felt a shiver of foreboding tickle her spine.

In short work they had all taken seats, and Grace was making a concentrated effort to sit straight, and follow the conversation without being distracted.

"Have you heard anything concerning the Duke of Chatterwood?" the viscount asked, diving right into the news that mattered most.

Lord Ramsey nodded, then leaned forward. "Some. It would seem he's keeping rather tight lipped about the whole situation, which is a boon. With his daughters properly married, I cannot imagine he would do more than to let his disapproval be known. To do anything further would risk his own reputation. The scandal follows you and Lord Heightfield, and if he wishes to remain clean of his new son-in-law's rather questionable reputations, he will wisely keep distance."

"Questionable reputation, hmm?" The viscount stroked his chin, an amused expression in his eyes. "I suppose that's more accurate than not."

"Indeed." Lord Sterling arched a brow, but his lips formed a small smirk. "A reputation that you're taking strides to improve?" he asked, his gaze darting to Grace.

Her eyes widened slightly and she cast her gaze to the viscount.

"If it's possible." He shrugged a shoulder. "But as it is, all of London's parties will be open to us if for no other reason than to gain the true story on how I came to marry the duke's youngest daughter. London and their love of gossip, you know."

"That and the husbands will all be vying for your favor."

"If they aren't already members." The viscount flicked a speck of lint from his coat sleeve and turned to Grace.

"You have nothing to worry about, Miss Grace. Don't let Lord Sterling intimidate you regarding your prospects."

Grace nodded, flickering her gaze to Samantha.

Samantha gave a supportive smile.

The sound of someone entering the room captured everyone's attention, and Mrs. Marilla curtseyed. "Dinner is served, my lord."

Again Grace was stricken with the beauty of the housekeeper, and she glanced to Samantha. Was she concerned about her husband having such a lovely lady on staff? Why had he hired her? All these questions filtered through her mind as she rose from her seat and turned her attention to the door.

The viscount escorted his wife, which left Grace with Lord Sterling. She took a hesitant step forward, waiting for him to offer his arm. He rounded the sofa, then paused, turning back to her. Grace moved to catch up, nearly tripping on the woven rug. His gaze was on her, studying her. It reminded her of the time she was in Egypt and watched a clockmaker. The man's bald head was bent over his desk, his expression focused, sharp, and intuitive as he studied the gears before slowly making adjustments, learning what worked, what didn't.

Lord Sterling was watching her as if trying to figure out how she worked, and why. She kept her expression neutral as she placed her hand on his offered arm, and waited for him to lead the way to the dining room. They fell into step easily enough, yet Grace couldn't help but notice that her head only reached the level of his jawline. In fact, as she hazarded a glance in his direction, she figured that even if she were to step on a footstool, she wouldn't be the same height as he. Of course, it would depend on the height of the footstool—

"Do you often stare at new acquaintances?" he asked, meeting her gaze.

Heat rushed to her cheeks, and her body grew feverish in embarrassment. She'd rather forgotten that her glance had turned into study, and that study had probably appeared like a rude stare. Well, nothing to do but walk through it.

"Pardon me. I was . . . well, I was deciding what height of footstool I'd need to compare with you in height." She glanced down the hall, a new wave of heat feeding the surely crimson blush on her face.

"Footstool?" He asked, his tone disbelieving and yet, diverted.

She risked a glance at his face, hoping to be able to read his expression. He didn't seem offended, just . . . curious. Curiosity she could work with without fear, or at least, much of it. "Yes, footstool. Since I've already made a cake of myself, if you don't mind me asking, just how tall are you?"

His lip twitched into a smile. "Six feet and three inches."

She returned the smile, only hers was far broader. "Ah, I wasn't far off. I was guessing around six feet, two inches."

"Very astute." He nodded, his grin widening. "And how tall are you, Miss Grace?"

"Not very common dinner conversation, is it?" she teased. "Five feet and six inches. Not much above average for England, but I was a veritable giant in India," she added with a daring smile.

"India you say?" He raised an eyebrow. "Yes, and I'm assuming if you're considered a giant, I cannot imagine the category to which I'd belong."

She tipped her chin upward, then narrowed her eyes. "A Titan."

He let out a loud laugh, then sobered slightly as if abashed by his unrestrained amusement. "A Titan?"

"Yes, you are aware of Greek mythology . . ." she asked with slight sarcasm, then regretted her bold move. Sarcasm wasn't ladylike.

Well, neither was telling a gentleman he was a Titan, she supposed.

She glanced to Samantha as the viscount pulled out her chair for her. At least she couldn't hear the conversation.

"I'm very well versed in Greek mythology and history," he answered. "And it's obvious that you know your studies as well."

She glanced at him, curious as to what his verdict on her education would be. In her experience, there were only two reactions: offense at a woman receiving such an extensive education, or begrudging respect—which was usually earned only on rare occasions.

She was rather expecting the first reaction.

He didn't reply, but simply pulled out a chair for her, then took a seat himself.

As the soup was served, the viscount turned to Lord Sterling. "We've received several invitations, but so far I haven't selected which event will be our first to attend. Do you have any suggestions?"

Grace sipped her beef barley soup and listened intently. It was an odd paradigm. Weren't women usually the ones who knew the answers to social questions? Yet, in her experience, both the viscount and Lord Heightfield were better versed in society, parties, planning, and gossip than any woman she'd ever met.

Of course, she had never been to London before, and all her conjecture might very well change once she met some of the ladies in residence. But for the moment, the truth still held.

Lord Sterling's brow furrowed slightly as he considered the question. "Can you tell me the invitations you've received?"

"Yes." The viscount nodded. "Herford, Longfitt, Sheffold, and . . ." He frowned then turned to his wife.

"Lord and Lady Drummel," Samantha supplied with a helpful smile.

The viscount nodded, then turned to his friend.

Lord Sterling took a spoonful of soup and ate it as he seemed to consider the names mentioned. "For the moment, ignore Longfitt and Sheffold. Both are grabbing for attention and all the focus will be on their daughters. Both families have girls in their first season."

"Noted," the viscount replied.

"You don't want to be vying for attention, though the season is especially well populated this year." He shook his head. "But the quality is low, if you gather my meaning."

The viscount arched a brow.

Samantha tipped her chin in an almost scolding manner, and then returned to her soup.

And Grace wondered if maybe Lord Sterling was placing her in that same group of low-quality debutants—whatever that meant. It most certainly wasn't a compliment.

"Herford is a good choice, and so is Drummel. Old, established titles and an appearance will be respectable, and they are sure to be well attended," Lord Sterling finished, his expression satisfied.

The viscount clapped his hands once. "Then we

shall start there. Thank you for your insight, it's quite valuable."

"I'm happy to assist." Lord Sterling gave a dismissive gesture.

The conversation lulled slightly, and Grace turned to Samantha, curious if this was a time for her to introduce a topic, or if she should wait. Blast, she could never quite remember when it was polite to speak and when she should keep her mouth shut.

It was a struggle, that.

Samantha gave her an encouraging smile.

Grace took a deep breath.

"When is Heightfield to arrive?" Lord Sterling asked a moment before Grace was about to speak.

She nearly choked on her words in an effort to stop them before she interrupted.

The footman removed the soup and soon brought another course, all the while the viscount answered Lord Sterling's inquiry.

"In the next month, or so he has said. I wouldn't be surprised if he arrived earlier."

"I'm quite surprised that he's stayed away as long as he has," Lord Sterling answered.

"He's quite . . . preoccupied." The viscount gave a sly glance to his wife, who blushed.

Grace turned her attention to the plate before her, slicing up a bite of potato.

"Ah yes, I'd imagine so," Lord Sterling replied.

At the next pause in conversation, Grace was ready to practice her table conversation skills. She breathed in, glanced to the side to make sure that Lord Sterling's body language didn't imply that he was about to speak, then, assured of her success, she spoke. "It was quite the rainstorm today," she stated.

Then she realized it wasn't a question, rather a very polite, very neutral, very unremarkable statement. She hastened to fix her error. "It reminded me of thunder. Is it quite common for it to rain in such a fashion?"

There, much better! She was pleased with her first attempt outside of the protective walls of Kilmarin in Scotland.

She turned to Samantha, and returned her warm, approving smile. The weather was always a safe topic, was it not?

The viscount nodded. "It rains like that more often than I'd like, but at least it usually doesn't last long."

"Were you ever in the monsoon season in India, Miss Grace?" Lord Sterling turned to her, his blue eyes alight with inquiry.

A smile bent her lips. "Why yes, I was. It's much different than rain here, at least in my very short experience of being in London. In Bangladesh, the monsoons sweep through slowly so that the rain seems as if it will never end, like a continuous circle of clouds that just repeats over and over. The air is so thick you feel as though you're not breathing it, but drinking it. The worst part is never being fully dry. If you're not wet from the rain, the humidity is enough to keep you damp." Grace grinned widely, the memories flooding her. In her mind's eye she could smell the fragrance of the rain on the parched earth, the sound of the first raindrops that signaled the need to take shelter, and the roar of the downpour when it finally hit.

"And did you enjoy it?" Lord Sterling asked.

She thought about it, then shook her head. "I hated it." She gave a soft laugh. "I'd far rather the desert than the rain."

"Ah, that will never do. We English are proud of our weather, as dreary as it is," Lord Sterling replied.

"It's good to be proud of one's home," Grace agreed. "But just because you find pride in something, doesn't mean it's the best option."

"How so?" the viscount asked, his smile wide, clearly enjoying the conversation. A swell of pride hit Grace, and she smiled at the irony of it. Hadn't she just mentioned that being proud of something didn't mean it was the best available? That was certainly the truth. She was proud of her conversation, but it most certainly had room for improvement!

"You're amused," Lord Sterling commented.

When Grace shared her irony, he grinned, then the grin gave way to laughter.

When she turned from Lord Sterling, she saw that the viscount's expression was somewhat astounded as he watched his friend. Grace wasn't sure how to interpret such a reaction, but decided it wasn't a bad one. She glanced to Samantha then, and upon seeing her approving smile, the first swells of hope danced through Grace.

She could do this.

She would do this.

London, look out . . . ready or not, Miss Iris Grace Morgan was about to make her mark.

For better.

Or worse.

Chapter Four

Ramsey couldn't remember the last time he'd laughed so much in one evening. In fact, it was entirely possible that he never *had* laughed that much in the span of a few hours.

Heathcliff's ward was a delight, a breath of fresh air. And he was certain of one thing regarding her: London society was going to eat her alive.

A tremor of fear shivered through him as he remembered her wide, innocent, wonder-filled gaze. She was utterly guileless, and as frank as they came.

And while those were good, even enviable character traits, they weren't ones that were safe.

She would offend some, gain the scorn of others, and be despised by all. He was sure of it, and he was also certain that he wasn't overreacting. Surely Heathcliff knew this, and certainly Lady Kilpatrick was aware and had taken some measures to help the poor girl protect herself.

Ramsey tapped his finger on his study desk. Maybe

he should check, at least warn them about his prediction for Miss Grace. At least then, when it all went to hell, he could at least feel less guilt because he was honorable and spoke up to his friend.

It was a bloody shame that the spark would be extinguished in Miss Grace's eyes, but it was the way of the world.

Sparks die.

Shame wins.

And people are fickle.

It was an undisputed truth in his world.

The rain pelted against his study window, and he turned absentmindedly to gaze at the light. The rainwater created small streams down the glass, distorting the view outside, but he wasn't looking further than the glass. It was oddly comforting, the rain. He'd grown up in Dorset, one of the wettest places in England, but rather than resent the near constant drizzle, he'd grown fond of the consistency of it. You could always count on the rain.

It was welcome when there was so much in his life that wasn't as consistent.

Or refreshing.

Or nourishing.

The sound of the raindrops softened, signaling the slow decline of the downpour, and Ramsey sighed.

It was only midday, but already he was exhausted, a bone deep exhaustion that never truly dissipated. He felt older than his thirty and two years. It was bloody disruptive to be so fatigued of heart, but it was expected when there was war always waging within one's soul. He shook his head to clear it, and thought back to the events of the previous evening.

Dinner was superb, and the company was dazzling,

but he simply couldn't move past Miss Grace. Miss *Iris* Grace. For the life of him he couldn't imagine why she'd wish to be called something other than Iris. It wasn't a common name, and it might distinguish her from the other ladies coming out that season. But, he reminded himself, it was none of his affair.

And he would be wise to wash his hands of the whole sordid business.

Lord only knew what could potentially go wrong with both Heathcliff and Lucas coming back into society. A smirk twisted his lips as he blew out a small chuckle. Perhaps *he* should head away to Scotland! Leave the whole mess to them to deal with.

But as tempting as the thought was, he knew he'd never act on it. The truth was, they might end up needing him. And he owed it to them to be around, to pay attention, and step in should they ever need him.

Not so long ago, they did the very same for him.

And their intervention saved his life.

So, it was with that sobering reminder, Ramsey made the decision to call upon Heathcliff, and at least give him some advice concerning his debuting ward.

And then he'd walk away from the mess.

Simply hide in the shadows, pay attention, and then if disaster struck, he would be waiting.

With a determined nod, Ramsey strode to the door. Tugging on his shirtsleeves, he ordered his carriage readied. And in less than ten minutes, he was sinking back into the soft leather of his well-appointed carriage and on his way to Heathcliff's residence.

The rain had let up, allowing for some orphan sunrays to pierce through the clouds and warm the earth. The air tasted.clean, a rare occurrence for London, and

Ramsey smiled in appreciation of the gift from the rain.

Soon, the carriage stopped at the curb of Heathcliff's home, and Ramsey stepped on to the wet earth before taking the steps two at a time to the door.

Before he could knock, John answered.

"My lord." He bowed. "I'll announce you." John didn't waste time, simply opened the door, stepped aside, and then proceeded down the hall to notify Heathcliff of his arrival.

Ramsey had the temptation to simply follow John down the hall; Lord only knew how many times Heathcliff had ignored Ramsey's butler and interjected himself into his home unannounced, and often even unwanted.

Bloody frustrating.

Ramsey waited, choosing manners over gratification. And his patience was rewarded by a quick return of John with an application for Ramsey to follow him down the hall to the parlor.

Heathcliff was in his study, as Ramsey had assumed due to the hour, and as such, Ramsey was quite at ease with the familiarity of his surroundings.

"What did you want, old chap? Since it's been less than twenty-four hours since I last saw you, I suspect there's something on your mind." Heathcliff leaned back in his chair, hands folded behind his head, the picture of utter ease.

Ramsey arched a brow, but took a seat across from his friend. The door clicked shut behind him, signaling the departure of John. "He's a far sight better than Wilkes," Ramsey started.

Heathcliff chuckled, his eyes squinting slightly with

the force of his grin. "Ach, don't be saying such things. You know that Wilkes has the best intentions. He's a good butler."

"He is, but I do think you made the right choice in employing John to take over his position temporarily. Wilkes is surely enjoying his little vacation in Bath."

"I'm sure I've ruined him for work forever, blast it all. It was Samantha's idea, you know. After I said I was planning on hiring a guard for the door, she inquired about the current butler, and well, she's a softhearted lass. Especially when I said how long he'd been with the family."

"I'm surprised he stepped down."

"I was too, but then I learned he was getting awfully arthritic. Of course, that was when Samantha decided on the whole season in Bath for him." Heathcliff shook his head. "Who ever heard of sending a butler to Bath?"

"Only us." Ramsey chuckled.

"Aye, only us. Let's keep it that way. Or else I'll have servants making demands."

"Yes, Mrs. Marilla. I still can't believe she puts up with you," Ramsey remarked with humor.

"She's dealt with far worse than I, though I think my wife was surprised by someone so fair and young."

"Age isn't always the number of your years, my friend."

"Isn't that the truth. Mrs. Marilla is at least eighty at heart. Poor lass. The least I can do is give her honest employment. She deserves far more."

"But she's happy with safety," Ramsey added, his mind flickering back to when they'd found her.

Literally.

It was after a particularly rowdy party at Temptations. They'd locked up after dispatching the last guest at dawn, and then taken account from the night before. They were finishing up their duties when a servant boy came in, his face white.

"There's a girl in the alley, dead!" The boy was panting, and Lucas stepped forward, asking the boy the particulars.

When the boy didn't answer, Lucas shared a look with the other two, and they all walked out into the morning light.

It wasn't a memory Ramsey liked to revisit.

Orphaned, abused, and then beaten, Mrs. Marilla had only made it as far as the alley before collapsing.

But that was long ago, and Mrs. Marilla had overcome much in the past ten years. Her loyalty was unwavering to each of them, and as such, she had proven many times an excellent spy. It wasn't the usual employment for a woman, but Mrs. Marilla had an uncanny ability to tear down people's defenses and ferret out information.

"Ramsey, are you even paying attention?" Heathcliff snapped his fingers, and Ramsey blinked.

"Sorry. Damn it all, I need to figure out a way to get some sleep."

Heathcliff paused, then tipped his head ever so slightly. His gaze grew empathetic. "Are you still having the dreams?"

Ramsey nodded.

"I'm sorry." Heathcliff stood and walked over to the sideboard, then poured himself a snifter of brandy, and then another one. He walked over to Ramsey. Holding the offering, he gave a small smile to his friend.

"Thank you." Ramsey accepted the snifter. "Starting early." Ramsey lifted the glass in a toast.

Heathcliff shook his head. "Depends on if you've slept, which it looks like you haven't. So for you, it's late my friend."

"Here, here." Ramsey agreed, taking a sip. The warm liquid was deliciously smooth. "French?" he asked.

Heathcliff gave a knowing grin. "Maybe."

"Traitor." Ramsey teased.

Heathcliff chuckled, then sat back down in his chair. "Now, what was it that you came to discuss with me?"

Ramsey took another sip of the exquisite brandy and then leaned forward.

"Your ward."

"Interested already?" Heathcliff leaned back, perfectly at ease, as if the words he'd just spoken weren't the most insane, idiotic thing he'd ever uttered.

Which was a feat in and of itself. Ramsey could name a great many things that his friend had said that were insane and idiotic but this, *this,* trumped them all.

"No," he replied, irritated.

"Oh, pity that. You would have made my life much easier." Heathcliff shrugged.

"A thousand apologies. I forgot that I live to make your life easier," Ramsey replied with heavy sarcasm.

"Don't work yourself into a lather," Heathcliff said. "What was it, then?"

Ramsey pursed his lips, then sighed. "I'm afraid that your ward, as refreshing as she is in face and character, will not make a good impression on her debut. It is my recommendation that you coach her further in keeping her peace around others, and not being so . . ." He searched for the right word. ". . . Altruistic," he finished.

Heathcliff blinked. "Just when I didn't think you could become more of a straight-laced idiot, you say something like that, which makes me think you're headed for Bedlam. Do you have any idea what you sound like when you say things like that? Good Lord, you'd put Lady Jersey to shame with your allegiance to propriety."

Ramsey glanced down at the rug, then back to his friend. "Am I wrong?"

Heathcliff opened his mouth to speak, then closed it. He sighed. "No."

Ramsey bit back a bit of a triumphant smile. "Then why the long-winded insult?"

Heathcliff tapped his finger on the desk. "Because you sounded like an arse when you said it that way."

"And you never sound like an ass." Ramsey rolled his eyes.

"I never said that," Heathcliff responded, leaning forward in his chair. "I'm often an arse, as my wife tells me."

"I have plenty experience of my own from which to glean proof," Ramsey added.

"True enough."

"So?"

"So . . . what?" Heathcliff asked.

"So, what are you going to do about her?" Ramsey asked impatiently. It would be a boon to be able to fix the problem before it actually became one.

"Nothing." Heathcliff shrugged.

Ramsey sighed. He should have known it wouldn't be that easy. Damn the man. "What do you mean, nothing?"

"I mean, nothing. There's nothing I can do. We're attending the Drummel rout tonight, and there's absolutely nothing I can do since we already indicated that we'd attend, and there's no way I can modify or try to modify Grace's behavior before this evening. At least any more than what my wife has already done. Good Lord, if you think she's frank now, you should have met her a month ago. But I must say, I rather liked her less restrained."

"You're Scottish, you think self-control is unnecessary."

"That's not fair." Heathcliff looked slightly offended.

"Perhaps not, but accurate at least of you." Ramsey didn't care a whit if he offended his friend. Lord only knew how many times the tables had been turned in his direction! Heathcliff wasn't truly offended anyway; Ramsey could tell by the way he was holding back a grin.

Pain in the ass.

"So, nothing. I gave my warning and nothing will come from it," Ramsey stated.

"Your advice is appreciated, but I'm afraid it can't be put into action."

"You're trying to make it sound better," Ramsey accused.

"Yes. Did it work?" Heathcliff smiled.

"Damn you," Ramsey replied without any heat in his tone.

"If I had a pound for every time you've said that to me—"

"It's still the truth," Ramsey replied, then stood. "Well, then I suppose that is all that is necessary. Keep a sharp eye on her, and I'll . . . ." Ramsey breathed out a slow breath, reconsidering the words he was about to say.

"Yes?" Heathcliff stood, preparing to walk his friend to the study door.

"I'll attend as well. To help keep an eye out. Between you and Lucas, we have more than enough drama and scandal for a decade. Your ward doesn't need to add to the equation. I'll help."

"That's not necessary," Heathcliff said in response, his expression frowning.

"I wasn't asking for permission." Ramsey arched a brow, meeting his friend's gaze.

Heathcliff sighed.

Ramsey waited.

"Very well. Just do me a favor?"

Ramsey nodded, but he was more than a little skeptical.

"Take a nap, you're no fun when you're like this."

Chapter Five

Grace slowly twirled, studying the reflection in the mirror.

Like a caterpillar just realizing it wasn't one any longer, she studied the beautiful dress that was like fragile butterfly wings, wondering if maybe, if she stepped out on that proverbial ledge, she could actually fly.

The dress made her think it was possible.

It made her want to think it was possible.

But what if she didn't fly, but simply fell?

The worst part? There was no way to know until after she jumped and tested her wings.

But the dress, dear Lord, she'd never had anything as beautiful. In the shop during the fittings, she'd looked at it, of course. She wasn't blind. But, the fit, the final stitching, the way the fabric seemed to shimmer . . . it transformed her.

Samantha had said that the pastel shades of purple were all the rage this season, and the modiste agreed. Grace wasn't sure why it mattered if she had one color purple over another. They all looked quite similar to her, but Samantha had insisted on the muted violet fabric, and now that everything was finished, Grace finally understood why.

Expressive green eyes came alive with the hue of the gown, and she almost didn't recognize her own gaze. Though never one to boast about thick lashes, for once her reddish-tinted brow and eyelashes didn't disappear into her pale skin, but came alive. Even her few freckles paled as the color enhanced the cream tones of her skin.

It was settled.

She would wear this dress for the rest of her life.

She twisted her lips at her own absurd thought. Maybe not wear the dress every day, but she *was* going to march down to Bond Street in the morning and order several other gowns made of the same fabric. Would Samantha protest if she requested to purchase the entire bolt of cloth?

Grace gave her head a slight shake and took a slow breath to ease her spinning mind. She needed to focus, to concentrate on not just looking the part of the lady, but actually being the lady. Her hair was woven with little seed pearls, and looped elegantly with just enough strands to frame her face. She fancied that she looked like one of the Greek goddesses she'd seen in a museum somewhere.

Perhaps a little more clothing, but just as hauntingly feminine.

A knock sounded on her door, and she straightened her posture a fraction more, and practiced a graceful walk to answer it.

Samantha was on the other end. Her expression widened, her breath caught ever so slightly just before a wide, approving smile illuminated her hazel eyes. "Breathtaking, my dear. Utterly beautiful."

Grace was surprised to see a shining tear gather in the corner of Samantha's eye.

"Are you well?" Grace asked, immediately on alert.

"So well, very well. Do not concern yourself over me. I'm just so . . . thrilled and proud of you. You look every inch the lady, but Grace—" Samantha paused, took a breath, then continued. "You're a lady at heart. I know how you think; at least I understand it enough to be able to conjecture how you're feeling. You're hoping that the outside will fool people into believing you're a lady inside as well. But I'm telling you, it's already true. You are every inch who you appear to be. It's not all smoke and mirrors, or trying to fool someone . . . you truly are a gently bred, well-trained, well-spoken, graceful, and vibrant lady. Don't question yourself; it is a great disservice to who you are," Samantha finished, reaching out gently to grasp Grace's hand.

Drat. Tears prickled Grace's eyes as well, and she was sure she was about to turn blotchy and ruin the effect of the dress. But Samantha's words, they were everything she needed to hear.

Everything she was already thinking.

And for her, Lady Samantha, daughter of the Duke of Chatterwood, a true lady of birth, character, and title, to say that she was one as well . . . it meant the world.

Especially since she had been the one to add the much needed polish to Grace's life.

"Thank you." It seemed so wretchedly insufficient a phrase, but it was all she could say. Words were simply not enough.

"It has been my pleasure. And we aren't finished yet. This is simply the next step, and you're ready."

Grace took in a deep breath. "I am."

"Then let us go, and show London all they are missing by not having made your acquaintance." Samantha gave a quick squeeze to Grace's hand and stepped back into the hall.

"Yes. They are missing so much," Grace replied with a little sarcasm, earning a mock glare from Samantha.

They traveled down the hall, down the stairs, and to the foyer, where the viscount waited for them. He was dressed in his evening kit, cutting a fine figure. He grinned at his wife, then kissed her hand when she reached him.

Turning his attention to Grace, he gave an approving smile. "You are going to be the name on everyone's lips tomorrow. Mark my words."

"Let's hope for a good reason, rather than a poor one," Grace added with a smile.

"Never fear. You've already won the battle. I can see it in your eyes. You know who you are, Grace. And the battle that is most fierce is always the battle within ourselves." The viscount gave her a sharp gaze, then turned to the door.

In short work they were driving down Mayfair toward the Drummel estate. Samantha had explained that Lord Drummel was an earl from a very old and established peerage. His family had retained the title for over three hundred years, and as such, they were very respected. The very elite of the ton would be in attendance, and only very select ladies would make their début at such an event.

No pressure.

Grace tugged on her gloves a little more tightly, and closed her eyes, focusing on her breathing, her heartbeat. In what seemed like too short a time, the carriage slowed, then stopped. Grace glanced out the window, watching as several carriages waited before them, making a line of waiting gentry to enter the party.

At least that meant she had a few moments to herself to mentally prepare herself.

Not that she hadn't been doing that all along. But now that the moment was closer, there was a slight edge of panic in her throat that she kept trying to swallow away.

"Breathe, dear." Samantha reached over and grasped her hand.

"Trying." Grace gave a tight smile.

"The worst you imagine is always worse than what will be," the viscount replied.

Oddly enough, that was quite helpful. The panic slowly eased away, and she didn't feel the need to breathe quite so shallowly. Their carriage pulled forward, and soon the door was opened by one of the Drummels' footmen.

As she waited for her turn to exit, she whispered a quick prayer, then put on a smile as the footman offered his hand in assistance.

Don't trip.

She put one foot down on the step, then set her other foot on the terra firma. When her other foot hit the gravel, she whispered a prayer of thanks. It shouldn't be so important, but falling from the carriage *had* happened before, and this was the last place on earth she wished to repeat such an event.

People would surely be talking about *that* in the morning.

"Come," Samantha whispered softly as they started toward the marble steps. Wide pillars framed the entrance, reminding her of the Grecian ruins she'd seen in a history book. The white marble was glistening, polished to a mirrorlike finish. Torches were lit beside the entrance to assist with illuminating the area, and the sound of music floated out past the door. Gentlemen and ladies all politely waited to go in and be announced. As the time came for their party to enter, she saw the viscount whisper their names to be announced.

She held her breath, walked behind Samantha, and then heard, "Lord and Lady Kilpatrick and Miss Grace Morgan."

The viscount continued on, taking the stairs down to a foyer that opened to a wide ballroom just to the left.

Nothing significant happened.

No one seemed to bat an eyelash.

It was oddly disappointing and yet relief flooded her.

She wasn't quite sure what she expected to happen. Maybe a glance, two perhaps. In her nightmares the whole ball would go silent and stare while crickets chirped in the background. She knew that wasn't going to happen, but she did expect . . . well . . . something.

But nothing was better than something bad, she figured.

She gave a mental shrug and then focused on the stairs. Of course there would be stairs. Biting her lip ever so slightly, she navigated one step after another, thankful that her slippers weren't overly prone to sliding. At the last stair, she breathed a sigh of relief and lifted her gaze to follow the viscount and Samantha. A few steps ahead, she picked up her pace to catch up, and nearly tripped on her hem, but righted the problem quickly before anyone was the wiser.

Or so she hoped.

Breathing deeply through her nose, she lifted her head high, and while her inclination was to smile wide and brave, she knew that she would be expected to remain impassive and neutral in expression. Schooling her features, she walked behind her guardians and into the ballroom, eyes wide. The sweet music of the string quartet added the perfect background to the wonder of the scene before her.

English lavender dusted the tables, the scent rising from vases on each table. White linen tablecloths accented the light purple buds and the fragrance was heavenly, immediately soothing and familiar. Grace couldn't stop the smile that tipped her lips from their carefully neutral position. Footmen in silver and navy livery offered orgeat and Madeira on silver platters, and the whole room moved as if alive. The dancers were their own accent to the kaleidoscope of color and movement, and for the first time in all her memory, Grace actually wanted to dance. Usually dancing was just a way to advertise her inability to perform the correct steps at the correct time.

Especially the waltz. Good Lord, she hated that dance.

But the way the people moved, their flowing steps, their turns and steps were lovely, engaging, and she wanted to be a part—even if she were to be the less graceful addition.

"You're doing perfectly." Samantha turned and whispered the encouraging words over her shoulder, just loud enough for Grace to hear.

After smiling in response, she continued studying

the room. The viscount shook the hand of some older gentleman. When she heard her name, she snapped her attention back to the viscount.

"And this, Lord Drummel, is my ward, Miss Grace Morgan."

This was her cue, and Grace bent into a practiced curtsey, offering a warm smile to their host. "A pleasure."

Lord Drummel was a full head shorter than the viscount, and far more well fed, but his features were kind, as was his smile. "The pleasure is all mine, Miss Morgan. Is this your first time in London?"

Grace nodded, holding her tongue, remembering that it was always wiser to keep her peace rather than prattle on.

"I see, and how do you like it?" he asked, his salt and pepper eyebrows arching in question.

She was saved having to answer by the arrival of a woman with regal stature. Nearly taller than Lord Drummel, she was as lean as he was well fed.

"Ah, Miss Morgan, allow me to introduce my wife, Lady Drummel."

Grace executed her curtsey once more, taking extra care to perform the action perfectly. Something told her that Lady Drummel would notice a misstep faster than a hawk would see a mouse in a field.

"An honor, Lady Drummel," Grace spoke softly.

"Miss Morgan." She nodded, then turned to the viscount. "And Lord and Lady Kilpatrick. We were thrilled to receive your acceptance of our invitation."

Her eyes were sharp and shrewd as she gave a quick study of Samantha, then dismissed whatever she was looking for as if not present.

Not that any part of that made sense. Grace made a mental note to ask Samantha later.

"It was our pleasure to attend, Lady Drummel," Samantha replied, all sweetness and light, but Grace noted the slight tightening around her eyes.

They made small talk for a few moments longer before moving on and allowing their host and hostess to greet other guests. As they moved from earshot, Grace saw the way the viscount protectively placed his arm around Samantha's waist.

Maybe, Grace thought, she wasn't the only one under scrutiny. And perhaps they weren't as unnoticed as she thought.

Maybe the ton were simply better at appearing disinterested when they were just the opposite.

The music ended, the dancers disappeared, and then the music restarted in the Scottish reel. Couples lined up to perform the dance, and Grace scanned their faces, knowing it was vain, but searching for something, someone familiar.

"Ah, just in time." The viscount gave a quick smile and strode forward.

Immediately Grace recognized the gentleman as Lord Sterling, but what caught her attention was the way the ton behind him followed him with their eyes.

Good Lord, is *that* how they did it? Wait till you turned your back and then stare? She gave a quick glance behind herself, just to check.

When it proved fruitless, she turned back to watch the approach and attention gained by Lord Sterling. Women scanned him from head to toe, while gentlemen tugged on their shirtsleeves and stood a little straighter.

In that moment, she decided she would never, not in a hundred million years, understand the way London Society worked.

Nor did she wish to.

"You made it." The viscount shook Lord Sterling's hand in greeting.

"I wasn't particularly given a choice," he remarked.

Grace wondered what *that* meant.

"You didn't want one. You like being bossed around."

"I live for your guidance," Lord Sterling replied dryly, then turned to Lady Kilpatrick. "A pleasure, my lady."

"So happy to see you, Lord Sterling. I trust you are well?" Samantha replied

"As well as can be expected in a crowded London ballroom with eyes boring into your back," he replied, not too quietly either.

So he knew about the staring. Interesting.

And Grace found it rather odd that he was willing to be so loud about his displeasure when the viscount said he was so concerned with propriety.

Just another mystery.

Oh well, it kept the evening interesting.

"And how are you faring, Miss Morgan?"

What she wanted to say was, *as well as can be expected in a London ballroom with eyes boring into your back.* But what she said was, "Far better than I was fearing."

He nodded, a grin tipped his lips and his gaze lingered a little longer on her face than it had last night, but he turned his attention back to the viscount before she could read much into his expression.

But there was something she'd never seen before in a man's gaze, at least while looking at her.

It was something dangerously akin to appreciation.

And it made her feel beautiful.

And for once in her life, she actually believed that it might be true.

Chapter Six

Ramsey resisted the urge to crack his knuckles as the quadrille began. Even though just a spectator, he watched each step carefully as if performing it himself.

He was on edge, restless and practically itching. Something bad was going to happen, he could feel it in his bones.

And damn it all, he had the sickening suspicion it was going to all center on Miss Grace Morgan.

He'd almost choked when he first saw her. In a word, she was transformed. He'd already noticed her beauty the night he'd first met her, but he was more distracted by her frank and fresh manner than her appearance.

Not so this evening.

If anything, it was the complete opposite.

Which didn't settle well. He didn't have time for women, or at least women of gentle breeding. He took a tumble now and then with one of the more discerning demimonde, but that was a business transaction, calculated and without attachments.

As soon as interest, affection, and emotions started coming into play, women became as distracting and disastrous as a hurricane in the Caribbean.

But his understanding of the trouble women caused didn't stop him from appreciating the view of Miss Grace. Once Heathcliff had begun the introductions, gentlemen had lined up to meet the fresh face of the ton. It hadn't taken more than a quarter hour for her dance card to be utterly filled. Even now as she lined up for the quadrille, he wondered if she were already speculating on who her suitors would be.

Women always did; it was in their nature to hedge their bets.

While men did it in the gentlemen clubs, women did it in the ballroom.

A wink here, a look over there—they were all methods of placing bets on different games, all hedging the prospect of gaining a husband, the wealthier the better.

It made him of the persuasion that gentlemen's gambling was nobler than the games played by the women. At least at the faro table, you always knew what you were betting and the rules of said game.

Yet even as he considered the moral aspects of it all, his eyes never left the form of Miss Grace. He bit back a smile as she nearly stepped on another gentleman's toes while turning a little too quickly. It was ironic for her to boast a namesake that didn't apply to her in any sort of fashion. It was clear that she wasn't graceful, and rather than find it offensive, he rather liked it. It added to her character.

Not that it was important to approve of her.

It was of no consequence.

He turned his attention to the ballroom, studying those in attendance. The party was well attended, with most of the more elite ton assembled in the stuffy ballroom. He resisted the urge to tug on his cravat, and glanced longingly toward a hall that ended in a path that led toward a small garden. He remembered that garden from a party nearly two years ago.

The garden kept its secrets well.

He could easily quit the party and head to Temptations, or even Whites. But he felt somewhat obligated to attend, loyalty to Heathcliff and all that. Bloody inconvenient.

The music for the quadrille ended and Ramsey turned back to watch the dancers abandon the center of the room. It wasn't hard to spot Miss Grace; with her bright red hair, she would be impossible to miss. Lord Mackey escorted her to the edge of the ballroom, depositing her back at Heathcliff's side without incident.

Ramsey frowned. Perhaps he was overreacting.

Then again, the night *was* young.

Damn it, he was going to be there for a while.

As the music started up for a Scottish reel, Ramsey watched as another gentleman collected Miss Grace for his reserved dance.

Good Lord, this is what people did all night, and on purpose. He couldn't imagine anything duller.

Seeking distraction, he noted a lady with a tall feather in her turban. She walked by him, catching his eye. There was a provocative sway to her hips and a welcoming smile on her lips that was a tempting diversion. He dipped his head, acknowledging her. When she smiled, he returned the gesture, only to have a gentleman come up beside her and gesture for her to precede him in the crowd.

Married.

That was a scandal and disaster waiting to happen. Hell, it could even end in a duel, something in which he had no inclination to participate.

Ramsey took a mental step back and turned instead to the dance floor.

So far Miss Morgan hadn't harmed anyone in this dance, and he was oddly growing hopeful that she'd make it through the song without incident.

Such had become his life.

He needed some air, and he'd only been at the ball for an hour.

Twisting his lips, he glanced back at the hall and made the decision to head that direction.

As the music ended, he made his way toward the hall and the promise of some fresher air found in the garden beyond.

The stars were visible from the stone patio, and he took a deep breath of the recently rain-soaked air. Various couples were milling about, some laughing loudly, others speaking softly, all self-involved and ignoring him, just as he liked it.

The music from the ballroom carried into the evening, and he found it soothing to his tight nerves. When the next song ended, he sighed, spun on his heel and headed back to the ballroom. Just as he was halfway down the hall, he heard the unmistakable sound of shattering crystal.

His blood froze, the sound echoing in his memory like a ricocheting bullet.

The sound reminded him of his father hurling the crystal port decanter at the wall.

The shattered fragments were a symbol of what his

life had become when he broke the news that fateful day.

Divorced.

Betrayed.

No heir.

Scandal.

Ramsey took a deep breath and pulled himself into the present, shaking his head to dispel the haunting memories. Striding forward, he tried to leave his thoughts behind him just as another sobering thought hit him.

Miss Grace. Bloody hell, *tell me it wasn't something she did*.

Why did he have the sneaking suspicion that she was at the heart of whatever just broke in the ballroom? The buzzing of people's words filtered through the hall like a beehive, and he could have sworn her name was on the breeze.

As he got to the edge of the ballroom, the sea of people parted just enough for him to get a quick glance at the activity that had caused all the fuss.

Miss Morgan was desperately trying to assist. Good Lord, was that Lady Downing? Damn it all to hell. This was going to be horrific. Ramsey searched desperately for Heathcliff and Lady Kilpatrick.

Samantha was pushing through the crowd, rather brazenly in fact, and was soon standing beside Miss Grace, helping Lady Downing right herself. Once the dowager was again seated, Lady Kilpatrick and Miss Grace handed several handkerchiefs to the woman, only to have a footman appear with more napkins to assist, while another footman bent to collect the scattered crystal.

Miss Morgan glanced up.

Pale skin was quickly turning a bright red of humiliation as she cast her eyes down in what was a classic expression of self-recrimination.

That was when the scolding started.

"Good Lord, girl. Why try to kill me? It won't get you noticed, I guarantee that! And where are your manners? What in heaven's name is the matter with you? Didn't you ever learn to walk slowly? And for Pete's sake, watch where you are going!" Lady Downing glared, her rheumy eyes boring through Miss Grace.

Ramsey gave a slight shiver.

He'd happily face down any loan shark over an offended dowager any day.

A loan shark can be bought.

A disgruntled dowager's wrath was as cold as a glacier, and just as severe.

Bloody hell, where the devil was Heathcliff?

The bastard was just arriving on the hellish scene. But Ramsey was quite certain that even Heathcliff's legendary charm was going to have a worthy foe in the face of Lady Downing's wrath.

If it weren't so damning to Miss Grace, the whole episode would have been diverting to watch.

But because of his loyalty, he thought it in bad form to reap any entertainment value from the situation.

Heathcliff began speaking to Lady Downing, his smile striking her with full force.

The old sour-faced woman actually gave a small smile in return.

This, this was why Heathcliff handled the disgruntled gamblers. He could charm the scales off a snake and then sell them back to it, for profit.

It was simply a stroke of some sort of benevolent

God that Heathcliff had a small semblance of moral compass; God save them all if he didn't.

Lady Kilpatrick slowly eased Miss Grace from the center of attention, after she'd, again, offered her apologies to the dowager. As they left the disaster zone, the spectating crowd parted for them, like Biblical Red Sea.

That, Ramsey decided, was not good.

He could almost hear the thoughts of the people watching their exodus.

Fool.

Don't touch them.

Serves her right.

Untouchable . . .

Hadn't he said that something was going to happen? He hated being right. Ramsey glanced back to Heathcliff, and seeing that he had the situation well in hand, Ramsey disappeared back into the crowd.

There was no further need for his presence and he started to head toward the exit, when he saw Lady Kilpatrick walk back into the ballroom, Miss Grace following close behind as they skirted the edge of the room. As Lady Kilpatrick continued, Ramsey noted that Miss Grace lagged further and further behind. The music had continued, the dancers were once again swirling about, but even with all the other distractions, he swore he could hear her thoughts.

They're right.

I don't belong.

What was I thinking?

Unworthy.

Maybe it was because he had spoken those words to himself for so long, believing them and owning them, that he understood the expression on her face. Maybe it was because somehow they were kindred souls.

Regardless, it compelled his feet to move, and before he could consider his actions, he found her at the edge of the ballroom, arms wrapped round her body as if protecting it.

"Come." He spoke softly, and didn't wait for a reply. Without a backward glance, he walked along the edge of the room, then paused in an alcove.

She wasn't far behind, and when she stepped into the alcove with him, he strategically situated them so that those looking into the alcove would see him, not her.

Propriety would be met, but she would be shielded. It was the least he could do.

"Don't." It was a single word, but it carried a wealth of meaning.

Miss Grace blinked, tipping her head just a fraction of an inch. "Pardon?"

He shook his head slightly. "Don't. I know what you are thinking, and it's wrong."

A bit of the spark he'd seen earlier flared to life in her eyes, and it pleased him. "I wasn't aware you were a mind reader."

"I'm not, but I am quite intuitive on certain things, and this is one of them. You're thinking you don't belong, that you knew you'd do something stupid like this, and that you are disappointing Heath—Viscount and Lady Kilpatrick." He finished, lifting his chin, daring her to contradict him.

Her defiant gaze flickered to the ground and he noted the way her jaw clenched. There was a slight sigh before she raised her gaze to his. "Am I wrong to think those things?"

He mentally applauded her willingness to be honest. "Yes. While it was unfortunate for you to . . . do whatever you did. I rather missed the whole mess, but only *you* can let it define you, Miss Grace. And I, for one . . ." He took a step closer to her. "Rather thought you stronger than that."

He issued the challenge, offering the opportunity to rise to the occasion rather than offer sympathy.

Sympathy was for fools, for those too weak to accept the challenge of rising above. And he was quite certain that Miss Grace needed the gauntlet thrown, rather than a soft word and kind pat.

Like a pet Yorkie.

Ramsey gave a slight shiver at the thought.

"I just made a cake of myself," she retorted with enough heat to warn him, but not loudly enough to draw attention.

"I know."

"And yet, you want me to waltz right out there—"

"I wouldn't waltz if I were you; *that* might draw attention. Most people simply walk, but . . ." He hitched a shoulder.

She glared, clearly not appreciating his attempt at humor.

Ladies were so irritatingly literal when they were angry. Annoying, that.

"Well, what are you going to do? Hide? Let them win? Cower? I guarantee that is exactly what they think you should do, and then they will whisper behind your back, and then to your face."

"They'll whisper regardless." Miss Grace shrugged, giving a very unladylike eye roll to punctuate her statement.

Even if it was unladylike, Ramsey had to agree with

the gesture. London elite had earned many an eye roll from him as well. "Yes, but the question is . . ." He took a step forward, met her gaze with a frank one of his own, and continued. "What do you want them to whisper about? How you ran, or how you had the bravery to rise above?"

Her green eyes sparkled, then kindled with what looked suspiciously like courage, but then she glanced down to the floor, hiding his view of her expression.

The first measures of the waltz started playing, and Ramsey turned to the ballroom, watching the dancers start to assemble in the middle of the floor.

Before he could second-guess his instincts, he held his hand out.

Miss Grace glanced from his hand, to his eyes, then back, her brows arching in a question.

"Or was I wrong? Are you not brave enough?" he challenged.

It wasn't a second later than her hand was firmly placed on his arm, following him from the alcove into the room.

As they stood in the frame of the waltz and began to melt into the other swirling dancers, it was only then that Ramsey realized that he had given the London Ton something entirely different to whisper about.

Himself.

Chapter Seven

"It could have gone much worse."

Grace sighed as she picked at her piece of toast on her white china plate. Normally more than happy to break her fast and enjoy whatever cook prepared for the morning meal, this morning she wasn't as inclined as usual.

Samantha's comment didn't exactly help, either.

"Yes, it could have been worse. I could have permanently injured Lady . . . whatever her name was," Grace replied, giving up her pretense at eating and instead lifting her teacup.

"I assure you there was no permanent damage."

"No, not to her at least, just my reputation." Grace sighed dramatically and took a long sip of tea.

"Lady Downing."

Grace lowered the teacup. "Pardon?"

"Lady Downing, that's the lady you, er, upset."

Grace set down her teacup. "Of course you'd be able to find a way to say it in such a delicate manner;

upset." Grace snorted, earning a glare from her former governess. "Pardon, but I did more than merely upset her."

Samantha cleared her throat delicately. "Well, it is of no consequence. No one will even remember that now. We need to thank Lord Sterling for that." Samantha lifted her teacup and shrugged a shoulder delicately.

Grace frowned. "Why? Not that I'm against thanking him, I'm just failing to understand what part he played."

Samantha lowered the teacup, then glanced to Grace with a questioning expression in her hazel eyes. "My dear, Lord Sterling doesn't dance with women."

Grace blinked, then tipped her head in confusion. She'd heard about men like that, and she was quite certain she met a few of them in India, but . . . "Oh, I had no idea. I suppose I wouldn't though." She blushed and glanced down. "I suppose many women in London are disappointed with his . . . alternative choices."

When Samantha didn't readily answer, Grace glanced up in confusion.

"Alternative choices?" Samantha blinked, then her eyes widened. "Good Lord, I didn't mean that." She set her napkin down, even though she'd just picked it up. "How do you even *know* about that . . ." Then she held up her hand. "Never mind, I don't need to hear." Samantha shook her head. "No, it's not that. It's that Lord Sterling doesn't dance with anyone. He's quite the confirmed bachelor and I'd be willing to guess that the last person he danced with was his wife."

It was Grace's turn to be surprised, and she nearly choked on the tea she'd just sipped.

"He's married?" She lifted her napkin and patted her lips, trying to process the information and think back to the conversations. Never once had he mentioned, or anyone else mentioned, his wife.

"Was, dear. *Was*." Samantha clarified. "It was a long time ago. She's passed since then, but it was quite an upset and scandal about six years ago. I wasn't even out in society and *I* knew about it." Samantha's gaze widened, and she shook her head slowly, as if mourning for whatever he'd endured.

"Oh. What was the scandal?" Grace asked, leaning forward expectantly. Absentmindedly, she picked at her toast and popped a corner into her mouth.

"Well, it's quite the long story, but it was one of the few cases of divorce I've ever actually known to take place. Most of the time, in the ton, if there is . . . unfaithfulness . . . in a marriage, it's kept secretive. But this . . . this kind of unfaithfulness was impossible to keep in the dark."

Grace leaned forward, eagerly anticipating the story. "Well?"

Samantha took a deep breath. "Lord Sterling met Rebecca Standson in her first season. I never saw her myself, but she was known as a great beauty. She was nearly an incomparable of the season that year. A lady of gentle breeding, very fine manners, and tolerable fortune, she was a very respectable prospect—which was the most enticing factor for Lord Sterling. Heathcl—Viscount Kilpatrick—has said much about his friend, but the most defining character trait used to describe Lord Sterling is the great weight he places on propriety and respectability." She nodded her head for emphasis.

"Yes, I've heard that," Grace agreed.

"So, it takes no great intelligence to see that a man searching for a respectable wife would find Miss Standson a very promising prospect."

"It would make sense," Grace agreed. "So, he offered, she accepted, and they were married."

"Yes." Samantha concurred.

"And then she was a strumpet?" Grace leaned back in her chair, crossing her arms in disapproval.

"No. Not in that way," Samantha answered.

Grace's brow furrowed. "*He* was a rogue?" That she hadn't expected. For someone so bent on propriety, it didn't follow that he'd be willing to risk his reputation by adultery.

"No. It's something quite different. I've never heard of it happening before, or since." Samantha whispered softly, but the intensity of her tone captivated Grace's attention.

"What happened?" Grace asked eagerly, leaning forward once more.

"Miss Rebecca Standson was actually Mrs. Nixwell." Samantha arched a brow.

Grace blinked. "I'm . . . confused. She wasn't who she said she was?"

Samantha lifted her teacup and took a sip, irritating Grace with the pause it created. "You're missing the first part. *Mrs.*"

"She wasn't widowed . . . Dear Lord. She was married?" Grace gasped in horror.

"Yes. Yes, she was."

"So she was married . . . twice? Goodness, how does such a thing occur without someone being the wiser?" Grace made a gesture with her hand and frowned in confusion.

"As the story goes, the winter before, she had run off with a gentleman of little means and low reputation to Gretna Green. Her father was determined to wash the whole business under the bridge, and paid off a rather corrupt local magistrate, and, as luck would have it, the gentleman she'd run off to marry was wanted for debtor's prison. He was locked up, which kept him silent on the true events. A few months later, the father, Lord Standson, presented his daughter at the London season with no one the wiser."

"It's like reading a gothic novel," Grace replied breathlessly. "What an arrogant attitude for the father to attempt such a thing."

"Very true. And it might have worked . . . but for two important people."

"The husband, no doubt. But who is the other?"

Samantha's lips bent into a sad smile, and Grace had the suspicion that the rest of the story was far sadder than the beginning. "The child."

"Dear God," Grace whispered with feeling.

Samantha gave a slow nod. "Miss Standson concealed the truth even from her father, and only after she had married Lord Sterling did the truth start to unravel. He might have been able to recover from a byblow, but when her first husband came to London . . ." Samantha gave her head a slow shake to emphasize her point.

"The scandal would be horrendous."

"It was. Lord Sterling attempted to set things right as quickly and quietly as possible, but his efforts weren't helped by the other parties involved. The first husband made his side of the story known, the father was implicated in concealing the truth, and then Miss Rebecca and the child she carried were known."

"Lord Sterling must have nearly died from mortification," Grace replied, blinkingly.

"I would imagine so. My husband says he has never quite recovered. There was some considerable fallout between him and his father after the situation was known, but I do not know the truth of it. Since then, Lord Sterling hasn't danced with anyone else . . . save you." Samantha punctuated her point by setting her cup down.

"It would seem that I owe him quite a debt of gratitude, then," Grace whispered. "It was truly a selfless act for him to take pity upon me."

"It was, my dear."

"What are we talking in whispered tones? Do I dare ask?" The viscount strode into the breakfast room, bending to place a quick kiss on Samantha's cheek.

"We were just—"

"Discussing last night—" Samantha interrupted Grace's statement, giving a quick shushing glance to her.

The viscount turned to Grace, his expression one of deep reflection. "It could have been worse."

"Good Lord, not you too." Grace slouched in her chair.

"What?" He replied, then walked to the side table to fill his plate. "How could such a statement cause offense?"

"Because it is exactly the same statement I said not a quarter hour earlier, my dear," Samantha replied, hiding a grin and attempting to suppress a giggle.

"Oh, I'm pleased we are of one mind, my love. That bodes well for us."

"Though I dare not expect it to happen always," Samantha replied saucily.

"Minx," he teased in return.

"I do believe that is my cue to leave," Grace replied, standing from the table. "If we're to attend Almack's today, then I best practice holding my peace, my curtsey, and all the other things I'm so very ill at performing." She rolled her eyes.

Samantha gave her a scolding look, but it was softened with a smile. "You'll do just fine."

Grace was just passing through the door when she turned slightly to reply. "As you said, it could be worse. I may achieve that today. We shall see." Grace grinned and walked away.

In spite of the fact that there was a serious amount of truth in the statement, she rather felt lighter. Because it could always be worse.

She could have Lord Sterling's past.

That was most certainly worse.

Chapter Eight

Ramsey added the figures once more, then set his pen down on the desk with a slight click. After checking his fingers for ink stains, he rubbed a hand down his face, all the while damning his friend Heathcliff to the seventh circle of hell.

Or lower, if that were an option.

What had started as a usual evening in Temptations had turned into a nightmare.

At least, *his* version of a nightmare. It started as a few whispers that carried his name.

The result was several bets placed in the betting book with his name in permanent ink.

All because of his damned oversensitive sense of responsibility to Heathcliff and his bloody, irritating, and clumsy ward.

If he hadn't attended the ball, then he wouldn't have witnessed the disaster that Miss Grace Morgan created. And if he didn't witness the scene, then he wouldn't have felt pity for the poor creature. And if he hadn't felt pity, then he wouldn't have marched over there and spoken with her and he bloody wouldn't have offered to dance.

A waltz no less.

It was as injuring to his toes as it was to his reputation.

Which, clearly, was in tatters. Again. As if he needed help in that department. Though, this time around the whispers were of lesser damage than before with that whole sordid mess with Rebecca. Dear Lord, now *that* was a disaster of traumatic proportions.

But, as it were, he was once again the object of scrutiny, suspicion, and whisperings, which he utterly hated to the core of his being. All because he attended the ball and bloody danced.

He glanced back to the betting book, reading the wagers. His eyes grew unfocused as he read through the five wagers placed on whether he, Ramsey Scott, Marquess of Sterling, would marry the mysterious and quite accident-prone chit.

Five. It might not seem like many, but it was five more than he wanted, that was for sure. And if there were five last night, then there would certainly be more tomorrow, and the next day, and so forth and so on until the girl married someone else.

The only upside was that Temptations would turn a tidy profit from all the losers of the betting pool.

Though that wasn't much of a silver lining in his opinion.

He slammed the book shut, then stood from his desk. The chair made a scraping noise on the floor as he abruptly scooted it back. He paced the floor, his gaze flickering back to the betting book, and then forward. What was he to do? Truly there was nothing he *could* do except wait it out.

Damn.

And he blamed Heathcliff. If he hadn't requested his help, if he didn't have some misbegotten sense of loyalty—he started all over, grumbling. But even as he held the grudge against his friend, he knew that the next ball would find him in attendance and he would once again take vigil over Heathcliff's ward. He wasn't sure why his loyalty was so excruciatingly demanding, but it was, and it wasn't about to change.

Damn the consequences.

The night was over, and to confirm it, he pulled out his pocket watch while suppressing a yawn. Yes, it was after dawn and as such, his optimum time for catching whatever sleep he could attain.

After giving one last glare to the betting book, he quit his office, locked the bolt, and strode from the hall into the foyer of the Barrots' residence, also the location of Temptations. With a determined stride, he took the back exit and, in no less than five minutes, was riding his gelding home.

However, even though he was soon comfortably situated in his rooms there was no rest to be found. He should be exhausted, he should be falling asleep the moment his head hit the pillow. Yet he was not; rather he was tossing, turning, and sticking one foot from under the bedclothes in an effort to keep from being too hot, only to discover that the single foot outside the bedclothes made him entirely too cold.

Blast it all.

And to top it off, his bloody mind wouldn't stop spinning. He considered a snifter of brandy, but decided against it. He was too tired to actually rise from bed and get it. He was too tired to sleep; that *had* to be it. It didn't happen often, but when it did, it was hell.

He should have expected the day would simply continue to be as wretched as the night had been.

No rest for the wicked and all.

At some point in the early afternoon, he opened his eyes, thankful to have fallen asleep for at least a few hours, though, it was the kind of sleep that made one imagine they were only thinking of sleeping, rather than actually falling under the spell of unconsciousness.

Whatever the case, he'd take it, and with a sigh, he rose from bed and rang for his valet.

In short work he was dressed for the day, or rather the afternoon, and he quit his room in search of some sustenance. It was his custom to take tea once he woke up; it was usually that time of the day anyway, and he found the tea service awaiting his leisure in the breakfast room. Beside the teapot was a plate of biscuits, and an assortment of sandwiches. He lifted one from the plate and took a bite as his eyes scanned for the correspondence that would be waiting for his attention. He took another bite of the cucumber sandwich, set it to the side, and then lifted a small stack of thick envelopes—invitations, no doubt.

He smirked. It had been quite some time since he'd received so many invitations. Usually he avoided the London social sphere like the plague, and only when absolutely necessary would he darken the door of a ballroom. If he needed an invitation, he simply hinted at it while at Temptations, and the invitation would appear the next day. It was quite simple really.

But overnight, that had all changed.

Which only meant one thing.

The matchmaking mamas of the ton thought he was in search of a wife.

Another wife.

Good Lord.

The day had gone from wretched to bloody horrific.

He could practically feel their assessing stares boring into his back. He glanced about the vacant room, then shuddered. It was his exact description of hell, to have those women circle him like vultures.

Well, he'd have to put a stop to that notion right quick.

But he wasn't exactly sure how to do such a thing.

Denial wouldn't work.

And if he showed any favor to any lady, Miss Grace included, it would only make matters worse.

He could, however, escape to Scotland . . . or India. Though even *that* didn't seem far enough.

And he wasn't keen on the idea of traveling just now, not with the silver masquerade approaching at the end of the season. There was much to do to prepare Temptations for the exclusive event. Certainly not the time to be gallivanting about the continent.

He gave a mental glare to Lucas, who was still gallivanting.

Ramsey had a stronger sense of responsibility. He always had.

Even when it cost him everything.

Duty and honor coming first in all things. It was how he was raised, how he was indoctrinated. And it felt as if he were constantly making amends for all the ways he had failed to live up to his father's expectations of those virtues.

Even with his father deceased these five years, Ramsey had never been able to release the need to achieve his father's impossible standards. It was a drive, it was a necessity, it was also . . . impossible. Yet that hadn't stopped him, and he didn't see how he'd stop any time soon. Pity, but the truth.

He could never restore the lost honor to name or title, but he'd be damned if he didn't at least try.

Never once had he ever considered that it wasn't a worthwhile endeavor. It simply was a necessity, like breathing. And since he must breathe, he must also strive.

He tossed the envelopes to the side of the table and served himself tea in the beloved silence of the breakfast room. The light was anemic as it filtered through the windows, signaling a certain rain in the near future. He sipped his tea, ignored the missives, and rather chose to think of . . . nothing at all.

But his mind resisted such a vacation from exertion and soon his eyes flickered back to the invitations. He wondered which event would be selected by Heathcliff to attend that evening. After considering the options, he rather believed it would be none of the above.

It was Wednesday, after all. The proper thing to do would be attend Almack's.

Good Lord, he could think of a million things he'd rather do than darken that door.

Leeches, a toothache, hell, a broken carriage wheel in the middle of nowhere, all sounded blissful in contrast to the prospect of the society present at Almack's.

But it was likely going to be a necessary evil, and, as his honor would demand, he would likely call on Heathcliff and ascertain their plans and do his best to assist.

More often than not, he rather hated his sense of honor, and the situations it created.

But to deny it would be like denying a part of him-self—impossible.

So it was with a reluctant heart that he finished his tea and the small meal accompanying it, and then ordered his carriage readied.

Sometimes the best way to deal with unsavory circumstances was simply to get them over with, and that was certainly the approach he decided to use today. With any luck, he would find Heathcliff planning to attend Almack's on the earlier side of the evening, and as such, Ramsey would be able to vacate the premises with alacrity, having the rest of the evening open for other orders of business.

But of course, hope, which sprang eternal, was not as eternally promised to bring about the desired outcome.

Chapter Nine

Grace studied the building before her as she cautiously stepped from the carriage. The building didn't appear as formidable as the occasion seemed to call for, but she hadn't exactly darkened the door as of yet. Almack's was supposedly such a rite of passage into the London marriage mart, but she couldn't see what all the fuss was about. It was a stone building, like much of the other buildings of London, but, also like much of London, the worth was not based on the building as much as the people inhabiting it.

Samantha followed her out of the carriage and gave her an encouraging smile. "You'll be wonderful. I'm not particularly familiar to Lady Jersey, so I requested for my sister to contact a dear friend of hers, Lady Grace. You shall not forget her name since you share it, I dare say. She is married to the Earl of Greywick. He recently inherited the title upon his father's death. Wretched man, but a delightful son. It goes to show that a child always has the choice to rise above the character of the parents," Samantha said with a firm nod. "And Lord Greywick is certainly of that variety."

Grace smiled. "Thank you for securing the introduction."

"Of course. It was easily done." Samantha gave a slight flick of her fingers and then led the way into the building.

Grace followed, the music greeting her ears before she was even fully through the door. Samantha graciously nodded to the ladies who were in the hall, calling a few by name before she and Grace entered what was certainly the main ballroom.

The first thing Grace noted was the humidity. Certainly someone could open a door or window? It was stifling, but there seemed to be no relief in sight. She had noted that it was a warmer day than usual, but this still seemed unexpected.

"Over there, that is Lady Jersey." Samantha flickered her eyes in the direction of several dowagers sitting in chairs, almost as if they were holding court in the corner of the ballroom. "We shall introduce you after a few minutes. I see Lady Greywick, and that is the first introduction we must make."

Grace glanced in the other direction to observe the other lady in question. She was tall and elegant, her dark eyes and hair a lovely complement to her light yellow gown. As if noting their regard, she turned and met Samantha's smile with one of her own. After making her excuses to her conversation partners, she began to cross the ballroom to meet them.

As she approached, Grace swallowed her slight apprehension and waited to be formally introduced.

"Lady Greywick, it is a pleasure to see you again."

"Ah, dear Samantha." Lady Greywick held out her gloved hand to squeeze Samantha's affectionately. "And how is your sister?" Lady Greywick's eyes danced with delight upon mentioning her.

"Quite well, as I'm sure you can imagine." Samantha's smile was broad, unreserved and delighted as she spoke of her sister. "And you appear to be very happily situated yourself."

"I am, indeed. All due to your sister and that charming husband of hers," Lady Greywick murmured softly.

Grace's gaze flickered back to Samantha; that would be a story she wanted to hear later.

"Allow me to introduce Miss Iris Grace Morgan, who also goes by Miss Grace." Samantha made a small sweeping gesture to Grace, and she took the cue to dip in a curtsey.

"A pleasure to make your acquaintance," Grace murmured softly, trying to be as ladylike as possible.

"It is very good to meet you my dear," Lady Greywick replied, her smile kind and warm.

"Thank you," Grace replied.

Lady Greywick glanced over her shoulder and noted the situation of the dowagers in the other corner. "I do believe that now is as good a time as any for introductions. If you will allow me?"

Samantha nodded, and Grace quietly gave her thanks, and their small party started to cross the ballroom along the edge, so as not to disturb the dancers.

As Grace approached, her nerves grew tight. This introduction was important, and as such, she was of course terrified she would somehow make an unpardonable faux pas, sealing her fate as a failed debutant.

"Lady Jersey, Lady Drummel, and Lady Markson, allow me to introduce Miss Grace Morgan, ward of the Viscount Kilpatrick. She is new to London this season and wished to make your acquaintance." Lady Greywick made the smooth introduction, and on cue, Grace dipped a curtsey.

"A pleasure," she murmured softly, meeting the unmoved gaze of Lady Jersey.

The dowager gave a slight nod, and the other ladies present followed suit.

"And of course, you're familiar with Lady Kilpatrick, the daughter of the Duke of Chatterwood." Lady Greywick continued with the introductions.

"Ah, yes. We're quite familiar with you, Lady Kilpatrick," Lady Jersey remarked, and Grace studied her tone and expression for a hint of distain, but found none, just plenty of curiosity.

"A pleasure." Samantha was as sweet as ever, and Grace admired her poise.

"Tell me, Miss Grace, how do you find London?" Lady Markson asked.

Grace paused. Did she answer honestly or how she thought they wanted her to answer? She chose a blend of the two options. "It has its charms, my lady."

"A diplomatic response if I've ever heard one," Lady Jersey remarked. "Do you somehow find it wanting?"

Grace felt like a rabbit stuck in a snare. If she lied, certainly they would be able to discern it; if she spoke the truth, she risked offense.

"I have only been here a short amount of time, and as such, haven't had the time to develop a firm opinion, my lady," she answered, quite pleased with how she negotiated such a minefield.

She could almost feel the relieved sigh of Samantha.

"Wisely said," Lady Markson replied. "And where are you from?"

Grace continued, "My parents traveled much, my lady. While originally from Matlock, they rarely visited their hometown. Mostly we divided our time between India, the continent, and sometimes the Caribbean."

"My, so widely traveled for one so young," Lady Jersey replied.

Grace wasn't sure how to reply, so she kept her peace.

"Well, it is good of you to make the introductions, Lady Greywick. Thank you, and we will be watching your début with some interest, Miss Grace," Lady Drummel replied, effectively dismissing the small party.

Grace relaxed the moment she gave a bobbing curtsey and turned to leave. One disaster avoided; maybe she had gotten all the trouble out of her system last night. Regardless, she was thankful to have avoided a tragedy this time.

"Now, with that all finished, you will no doubt find some relief," Lady Greywick commented as they walked toward the refreshment table.

Good Lord, all Grace wanted in the world was a cool glass of lemonade.

As she reached for one, she was disappointed to feel the glass of the cup less than cool, and as she sipped, the lemonade merely tepid versus refreshing. Well, it was at least quenching her thirst, even if it was a little sour.

"Ah, it looks as if Lord Sterling is making the

rounds. He is quite determined to assist you, my dear," Samantha whispered.

"I find that interesting." Lady Greywick commented slyly.

"His loyalty knows no bounds, or so my husband says," Samantha replied.

"Or his interest." Lady Greywick gave a wink to Grace and then made her excuses.

Grace dismissed her comment, and watched Lord Sterling's approach.

"Good day." He bowed crisply.

There was a slight shadow under his eyes that hadn't been there the night before, and she wondered what had caused such a change in his appearance.

"Good day, Lord Sterling." Grace replied, as well as Samantha.

"I trust you've already made the necessary introductions?" he asked, then glanced to Samantha for confirmation.

"Yes, Lady Greywick was happy to assist."

"Good, that was quite kind of her. She was the one you applied to for vouchers as well, I assume?" he asked.

"Yes, she was quite helpful in all areas."

He nodded, and the conversation lulled. The music started back up into a reel, and Grace glanced about the room at the various gentlemen, none of whom approached her.

After a moment's pause, Lord Sterling cleared his throat. "If you will?" He offered his hand, and Grace accepted it. But rather than lead her to the dance floor, which was what she was expecting, he led her alongside the ballroom, toward a group of gentlemen. Before they approached, he whispered quietly, "The viscount needed to address some business, so I'm to provide you with adequate introductions."

Grace was saved from a reply by their arrival in the small circle of gentlemen, whose conversation came to a grinding halt at their approach. Heat flushed her face at their inquiring expression as each bowed.

"Miss Grace, allow me to introduce you to several gentlemen of my acquaintance." Lord Sterling gestured to each man in turn, naming them, five gentlemen in all.

"A pleasure, Miss Grace." One of them, a Mr. Smythe, stepped forward. "If you will allow me the pleasure of your next dance?"

Grace readily accepted, and soon she was promised to each gentleman for a dance. Lord Sterling left her in the care of Mr. Smythe as the music began, and, as she approached the dance floor, couldn't help but admire at how quickly, easily, and efficiently he'd neatly introduced her to several eligible men.

She danced in turn with each new gentleman, and as the time came to take their leave, Samantha collected her from the arm of the last gentleman, a Lord Garton, and made their excuses. By the time they were in the carriage on their way home, Grace realized she hadn't seen Lord Sterling's departure, nor thanked him.

"That was very generous of Lord Sterling," Grace commented to Samantha as they made their way home.

Samantha gave a small grin. "Yes, but it also benefited him as well."

Grace frowned. "In what way?"

Samantha lifted a shoulder. "It would seem that last night's dance with you created a stir, much like I said it would, and my husband mentioned that Lord Sterling was anxious to put to rest the suspicions of many."

"Meaning?" Grace still was unsure as to what she referred.

"Meaning, if others saw him put you in the path of eligible men, then they would cease in suspecting his interest in you."

Grace wasn't sure why, but her spirits deflated a little at such a revelation. "Oh, well . . . then I'm pleased that I could assist with what he needed to convey. No one watching us this afternoon would suspect that there was any attachment between us."

"No. No one would," Samantha agreed. "However, that begs the question, did you find any gentlemen that could encourage an attachment?"

Grace smiled at this. "They were all very kind, and good dancers. Better dancers than I, I admit."

Samantha giggled.

"I dare say that I might have a few call on me tomorrow, but it's far too quick for me to gauge my respect or affection for any."

"Wise girl," Samantha spoke. "And I do agree, I think tomorrow will present a few callers, and that will afford time for conversation. And conversation can easily lead to attachment and interest. We, my dear, have made a very important first step."

"And I didn't manage to ruin it," Grace couldn't help but mention.

"No, you did perfectly. As I knew you would. Have more faith in yourself, my dear. Don't mistake your strengths as being weaknesses simply because others don't share them."

"I understand, but I will triumph in today."

"As you should."

"Tomorrow has enough trouble. I shall not borrow it."

Samantha gave her a beleaguered look. "So much for faith in yourself."

"One step at a time."

"That is all I can ask."

Chapter Ten

Ramsey congratulated himself on such a brilliant plan. It seemed to work quite well! In introducing Miss Grace to eligible men yesterday, the betting book had seen no increase in wagers based on his interest. And it was a commonly known truth that the betting book had a finger on the pulse of the gossip of the ton. So, as far as he was concerned, it was a swimming success story.

He had bloody well racked his brain in efforts to find a way to discourage such gossip, and the answer was so simple, he nearly overlooked it.

And as long as he continued in such a fashion, he could neatly fulfill his honor and duty as a friend by assisting Heathcliff while simultaneously not bringing his bachelor status into question.

Today was certainly an improvement over yesterday!

He added up the sums in the book, as was his habit,

and was about to quit the office when there was a sharp knock on the door.

"Come in," he called.

Heathcliff opened the door, striding into the room with ease. "I see you are in a much better mood than yesterday. Good Lord, man. One of these days you'll be wound so tight everything in you will snap." Heathcliff helped himself to a chair and lounged in it.

"Well, my personal crisis is averted."

"It wasn't a crisis," Heathcliff replied with an exasperated tone.

"For you," Ramsey replied. "How may I assist you?"

"I'm not a patron, Ramsey." Heathcliff gave a chuckle. "I was just checking on you. You seemed so out of sorts I was concerned about that snapping actually taking place."

"Your concern is heartwarming," Ramsey replied with sarcasm.

"I try," Heathcliff replied. "In all truth, though, I've come to a decision."

"Good Lord, do I want to know?"

"Yes. Since it pertains to you."

"Now I'm quite certain I don't wish to know. And who gave you leave to make decisions for me?"

Heathcliff gave a disinterested shrug. "Someone has to help you."

"And, pray tell, why do I require help?"

"Because you're . . . well . . . you."

Ramsey gave a slow clap. "Your eloquence in conversation is humbling."

"Bastard. Just listen."

"I'd rather not."

"Too bad. I'm absolving you of any assistance with

my ward. There. That is all." Heathcliff dusted his hands off as if washing his hands of the whole mess.

Ramsey blinked, then cocked his head. "Pardon?"

"You take things too far, and with far too serious a notion. She is my responsibility, and as such, I'm the one to take it upon myself to introduce her to gentlemen, and then scare them off when I find them unsuitable until the right gentleman asks for her hand."

"You sound like a right and proper father, not a guardian. I thought you wanted to marry the girl off post haste?" Ramsey leaned forward on the desk, folding his hands, curious at this change of events.

"Ideally I'd marry her off quickly and to the right man, but I'm afraid I need both of those requirements met."

"Well, I dare say you'll be able to marry her off in a season or two, as long as no more events like what happened at the Drummels' ball take place."

"It's part of her charm."

"Spoken like a blind father."

Heathcliff made a rude gesture to Ramsey, and Ramsey chuckled. "So, you don't wish for my help?"

"No. You'll just take over, and your sense of loyalty is admirable, but not necessarily . . . healthy."

"I'm offended."

"It isn't the first time."

"True, still . . . I suppose I should thank you," Ramsey replied, furrowing his brow. Oddly he didn't feel relieved, or thankful. Rather, he felt slighted. It was worrisome and unwelcome to feel such a way.

"That is the response that I'd expect," Heathcliff said, "from anyone but you."

"And the offense continues," Ramsey sighed.

"Just . . . maybe take a break. Go travel. You've had more than your share of business and no pleasure."

"Pleasure is for the weak," Ramsey replied.

"Says the man in great need of it," Heathcliff replied swiftly. "Lucas will arrive in a week, and we shall have all things in hand here."

"I'm becoming obsolete, is what you're saying."

"No. I'm saying take some time to yourself before you do become obsolete and a pain in my arse with your highly overactive sense of control."

"I doubt I compare with Lucas's tight hold on it," Ramsey grumbled.

"You are on the path to becoming far more controlling than even he was at his peak, so that is why I'm suggesting you take a new path before it's too late."

Ramsey sighed. "Very well, I'll make a few arrangements. At least you didn't suggest I find a woman."

"I know better than to suggest such a thing. What woman would I wish you upon?" he teased.

To this, Ramsey had to chuckle. "Who indeed?"

It was after this conversation that Ramsey left for his residence, deep in thought and reflective of the previous conversation. There was much to be digested, and he found the idea of a break a welcome one.

Sleep was swift in coming, and upon waking, he decided that if he were going through with the idea of a sabbatical, he wished to spend a grand time of it in rest. Good Lord, heaven only knew how much sleep he'd missed because of Temptations and the quick departure of his two friends last year.

It was to their credit that they wished him a break from work, yet as he made the final arrangements for his time off, he felt a great restlessness overtake him.

What in heaven's name was he to do now, aside from catch up on sleep?

London held no attachment for him.

And he bloody well didn't wish to go back to Glenwood Manor. It had been nearly five years since he'd returned.

Which only punctuated the point that it was beyond time for him to return and address business in his country seat.

But he was loath to do it. Returning to Glenwood Manor would most certainly not constitute a vacation. Rather, it would be the severest of punishment.

Which was probably why he was already planning to go.

When guilt plagued you, punishment was always the answer.

And there could be no more severe punishment than to return to the place that sealed his estimation in his father's eyes.

Glenwood Manor.

Where his father, and Ramsey's honor, died the same day.

As arrangements were made for him to depart within a few days' time, he sent off a letter that notified the staff of his upcoming return. The housekeeper would likely have a heart spasm from shock at the news, and the steward would probably call it an answer to a prayer. He was half tempted to rid himself of the place, but it had been in his family for generations, and such legacy wasn't so easily dismissed.

Ramsey also sent word to Heathcliff to notify him of the upcoming departure, and only on the last line left the destination of his venture. He could almost hear the groan and displeasure of his friend at reading his intentions. But Heathcliff, while loyal, never had the same drive in sense of honor that Ramsey experienced.

No, Heathcliff was far more jovial, flexible, and dismissive of the harsh truths of propriety. It was times like these that Ramsey wished he were more like his friend.

And other times, he wished his friend was more like him.

But, as in most good friendships, they balanced each other out in a beneficial way.

The few days' time before his departure passed quickly under the constant details that needed attending to in order for the trip to be made smoothly. And far quicker than he would have wished, Ramsey found himself in a carriage on the way to Glenwood Manor in northern England. He could only praise God that it would take him a full two days on the road to get to his destination.

He'd need that much time to resign himself to the fact that he was returning.

Returning to the place that should have been called home, but never felt like it.

No. Prison would have been a better description.

With shackles that he still wore, regardless of where he lived.

Shackles with his father's name engraved on every inch.

Chapter Eleven

"**H**e's a bloody fool."

Grace sipped her tea quietly as Viscount Kilpatrick sat back on the sofa with a disgruntled expression.

"Perhaps it's for the best?" Samantha asked delicately as she set her teacup down on the coffee table.

"I've never met a man so bent on self-punishment. As if his father didn't give him enough of it growing up." Heathcliff wiped a hand down his face. "Of all the places in all the world, he returns to his prison."

Samantha's brow pinched and she laid a soft hand on her husband's shoulder. "Could it be that he needs to face his demons rather than run from them?"

The viscount blinked, then bit his lip as if considering her words. "That may be, but not alone."

"With whom?" Samantha asked. "It's been five years, that's not an overmuch amount of time, but it is significant enough to gain perspective."

"True, but I doubt he's gained said perspective."

"That may be the case, but he may gain it upon his return," Samantha replied.

Grace held her peace, listening with attentiveness to the conversation. Ever since Lord Sterling had sent the missive on his departure to the viscount, this had been a common conversation. She was pleased to have the viscount and Samantha feel the liberty to have such an open discussion in her company, and it continued to feed her curiosity concerning the quandary that was Lord Sterling.

"Enough. If we don't hear from him in a month's time, I'll send word."

"Word of?" Samantha asked, a small smile teasing her lips. "Will you demand he come back to London?"

"Yes. I'd be so bold as to mention as such. But I find it highly unlikely he will remain gone that long. We shall see." He sighed, as if using the deep breath to conclude the conversation, and then turned to Grace. "Well, do you think we shall have as many callers today as we have had the past few days? It seems as if you have a loyal following amongst the eligible men." He gave her an approving smile.

"It would seem as if my luck is holding fast . . . for the moment." She dipped a shoulder.

"When we attend the Rinehardt ball this evening, I dare say you won't sit out even a single dance," Samantha asserted, a knowing smile peeking over her teacup as she sipped.

"Perhaps. But it is dreadfully hard to get to know the character of these men from a single dance or from one afternoon's conversation."

"What do you wish to know? Tell me your favorites

and I'll dispatch John to find out the necessary information on the gentlemen in question." Heathcliff leaned forward, a determined gleam in his eye.

"I thank you, but so far I have no favorites. But when I do I'll certainly take you up on your kind offer."

"Remember this, Miss Grace. It is always *who* you know," the viscount said significantly.

"I'll try to remember that," Grace replied.

"It's almost time for our at-home hours. Do you wish to change before you hold court?" Samantha asked, teasing Grace with her words.

Grace grinned in reply. Samantha was enjoying the success of her former charge, and it was gratifying to Grace to know she had met and even perhaps exceeded her expectations. "What do you suggest?"

Samantha tipped her chin thoughtfully as she stood. "Your green day dress should do nicely. It will complement your eyes."

"Done," Grace replied, standing as well to take her leave and change.

It was less than an hour later that Grace was in a different parlor, speaking with no less than three gentlemen who had come to call upon her.

They were witty, kind, and even handsome.

Yet, if pressed, she could hardly remember their names.

Because amongst all things, they were forgettable. None of them sparked her curiosity, and in turn, didn't spark her fancy.

It was the same that evening at the Rinehardt ball. Just as Samantha predicted, her dance card was quite full and she entertained several gentlemen in conversation between dances. Lord Reinhardt's son was amongst their ranks, and he seemed the most promising, but again she didn't feel as though her tender feelings were engaged.

Was it wrong to want something more than just a flicker of flattery from a gentleman's attention? She knew it was nearly ungrateful to have the attention of suitors and not appreciate it, but she was . . . well, bored.

There was no adventure.

No mystery.

There wasn't even a true sense of emotion.

Even the colors were muted, in shades of pastel and white, and she wondered if maybe that was to be her life.

She should want it. She should be thankful and agreeable and settle down with a nice, titled gentleman who could provide for her and their children. There was nothing wrong with such a thing.

But there wasn't anything right about it either.

So it was that after the Rinehardt ball that she made the choice to speak with Samantha.

Because if anyone knew about taking a risk, it was she.

And Grace was just reckless enough to try something, if not adventuresome, then most certainly stupid.

And it would either make or break her.

But how can someone ever find out if they can fly, if they can reach higher, unless they actually try?

So it was with not a small amount of trepidation that Grace requested the company of Samantha in the green parlor after tea. It was an uncommonly beautiful day in London, and Grace started to second-guess her decision to stay indoors.

Samantha walked into the room, her lips bending

into a welcoming smile as she met Grace's gaze. "Good afternoon, dear."

Grace stood and returned the greeting. But rather than sit, she started to walk about the room, collecting her thoughts as if they had run away from her.

"Ah, this must be serious if you're pacing," Samantha said, taking a seat as if nothing in the world were amiss. And, actually, nothing was wrong, but Grace felt as if things were in disarray. She should be happy with such attentions, yet she felt even more ill at ease as she thought about them. Was it so wrong to want more? She had to start the conversation, but how? She bit her lip.

"First you should take a deep breath," Samantha replied. "Then start from the beginning. I do not imagine it is truly terrible."

Grace took the encouraged breath, and then turned to face her former governess. "I feel . . . ungrateful."

Samantha didn't reply, but simply waited.

Grace continued her pacing where she left off. "I should be thankful to have the attentions of even one, let alone as many suitors as have shown interest and yet I find the prospect of their interest less than welcome. I do not wish to be a burden to you or the viscount by being under your guardianship for long. I realize that it is a great service to me that you are taking such great pains to find me a suitable husband and not just marrying me off to the first available gentleman—"

"We would never do such a thing!" Samantha interjected.

"And that is to your profound credit, but I do not feel equal to such credit as you offer because I cannot find even one of the men in question the least bit fascinating. I'm bored with them all, which sounds horribly ungrateful and even imprudent. But I . . . I saw my parents' marriage and they not only loved one another, but they liked each other too. They spent all their time together, traveling, exploring, having one adventure after another, and even when it wouldn't turn out like they planned, it would be alright, because they were together. Then I see you and the viscount and the deep affection you have for each other, and I do not want to miss out on such a blessing." Grace took a deep breath, conscious that she was rambling.

"Why don't you wait a moment and sit down," Samantha encouraged.

Grace all but flopped into a chair in her exasperation with herself.

Samantha arched a brow but didn't offer any reproof to her behavior. "You are not being ungrateful; you are learning that this isn't as simple as you imagined."

Grace tipped her head, considering her words. Never once had she thought it simple, but her attention was stressed on the formalities that she was to perfect—the dancing, the curtsey, and the like—not on the gentlemen involved. She rather assumed that if any were interested in her, she would be pleased. Simple as that.

Or rather, not as simple as that.

Samantha continued, "The viscount and I have spoken on this topic at length, and neither of us are inclined to have you enter marriage on so small a temptation as mere flattery of receiving an offer. To have your adventuresome spirit not attain its potential would be a tragedy. So, take it from me, you have more than adequate time to find a suitor whom you can both love and find equal to your challenge. We would have you do

nothing less." Samantha folded her hands on her lap
and gave a small smile. "Now then, was there anything
else?"

Grace frowned slightly. "No, it was simply . . . that."

"Good, then. I suggest you take advantage of this
beautiful day and take the opportunity to explore Hyde
Park. Be sure to take Regina or another maid with you
when you embark, however. Propriety and all," Samantha
reminded gently.

"Of course," Grace replied, still quite surprised at
the neat way Samantha had tidied up all her mixed
emotions.

"Good day, then." Samantha stood, reached over,
squeezed her hand, and then quit the room, leaving
Grace still somewhat surprised at the quickness of the
conversation that she had been so loathe to begin.

A bird's song came from the direction of the window, effectively distracting Grace from her musings,
and as she noted the sunshine, she spun on her heel to
go and change into a walking dress.

Samantha was correct in many things; however, at
the moment she was most inclined to obey her suggestion to get some air at the park.

A half hour later, Grace ambled through the streets
of Mayfair with Sally at her heels accompanying her.
Regina was otherwise engaged with other duties, and
Sally was perfectly happy to chaperone the occasion.
The sunlight filtered through the leaves of the birch
trees, and even the hedgerows seemed a brighter green.
A few sparrows darted across the sky, adding to the
merriment of the walk, and for the first time in several
weeks, Grace was at peace.

She was still striving to comprehend the degree of
understanding Samantha had given her earlier; it was a

gift of the most precious variety. It had utterly set her free from the stress she'd put herself under, and now it seemed as if the future held more promise.

Or at least, more promise than anxiety.

She would take whatever she could get.

It wasn't a long walk to Hyde Park, and as she wound around the final bend she crossed Park Lane, and entered through a gate of some importance. The park was humming with activity, with ladies riding their horses at a sedate pace while gentlemen ambled about, conversation abounding between the two sexes. It was as much of a meeting place as the London Ballroom, Grace decided. And far more beautiful as well. She started down the path that indicated it led toward the Serpentine, and used the moments to be a student to human nature. A gentleman kissed a lady's hand, smiling charmingly as he released her, and Grace felt a grin tip her lips as the lady seemed to simper—Grace was too far away to see much detail—and appreciate the attention. Just then a pair of doves flew overhead, in pursuit of each other.

It most certainly was the season for love.

Pity she was already bored with the London season.

Grace continued in that manner for several minutes, taking in the behavior of the people in the park as well as the wildlife when she heard a shout. Curious, she turned to see a gentleman chasing a runaway horse. The beautiful animal was obviously riderless and cantering in her direction. She paused, indecision freezing her as she debated whether to zig or zag, when she was lifted from behind and carried several feet from where she had stood. The horse thundered by, and Grace spun around the moment the strong arms left her waist.

"A thousand apologies, my lady." The gentleman nodded and took a step back to give her room. "I wasn't sure if you were going to move, and I didn't want to risk your injury." He lowered his eyes for a moment, then met her gaze with the full regard of his own. Deep blue eyes studied her, his expression properly apologetic. Grace couldn't fault his decision so she simply smoothed her skirt and nodded.

"No apology is necessary," she replied, but, oh my, his eyes were fascinating. Just light enough to see the color, but dark enough to hide whatever thoughts spun through his mind. Immediately her fancy was caught, and rather than find a way to excuse herself, she sought for a way to keep him in company.

Belatedly, she realized that an introduction would be the next step, but he had already anticipated such a step.

"Forgive me. I haven't even given my name. I'm Julian Lambton, sixth Earl of Westhouse. It is a pleasure to meet you . . ."

"Grace. Miss Grace Morgan." Grace spoke smoothly, for once not stuttering under pressure. She silently congratulated herself.

"A pleasure, Miss Grace Morgan." He bowed crisply.

Grace curtsied in return, all the while thinking of something suitable to say to extend the conversation. "I do believe a thank you is in order. I was quite surprised by the charging animal and I was debating on whether to zig or zag, but my deliberation halted my progress. Thank you for your help."

"It was of no consequence." He made a dismissive gesture with his hand, and then seemed to consider whatever he was thinking about saying. "Would . . . would you like to take a turn about the park with me?"

Grace grinned, unable to restrain her enthusiasm. "Of course. As I have not had the pleasure of making your acquaintance, I'm sure there are plenty of conversational topics we can explore."

He gave a small chuckle. "Quite true. Why don't you start with your family? I don't believe I've heard of the Morgans," Lord Westhouse said as he extended his arm to her.

Grace took it, feeling a jolt of electricity hum through her at the contact. Her lips twitched in delight. "I'm originally from Matlock, but my family didn't keep residence there. We traveled much of my childhood. This is my first time to London."

"Ah, and how do you find it? Is it to your liking?" he asked, all gentlemanly manners.

Grace inwardly sighed. Though it was a natural question to ask, she would really rather people stop asking it. It put her in the most horrid position of lying, or at the very least, telling a half-truth. But as she turned to Lord Westhouse to answer, she decided that perhaps London wasn't so bad after all.

"It improves more each day," she replied, conscious that her words could be taken as a flirtation.

Samantha would be proud.

"Ha! A very cautious answer. Are your parents in residence?" He moved on in the conversation.

Grace was just evaluating his height. He was not as tall as the viscount, and not nearly the height of Lord Sterling, but he wasn't short either. Somewhere in the middle.

Somewhere just right.

But his inquiry into her parents sent a pang of sorrow through her heart and her gaze fell to the path before them. "They passed almost two years ago."

"My condolences. I should not have asked," he added kindly.

Her gaze shot up to his. "How could you have known? Please, I'm much too even tempered a person to be so willing to blame others for what they cannot have foreseen." She gave a small, brave smile.

"I shall remember that." His blue eyes sparkled when he smiled, and Grace was very pleased in saying something that provoked such a reaction.

"And what of you? Do you live in London?" she asked, returning to the conversation.

"That I do, my lady. I'm quite fond of it here, especially on beautiful days such as these," he added.

"Oh yes, today is lovely. It's why my guardian suggested I take in the air. We walked quite often when were in residence in Scotland, but I haven't had the pleasure as much since we've arrived in London."

"Scotland, you say?" He glanced to her, awaiting confirmation. "Who is your guardian, if you don't mind me asking?"

"Certainly not. It's the Viscount Kilpatrick," she answered. His brow furrowed for a moment then smoothed out as if it never happened.

"I see. I'm assuming he's in residence then?"

Grace thought this was a strange question. If she were in London, then it would follow that her guardian would be as well. She filed the oddity away in her mind and answered.

"Yes, he and his wife are in residence."

"Will you be attending the Morris ball tomorrow night?" he asked, his tone kind and warm.

Flattered that he would inquire to her social schedule, she nodded. "Indeed."

"Would it be overly presumptuous to request a dance?" he asked, turning to meet her gaze.

"Not at all. You did save me from a runaway horse," she added, mentally rolling her eyes at how silly it sounded, regardless of its truth.

"Ah, then I'd almost think that such a feat deserves maybe . . . two dances?" he stated boldly, his white smile distracting against the olive tone of his skin.

Grace took a moment to appreciate his handsome features, from his chestnut hair to the full spread of his smile. For a moment she deliberated on how to answer.

"We will have to find out, won't we?" she answered vaguely, hoping it would come across as sophisticated and flirtatious rather than awkward and unsure.

She must have done it right, because Lord Westhouse chuckled, kissed her hand, and then begged his leave of her, with a promise that he would be looking forward to the ball with great anticipation.

Grace watched him depart, her smile wide and free.

Perhaps the suitors she'd found tedious only meant that she hadn't yet met the right one.

She couldn't wait to tell Samantha.

Chapter Twelve

One week. He'd been in residence in Glenwood Manor for one week and he was ready to bloody kill himself.

Maybe not that extreme, but he was dangerously close. He'd always heard stories of haunted castles; he never realized he owned one.

But he was quite certain that the ghosts haunted only him.

And that the haunting was in his own memory.

Everywhere he turned, some reminiscence surfaced. He couldn't walk into the breakfast room in peace without some damn word from his father floating through his memory, reminding him of all the ways he'd failed. Every mirror he'd pass would reflect the man he used to be, not the man he was.

And the bloody silence.

It was like the inside of a crypt.

The servants walked around silently, whispering in

soft tones only when absolutely necessary, a result of decades of training to be invisible to avoid wrath.

It was as if they expected him to be his father, and as such, had reverted to walking on eggshells that had defined the way of life at Glenwood Manor.

Ramsey knew it all too well. Like walking on fragile ice, you stepped cautiously, trying to remain unseen, unnoticed, to simply blend in.

It was easy for the servants. They were imagined so far below his father's station that they were only spoken to when absolutely necessary. Almost as if the man thought just speaking to them muddied his hands from their lower station. Ramsey shook his head in memory.

But as a child, the only child, the heir, Ramsey couldn't hide from his father's view or scrutiny.

He stood from the chair in his study and walked over to the window. The hill behind the manor was stately, an ancient wood pointed to the heavens like tiny green arrows, while the white puffy clouds made the sky a richer blue in contrast. But the beauty was lost to him. He felt like a prisoner looking through bars of a jail cell at a sight that was just a reminder of freedom out of reach.

Facing his demons had been harder than he had anticipated. He closed his eyes and leaned a hand on the window frame.

A timid knock came at the door, and Ramsey welcomed the intrusion on his bleak thoughts. "Yes?" He turned.

"Pardon, my lord. But I took the liberty of bringing you tea." The longtime housekeeper, Mrs. White, cautiously walked into the room with a servant girl following her with a tray laden with tea things.

"Thank you, how very kind," Ramsey replied, trying to be everything his father was not. In a word, he wanted to be gentle.

Such a simple word with such complicated execution.

"You're quite welcome, my lord. Shall I pour for you?" she asked after dismissing the servant girl.

"Yes, please." He was grateful for her thoughtfulness. Growing up, she had always been the one he could count on for a word of encouragement.

"Still two sugars?" she asked, a twinkle in her green eyes, a touch cloudier in complexion than he remembered.

"Yes, of course," he replied. Then proceeded to do something his father would never have supported. "Thank you, Mrs. White. You've been loyal and kind and often the only encouraging voice I can remember. I don't know that I ever said how much I appreciated you, but I give you my thanks now." He bowed his head respectfully.

Mrs. White blinked, handed him the cup of tea, and then withdrew a handkerchief and dabbed her eyes. "Oh, my lord. I cannot tell you how that blesses my heart." She paused, then tilted her head as if considering him.

"Yes?" he encouraged.

"May I be frank, my lord?" she asked, albeit a bit insecure.

"I would treasure your frank opinion, Mrs. White." He took a tentative sip of tea. Perfect.

Mrs. White twisted her wrinkled lips and then took a breath. "From the day you were born, we knew there was only two options for you."

Ramsey blinked, intrigued. "Yes?"

"You would either be worse than your father, God rest his soul, or you'd never measure up to whatever forsaken standard he created for you. Regardless, you would lose either way. You were born without hope, my lord. I cannot tell you how it has plagued me to watch you grow, and be helpless to offer any solace to your young heart."

Ramsey was moved by her insight and care, but was also practical enough to understand it was impossible for anyone to combat the powerful influence of his father's will, let alone for a servant even to try. He appreciated her heart, however, and felt it necessary to mention as much. "You did what you could, and I appreciate every effort. My father was not a man to be challenged, and in your way, you assisted more than you can ever know."

The housekeeper, clearly relaxing as she hitched a shoulder, continued. "We tried ever so hard, my lord. We took extra caution not to excite the master or stir his wrath in any way. We kept quiet, moving about the house as ghosts, we did. It seemed the smoother things ran at the estate, the less anxious and . . . exacting he would be to you." She sighed. "But I'm afraid all our efforts only amounted to a small help, and for that I have deep regret, my lord."

Ramsey considered her words, mulled them about in his mind as he looked at their hidden meaning.

The silence.

The walking on eggshells.

The blending in.

The ghosting of the servants . . . was all for him.

For his benefit.

To ease the wrath of a tyrannical father on his only son, an entire household of servants had mobilized to do anything they could to provide whatever protection they could offer him.

It was humbling.

It was startling.

It was . . . healing.

"Mrs. White. I don't know what to say," he answered inarticulately. "I had no idea that you had all taken such great pains."

"It was happily done sir. You always were such a kind, good boy," she answered.

And of all the things she had said, that was the most profound. Good? Kind? Never once had he used those words to identify himself, let alone his childhood.

Inadequate.

Imperfect.

Lazy.

Those were the words that bore his name as a child. Yet in a swift turn, he wondered if maybe Mrs. White spoke the truth.

"I can see you don't believe me, my lord. And after all the times your father spoke such opposite things over you, I can comprehend why." She paused, as if just stopping herself from going further. Her eyes sharpened, and some sort of resolution was fixed. She gave a slight shake of her head, then continued. "But it's the truth. Never once can I remember anyone having a harsh word from you. Rather, remember the time you took a beating because you said thank you to the butler for finding your lost boot? I can't tell you how Salberry was tortured for feeling he aided in such a cruel treatment of you. And then the time you found cook's little one above stairs, nearly toddling into your father's library. Good Lord, I can't even imagine what would have happened had you not scooped up the little boy and carried him to the kitchens. Cook is convinced you saved her position in the household. My lord, I could name time and time again." She paused, considering him.

It was too much.

It was one thing to think that your father could be wrong in all the horrible things spoken over you, and your future as a child. But to have someone who lived in the same hell, who knew the man behind the title, and confirm those same helpless feelings. . . . He scarcely knew how to fathom such a thing.

And rather than feel alone, he felt all the weight of an entire staff supporting him, pulling for him, supplying him with assistance whenever in their power to give it. In a five-minute stretch, so much of what he had known as a child had turned on its ear, in the most helpful way.

"Will there be anything else, my lord?" Mrs. White asked.

Ramsey didn't trust his voice, so he simply shook his head. The housekeeper curtsied, and then quit the room.

Leaving him with his spinning thoughts, though, this time he wasn't as haunted by them. Like looking through the backside of a mirror, he reflected on his childhood, and saw things differently. He wouldn't put it past Mrs. White to embellish the truth about his character as a boy, but he certainly didn't believe her to be dishonest about such a thing. That being the case, what she said had to carry some weight, had to be built upon truth.

Why was it that one could go throughout life knowing that they were more than what they'd been told they were, but it never fully took root till someone else, someone who had walked that similar road, came alongside to affirm it? How long had he tried to convince himself that he was worthy, honorable in spite of the many failures and especially the sham that was his marriage? Yet all his efforts were to no avail.

A simply violent, desperate attempt to validate himself, only to fall short time and time again.

Only to prove his father right, again and again.

It was a whirlpool, pulling him lower and lower without any aid to rise above the torrent.

Heathcliff and Lucas had many times encouraged, affirmed, and even stated frankly that his father was a bastard. And Ramsey agreed that his father was one of the cruelest men, but certainly some of that leaked into him. He was, after all, his father's son. So as such, Ramsey had seen himself with the truth that not only did his father's cruelty lurk deep within him, but he carried what his father never seemed to touch—shame.

In turn that only equaled one thing: utter and complete failure.

But Mrs. White's words were like a balm to the gaping wound of his soul. Because she *knew*. She had lived in the manor, seen the fits of rage that would send crystal to shattering, walls to shaking, and often, Ramsey to his room with welts, bleeding and bruised. And for her to say it wasn't deserved. For her to tell him that he wasn't his father . . . well, if anyone knew it, it would be she.

And the weight of three decades of self-recrimination fell off his shoulders like unloading a heavily laden cart. He breathed deeply, this new freedom from within, and gave his head a slightly astounded shake.

All this time, he thought the demons he needed to face bore his father's name.

But in truth, the demons were far closer. They were within his own heart, believing the lies his father spoke, owning those lies, living them out.

No more.

He glanced to the window and then strode over to it, for the first time appreciating the view.

Because he was no longer that prisoner; he was set free.

And freedom was a beautiful thing, indeed.

Chapter Thirteen

Grace bit back a smile of anticipation as they arrived at the Morris ball that evening. She hadn't said much to Samantha by way of her new acquaintance, but had implied that she was excited for the evening. She was sure that Samantha and the viscount would be watching with interest, but she didn't concern herself with it.

The Morris estate was a beautiful residence on Park Lane, with great stone pillars guarding the entrance. The grandeur of the entrance was built upon by the high-rising balcony overlooking the beautiful ballroom of their residence. It was a well-attended party, and Grace heard Samantha mention "crush" to describe it. It was an accurate representation of the collection of people, but rather than feel suffocated, she was too excited as she looked for a particular individual. The music floated through the air while footmen in scarlet offered lemonade to those who forwent the current dance.

Lord Wiltmen approached their party and asked for the next dance. Grace could feel Samantha's scrutiny, probably wondering if this were the gentleman who had caught her fancy. Grace ignored her attention and graciously accepted Lord Wiltmen's invitation. He gave a crisp bow and promised to return.

When Grace turned to Samantha, her eyebrows raised in silent question. Grace gave a definitive shake of her head and lifted a glass of lemonade from the passing footman's tray.

"Would it be unforgivable for me to say I'm quite exhausted with the London scene?" the viscount commented quietly to his wife, but Grace overheard and gave a slight grin.

"Yes." Samantha replied succinctly. "Especially here." She gave a slightly arched brow expression. "You may seek refuge in your sanctuary later on." She gave shake to her head as she smiled.

Grace bit back a grin. She'd often wished to know more about the mentioned "sanctuary," but hadn't been able to learn much. All she knew was that it was a place of business of some sort, and that it brought the viscount back early in the morning. When she asked Samantha, she was given a very short, curt answer.

Which had to mean it was scandalous or off limits. But she couldn't imagine anything too scandalous since Lord Ramsey was involved. Wasn't he utterly terrified of scandal?

And for good reason.

If half of what happened to him had plagued her, she would be terrified it of it as well.

The music ended and the musicians paused before beginning once again. Grace turned to find Lord Wiltmen approaching. He offered his arm, which she accepted, and they were off to the dance floor.

It was the cotillion, which was one of her more graceful dances, and belatedly she felt a shiver of apprehension. What if Lord Westhouse requested a waltz? Good Lord, she'd be forced to warn him to watch his feet. It was only the kind thing to do, wasn't it? But it was humiliating, too. Just the thought made her stumble on the turn for the current dance.

The cotillion made conversation difficult, but to Lord Wiltmen's credit, he tried to engage her as much as possible. He was a kind man, but there wasn't any spark that set her to seeking further acquaintance. And when the dance ended, he took her back to the viscount and then took his leave.

"He's a nice gentleman." Samantha remarked, watching him leave.

"Yes." Grace couldn't deny it.

She waited for Samantha's reply, but instead was met by silence. As she turned to her friend, her attention was engaged just over Grace's shoulder. A shiver of awareness tickled down her spine, and before she could identity it, a somewhat familiar voice spoke her name.

"Ah, Miss Grace, what a pleasure to see you again."

Grace couldn't restrain her grin, but tried to at least temper it before she turned and met the engaging blue gaze of Lord Westhouse. "A pleasure to see you as well. I had no idea you'd be here!" she teased, then laughed softly,

"Imagine that!" he played along. "I do love to surprise unsuspecting ladies."

"You're all charm and delight, Lord Westhouse," Grace remarked, her breath catching as he reached out to grasp her hand and kiss it. His blue eyes searched hers, and breathlessness overcame her.

A gentle touch at her back made Grace remember her place, and she slowly withdrew her hand and turned enough to allow for introductions. After swallowing back her response to Lord Westhouse, she turned to meet Samantha's inquiring gaze.

"Lady Kilpatrick, allow me to introduce you to Lord Westhouse." Grace stepped back slightly to allow for a better situation.

Samantha offered her hand and Lord Westhouse bowed over it, then released her.

Grace fancied that he held her hand much longer, and she hoped that it indicated his interest in her.

"A pleasure to meet you," Samantha replied. "My husband just departed to speak with a friend. I'll have to make the introductions later, I'm afraid."

Grace glanced behind Samantha and noted that the viscount had his back turned to them, speaking to another gentleman, one she didn't recognize.

But then of course, she didn't recognize many of the ton.

"I was hoping to collect on one of the dances you promised." Lord Westhouse turned back to Grace, his smile welcoming.

"Of course, I'd be honored." Grace replied. *Please don't ask for a waltz!* she thought furiously as she forced her expression to remain calm while he continued.

"Would you honor me with the supper waltz?" he asked, his blue eyes regarding her eagerly.

Grace silently groaned, but she gave a bright smile and nodded. "Of course."

"Then I shall be back a little later to collect on that

dance," he remarked, then with a swift bow and a lingering look, he turned and left.

Grace watched his departure with interest, regarding the way that several ladies followed him with their gazes, and noting the way he cut a fine figure in his evening kit.

"So, I'm assuming that the reason you found the prospect of this ball more promising just walked away," Samantha remarked quietly, her voice soft to keep from eavesdroppers.

Grace gave a slow nod, not quite ready to cease watching his departure. When he was hidden from view behind several people, she finally turned to face Samantha.

"Is he not charming?" Grace asked.

Samantha gave an amused grin. "He is indeed. His name sounds familiar, but I cannot place it," she added thoughtfully. "Once the viscount ends his conversation and returns, I'll have to inquire about him."

After a moment's pause, Grace watched while Samantha took a breath, then paused, her expression full of a question. "A waltz," she simply stated.

Grace nodded slowly, understanding all the implications beneath the simple statement. "A waltz," she repeated.

Samantha looked as if she wished to say something more, but then thought better of it and simply reached over and patted Grace's shoulder. "It will be just fine."

Grace gave her a rueful smile. "Oh, I know I'll be fine. I rarely step on my own toes; it's his toes for which I'm concerned."

Samantha covered her lips with her gloved fingers to stifle a laugh. "You've improved."

"Not nearly enough to cease being a danger," Grace mumbled softly, then glanced back to where Lord West-house had disappeared. Just over the crowd, she could see a profile of his face before he turned to face the other direction.

Dear lord, he was handsome.

The next few dances began, and Grace was engaged for each by a different partner. Each dance left her with more nervous energy than when she had begun, and as the supper waltz music began, her hands were perspiring under her gloves.

Lord Westhouse approached as she waited with the viscount and Samantha. The viscount had just returned to their party, and as such, Samantha hadn't the opportunity to ask him about Lord Westhouse. However, it was made abundantly clear that the viscount knew of Westhouse. As the gentleman in question closed the distance, the viscount swore quietly, his voice carrying a venom Grace had seldom heard. Her senses tingled, and she wondered what the next few moments would hold.

"Viscount Kilpatrick." Lord Westhouse bowed respectfully, offering a gracious smile.

"Westhouse," the viscount returned, his expression stoically void of emotion.

"It's good to see you again. I haven't seen much of your society of late," Lord Westhouse said by way of conversation.

"I'm sure I was sorely missed," the viscount returned.

Grace's gaze shot to Samantha, who was also watching the interchange with great interest.

"I requested this dance with your lovely ward, if I

may?" While the words were framed to be a question, Lord Westhouse reached his arm out to Grace, not waiting for an answer from her guardian.

Grace deliberated for a moment, but as they had gained the attention of those around them, she decided that it would be best to simply smooth things out.

Lord Westhouse bestowed upon her the most charming smile and led her away, clearly not interested in the viscount's response.

Not that the viscount ever gave one.

It was strange, and a shiver of trepidation tickled her back as Westhouse led her onto the ballroom floor.

As he held her in the frame of the waltz and led her into the swirling dancers, he spoke. "Please forgive me. There was one time that I called Kilpatrick a friend, but there was a . . . situation . . . that was misunderstood and I'm afraid we haven't gotten past it as of yet. It is hard for me to be at such odds with a great man such as he, but I confess, I haven't made efforts to mend the rift either," he sighed, his gaze open and honest.

Grace felt her lips twitch in a sympathetic smile. "That must be very difficult. I did sense some . . . tension. . . . It's good to know that you don't bear him any ill will. He is truly a wonderful man and kind guardian."

"He would be the best of guardians, I'm sure," Westhouse replied, and to his credit, didn't wince when she stepped on his toe.

"Pardon," she murmured.

"For?" he asked, tipping his head as they continued to dance.

"For stepping on your toes," Grace nearly mumbled, hating that she needed to mention it out loud. Maybe she shouldn't have apologized. But it was pointless to pretend that it had not happened. Wasn't it?

"Oh, that. It's less than nothing. My youngest sister used to do the same thing." He gave a quick smile.

Grace's heart melted a little bit more. Someone who didn't mind when she stepped on their toes? It could be love.

Leave it to her to find the one man who could tolerate her dancing the waltz and have him at odds with the very man in charge of her future.

They conversed throughout the dance, and when the waltz ended, she was escorted back to the side of the viscount, and Lord Westhouse requested to speak with the viscount privately.

Samantha watched the men leave, then turned to Grace. "I do not know much, but what I do know I do not like."

Grace's soaring heart deflated, and she met Samantha's gaze. "He said that there was a bit of a problem with their former friendship."

Samantha frowned. "Well, I suppose that it is very respectable for him to admit as such. Perhaps he is not who he once was."

Grace watched as the men disappeared into the crowed and hoped sincerely that Samantha was right.

But only time would tell.

Which was the devil when you were born impatient, like her.

Chapter Fourteen

Ramsey dispatched the missive to Heathcliff that he was returning to London, and then for good measure, sent one to Lucas's residence as well. He wasn't entirely certain that Lucas would have returned to London as of yet, considering that Ramsey was cutting his trip a bit short, but he wished to be thorough in all things.

And what a blessing to be through, not out of obligation but because he wished to be. What freedom he had experienced in the past week, and it was high time he moved on from this horrific past, and onward to a future that held hope.

Tomorrow he would depart from Glenwood Manor and start the journey to London. And as the sun set and he retired to his rooms, he inhaled deeply, savoring the feeling of the absent ghosts that haunted his memories. His father was still a bastard; that would never change. What had changed was the elemental foundation of who Ramsey saw himself to be: *enough*.

One word could carry a universe of meaning.

It was the same word that lulled him into a deep sleep that night, with the thought that tomorrow promised continued hope.

So it was with that hope that he rose, bid farewell to Mrs. White with a promise to return sooner rather than later, and departed.

The trip was just as uneventful as the one that preceded it; the only change was the atmosphere of the carriage. It was merely one night on the road, and by the second day, they approached the city limits of London. The smoke greeted him first, then the constant buzz of activity that never slept in the busy capital. When he arrived at his residence, he sighed in a relieved manner, and stepped thankfully from the carriage. He regarded his home with more affection than before, but perhaps it was simply that he could hold other emotions in his heart, and that the bitterness and anger had vacated the real estate.

Regardless, he felt lighter, as if the weight of the world, his world, was no longer resting on his shoulders as if he were Atlas.

After greeting his butler, he took the stairs to his room and refreshed himself from the long trip, and in short work he was back in his study surveying the stack of correspondence that awaited his attention.

In keeping with the new theme when he departed, there were several invitations to social events, all of which held no interest for him. He tossed them to the side and selected the more important missives that required his attention. As he was finishing the last missive, a knock came at the door. Ramsey set the missives to the side and called, "Yes?"

His butler opened the door, allowing Heathcliff to all but stomp within.

"Good afternoon to you, too," Ramsey sighed. Whatever Heathcliff had to say, he was quite certain he wasn't going to like it, not with his friend acting as such.

"Do you remember when I said I didn't need your assistance with my ward?" Heathcliff said by way of greeting.

"Vaguely." He shrugged, enjoying how the tables had turned. Normally it was Heathcliff who was calm while Ramsey was in a dither.

Heathcliff paused at Ramsey's response, offering a quick glare. "Stop enjoying my agitation. Once I tell you what, or should I say, whom, she is associating with, you'll be just as frustrated. More so, if I'm assuming correctly."

"What concern do I have over whom your ward associates with? What is it to me?"

"Oh, it's something to you." Heathcliff sank into a chair.

"Am I to wait in suspense or are you going to tell me?" Ramsey inquired.

"Westhouse."

Ramsey felt the blood drain from his face, only to surge to his fists as he clenched them, wanting to pound Westhouse's face with a rounder. He wasn't usually a violent sort, but that man brought out every combative fiber in Ramsey's being.

"How in the hell?" Ramsey asked.

"I don't know, the bastard already knew her at the ball the other night and they've been in close confederacy since. Each ball she attends, he is there paying her court. I've given John strict instructions that he is not to be admitted into the house for calling hours—a detail I haven't shared with my wife or ward, but I want no part of him."

Ramsey nodded in agreement. "Does he know? Is it possible that he knew her association with you, and in turn me?"

"I'm not sure. 'Twould be quite a stretch."

Ramsey stood and paced about the room, the rhythmic footfalls helping him think. "What of Miss Grace? Have you tried to reason with her, let her know that he is not a man to be trusted?"

Heathcliff gave his head a shake. At first Ramsey though it meant he hadn't discussed it with Grace, but as Heathcliff spoke, Ramsey's blood boiled hot against that bastard, Lord Westhouse.

"I tried to inform her of his character but it would seem that he circumvented that quite well. He already had mentioned to her his 'tentative' relationship with you, and how he had done you a disservice, et cetera, basically bled all over her and she bought it. In her opinion, he is a changed man."

"Bloody hell," Ramsey swore.

"It's a miserable mess. And my wife agrees with me, and has tried to speak with Grace as well, but, in case you hadn't noticed, my ward can be quite . . . stubborn when her mind is set. And I'm afraid it's quite set on Lord Westhouse."

Ramsey paused his pacing and sighed. "All reasonable efforts have been attempted, so that leaves the more unreasonable ones. Is Lucas in town yet?"

"Next week. You came back early, thank God."

"It's nice to be missed." Ramsey gave a tight smile. "But I must confess I don't cherish the idea of dealing with the devil. Yet it must be done. There has to be some sort of underlying reason for him to single her out." Ramsey frowned.

"That is what I suspect, but so far John has been unable to come up with any motive."

"Aside from me, you mean," Ramsey remarked.

"Yes, but what does Grace have to do with you? Nothing."

"True. I don't understand. Keep John on the task."

Heathcliff nodded. "Any other suggestions in the meantime?"

Ramsey sighed. "Well, my social calendar just filled up. When is the next event you'll attend?"

Heathcliff gave a shrug. "Tonight, of course, though I'd much rather rescind our invitation. No doubt the devil will be in attendance."

"No doubt. Tell your ward that I'm in town and wish to have the supper dance. Ask Lord Greywick to dance with her for the second waltz; his wife, Lady Greywick was instrumental in your vouchers for Almack's, correct? Certainly he will not mind."

"I'll send a missive to him directly once I get home. He's an affable sort of fellow, I always liked him, not a thing like his bastard of a father."

"I know all about that, sadly. The former Lord Greywick was a pain in the ass, nearly destroyed Lucas's chances with his wife." Ramsey shook his head. "I doubt a tear was shed at that man's funeral."

"I wasn't there to witness it, but I'm of the same conviction. It's a bloody boon that his son is a good egg."

Ramsey nodded. "Good, that takes care of both waltzes, and that way we can stifle any chatter about a match. That's enough damage control for one night. And it will buy us some time to try and ascertain his motives."

Heathcliff nodded, his expression pensive. "One question, and I'm only asking because my wife will certainly ask and I want to hear it from you."

"Go on."

"Is it possible that Lord Westhouse has turned over a new leaf?"

Ramsey gave his most disbelieving expression and then sighed in a frustrated manner. "Does a leopard change its spots? Can you dress a pig and make it a lady? No. Since Eton he's been a bastard, and there's nothing material to prove he's otherwise changed. Have John double check on that, if you wish for a second council on the subject. I'm sure he's left not only ruin in his wake, but much more."

"I'll notify John as well. That's a good idea, I should have thought of it."

"You're preoccupied."

"Clearly."

"Now, is there anything else?" Ramsey asked.

Heathcliff shook his head. "No, thank the Lord. Isn't this enough?"

Ramsey gave a small smile. "Well, until this evening then."

"Yes. We're attending the Rohners' Ball."

"Ah, yes. I just tossed the invitation away. I'll be sure to accept it immediately."

Heathcliff paused and regarded Ramsey. "You're a good friend, Ramsey. Thank you."

Ramsey accepted the compliment, for the first time feeling like it might be true. "Thank you."

With a swift nod, Heathcliff quit the room, leaving Ramsey with the unpleasant expectation of meeting an old enemy.

Apparently it was the season of facing the ghosts of the past.

But Westhouse was certainly one he could go without ever seeing again.

Chapter Fifteen

Grace was exceptionally careful to pay attention to each detail of her dress for the evening. Her hair was pinned perfectly, and her maid had tucked several soft white feathers into her coiffure to add a little more elegance. Her dress was a lovely shade of cream, just the perfect hue that set off her fiery red hair without washing out her complexion, or making it pink—or so the modiste had said when she'd picked out the fabric. Honestly, she couldn't figure out if the modiste was completely accurate, but she did feel beautiful as she gazed at her reflection, so that certainly had to mean *something*. It wasn't every night that she felt like she belonged in a crowded London ballroom with the most elite of the society, but tonight . . . tonight she did.

The carriage was waiting out front as she passed through the foyer and met up with Samantha and the viscount. She regarded him with a slight uneasiness. He'd been quite assertive in his statements regarding

Lord Westhouse, and as such, she felt obligated to give his words weight. However, it fought against every instinct in her mind and heart, so she constantly felt at war within, making her edgy whenever the viscount was around. It wasn't the best of feelings, but it was tolerable. And the elation that overtook her when with Lord Westhouse far overcompensated for the uneasiness from the viscount's disapproval.

As they all entered the carriage, she smoothed her skirt and turned to the window, preparing for a mostly silent ride.

"Did I mention that Lord Sterling was back in residence?" the viscount offered as they started down the road.

Grace turned her gaze to him. "No, I wasn't aware."

The viscount gave a dismissive nod. "He requested the supper waltz with you, and I agreed. I assumed you'd wish to see him since he's been gone for several weeks."

Grace gave a slow nod. Something felt a little off. "Of course, I'm happy to oblige." And she was, but as she thought about it, it smacked of planning.

"And I spoke with Lord Greywick earlier today, he mentioned that he hadn't made your acquaintance yet, and requested the second waltz." The viscount gave an innocent smile. "You know, his wife is the one to thank for the Almack vouchers."

Grace was sure her suspicions were well-founded by this point. He was most certainly trying to control her waltz dances, keeping them occupied so that she couldn't dance with Lord Westhouse.

Her anger simmered just below the surface as she took a breath to calm herself. A temper to match her hair—her father had always said that and it was more than accurate.

As his ward, she understood that he had the power and obligation to oversee her transition into independence, or rather marriage, but that didn't mean that she needed to appreciate that, at least now. Most times she did appreciate it, but not at the moment.

No.

At the moment she wanted to give him an earful.

But that wouldn't help her cause.

What she needed—she thought about it for a moment while the viscount awaited her response. Let him wait.

What she needed was Lord Westhouse to *prove* that he was a changed man. Not that she fully understood the nature of the huge trespass for which he had to atone, but apparently there was more to the story than either side had shared. But, *but,* if Lord Westhouse could prove to them that he was a man of honor, a man of good principles, then they would not meddle so. That had to be the answer.

She'd suggest it tonight.

After all, if he were everything he said, then it would be no effort at all. Would it?

Her temper abated, she turned back to the viscount and realized that he was still awaiting her response. He raised an eyebrow.

Samantha cleared her throat.

"Yes, of course. I'd be honored," Grace replied, quickly searching her memory for the image of Lord Greywick. Certainly she'd at least seen him before, even it if were just across the crowded ballroom.

"Brilliant." He nodded in a very satisfied manner.

Grace had the urge to raise a brow in sarcastic query, but stifled the impulse.

"That dress is so very lovely on you, Grace. I'm very pleased with the modiste's recommendations on the color. It suits you perfectly."

"Thank you." Grace nodded graciously. "I rather thought it was quite beautiful as well."

They continued in polite conversation till they reached the Rohner residence. After they stepped from their conveyance, the music from the ballroom greeted them as if floating on the air. Its welcoming sound beckoned them into the ballroom, which was already crowded with people in conversation. In the middle of the ballroom, the cotillion was being danced, and Grace searched the dancers for Lord Westhouse's familiar face. He had mentioned in passing that the cotillion was one of his favorites.

When she didn't see him, she regarded the rest of the ballroom, her eager eyes searching for his dear face. As one who had never been in love, or even experienced infatuation, it was a delicious, heady feeling to have that special connection, that need to see another person.

The viscount excused himself to speak with another gentleman several yards away. Samantha took her arm and led her toward Lady Greywick. She was standing beside a classically handsome gentleman, and judging by the protective arm at her back, Grace made the assumption he was Lord Greywick.

Lady Greywick gave a wide smile as they approached where they stood, just on the edge of the dance floor.

"Lady Greywick." Samantha gave a welcoming smile.

"Ah, Lady Kilpatrick, a pleasure to see you again." She glanced to her husband, a secretive smile on her lovely face as she looked at the man beside her.

"Ah, Lady Kilpatrick." Lord Greywick gave a knowing grin. "I do believe this is the first time I've had the pleasure of calling you by your married name." He arched his brows meaningfully.

Grace decided that there was more to the story of their acquaintance than she had previously thought.

"Yes, and it's a delight to hear you say it."

"I would think so," he replied. "And this must be your husband's ward?" He turned to Grace with a charming smile.

"Indeed. Please allow me to introduce Miss Grace." Samantha released Grace's hand so that she could curtsey.

Grace smiled as she stood from the formality. "A pleasure, Lord Greywick. We are deeply indebted to you and your lovely wife for the vouchers, thank you."

He gave a dismissive wave of his hand. "It was merely convenient for us to obtain them; you didn't need our help. Not with your connections." He gave a smile to Samantha. "But we were happy to be of service."

The conversation continued, and Grace tried to keep invested in it, but her eyes continued to wander, searching for one man.

The music ended for the cotillion, and a reel began to play. It was then that a shiver ran down her back and she caught her breath, a smile teasing her lips as she turned.

How was it that she knew? Was she already so aware of him to realize his presence before she even saw him?

Was that love? It was devilishly good whatever it was, and she couldn't help but widen her grin when she met his familiar gaze.

"Good evening," he said, but his expression conveyed so much more than just a mere greeting. His gaze was warm, consuming, and made her feverish.

"Good evening," she returned, biting her lip as he took her hand to kiss it. He lingered in the welcoming kiss, then slowly released her. "Dare I hope you're pleased to see me?"

Grace's face flushed with heat as she tried to remain composed. "You're free to think whatever you wish. I, however, am free to conceal my reactions if I please," she teased, flirting.

"A woman who knows her mind—what a pleasure to discover so rare a creature."

"Sir! I cry foul. How dare you be so harsh on my sex. We ladies are not so easily lumped into one category," she countered with a smile.

"You simply outshine them all." He bowed graciously, as if apologizing.

"Such flattery." She glanced up, then returned his affectionate gaze. "I'm rather fond of it."

"I am well versed in finding ways to flatter, my lady. It turns out you make it simple," he returned.

An arm grasped hers, and she turned, expecting to find Samantha, only the arm she grasped was that of the viscount. "Westhouse," he greeted soberly.

"Kilpatrick," Westhouse offered with more than necessary graciousness in his tone.

Grace was proud of such humility in his expression, and turned to the viscount, curious as if such a display could touch his heart concerning his ideas on Lord Westhouse's merit.

The viscount's expression remained unchanged. "If you'll excuse us." The viscount returned, beginning to lead Grace away when Lord Westhouse stepped forward. "Would it be too bold to request the next dance from Miss Grace, that is, if she is not already engaged for it?" he asked the viscount, his expression openness and kindness itself.

Grace's heart melted a bit more. It was one thing to be kind to someone who returned the kindness, but for Westhouse to continue to be graciousness itself to the viscount when he was so stoic and cold in his replies, that was truly well bred of Lord Westhouse. It spoke of his character, and she adored him for it.

"Of course," the viscount replied after a few moments. "If you'll excuse us."

Lord Westhouse bowed, then gave a quick wink to Grace before stepping aside to allow them more room to pass by.

She held her head high as she navigated the ballroom beside the viscount. His demeanor was kind and friendly to everyone else he greeted. How was it that he was so utterly unable to spare such equanimity on Lord Westhouse? It was irritating. He released his hold and offered his arm to Samantha as they came up beside her as she spoke with another acquaintance. When had Samantha left the conversation with Lord and Lady Greywick? Her quick mind put the puzzle pieces together and she was tempted to give Samantha a disbelieving stare. As soon as Lord Westhouse approached, Samantha must have excused herself to find the viscount! That's how he found her so quickly and whisked her away! It was quite efficient, even if it was frustrating. The music shifted, and her heart picked up his cadence. Forgotten was the meddling of her beloved guardians, and all that remained in her mind was the glorious expectation of a dance with Lord Westhouse.

She turned and watched him approach, appreciating the fine figure he cut in his dark evening kit, and offered her most engaging smile—or so she hoped. He bowed smartly when he arrived and took her hand with the utmost tenderness, and led her to the dance floor. She could almost feel the tension in the viscount, but she disregarded it immediately, focused on only the pleasure ahead that was sure to come when dancing with a promising suitor.

The fast-paced dance didn't offer much opportunity for conversation, but it was fascinating how much a mere glance, a simple look could convey without any words. Lord Westhouse's gaze was warm, appreciative, and made her heart feel light. Far too soon the dance ended, and as he led her from the dance floor, he circled in the opposite direction from where they entered.

Grace glanced over her shoulder to see if the viscount was watching them, but his back was turned and a shiver of excitement flickered through her body at the prospect of a few stolen moments with Lord Westhouse. She expected him to lead her along the back wall of the ballroom, maybe circle back leisurely to the viscount so that they might engage in some conversation. Delight filled her, but Lord Westhouse simply gave her a wink, then led them past the ballroom doors into a darker hall.

Several people milled about in the hall, so it was perfectly respectable, but Lord Westhouse didn't linger in the hall; rather, he continued toward the exit of the hall, and for the first time since meeting Lord Westhouse, trepidation mixed with excitement and she wasn't sure which emotion was strongest.

"Forgive me my forwardness, but I'm quite certain that your guardian won't let you out of his sight, and I'm convinced that he's told your butler never to admit me to your residence either. So I've resorted to rather bold behaviors." Lord Westhouse spoke in gentle tones, abating her trepidation. As his words sank in, anger burned in its place.

"Not admit you?" She paused before the door that opened to a lovely garden with a few other couples in quiet conversation.

Her words carried louder than she expected, and several of the couples paused, glancing at her with various levels of disapproval.

She gave an apologetic expression to each and then calmly walked through the door to the stone patio of the gardens. Two of the couples regarded her then left, implying that she was rather loud for their quiet tête-à-tête.

So be it.

Grace still had enough residual anger from the revelation that she wasn't in any mood to be accommodating for anyone.

"I'm making an assumption, and it could be incorrect," Lord Westhouse responded softly, as if wounded.

Grace frowned. How could the viscount not see how his actions wounded others? Especially Lord Westhouse! It was horrific.

"You can be sure that I will mention—"

"Shh . . ." he whispered and stepped closer to her, his other hand grasping hers and facing her fully. "I didn't risk his wrath in stealing you away that I might tattle on him like a child. I simply wanted time with you. It seems to be rarer than a fine emerald, and just as precious." He whispered the words like a caress.

Her temper melted, and a new fire took the place of the frustration. Out of the corner of her eye she noted the last couple leaving them, making the garden area quite private, quite secluded, quite tempting.

Would he kiss her? It would be a terrible risk, to her reputation and to his health, if she assumed the viscount's reactions correctly, but the real question was: did she want him to?

The moonlight made his eyes seem darker, deeper and more mysterious. The gentle circles he drew in her gloved hands were invitingly sweet, and his voice was like a spell, woven over her as he spoke her name so softly.

Grace.

He took the smallest step forward, meeting her gaze with intensity, with purpose, with resolution as his head lowered ever so slightly.

Yes!

No!

Yes!

No!

She couldn't make up her mind. For this to be her first kiss, she wanted it badly, but the implications and the risk if they were to be caught . . . as much as she was angry with the viscount and Samantha for their treatment of Lord Westhouse, she didn't want to let them down by behaving poorly; she loved them too much.

She had only a moment to make a final decision.

Licking her lips, she took a breath and parted her lips.

"Beautiful evening, is it not?" an oddly familiar voice asked, startling Grace as she nearly hopped back from Lord Westhouse to see Lord Sterling lazily leaning against the door frame of the garden entrance. He was regarding her coolly, studying her for a moment as if assessing her worth.

Shame flooded her, not because she had done something wrong, but because she had the sinking suspicion that her estimation in his eyes had just plummeted. And his approval was surely not given easily.

And another reason filtered through her mind a moment later.

He would most certainly tell the viscount.

It wouldn't matter that she was going to step back anyway. It wouldn't matter that she wasn't going to let him kiss her.

She let out a deep sigh, keeping it as silent as possible. She turned to Lord Westhouse, but his attention wasn't on her, it was on Lord Sterling. His kind and open expression was closed off like a vault, and she could almost feel the animosity radiating from him.

Curious, she glanced to Lord Sterling again, wondering if he would radiate the same perturbation. But his stance remained relaxed; the only telltale indication of his intensity was the clench of his jaw as he regarded Lord Westhouse with a placid expression.

"If you'll excuse me." Lord Westhouse bowed slowly, then with very deliberate movements offered his arm to Grace.

She glanced to it, then turned to Lord Sterling, raising her brows as if asking for his opinion on whether she should take it or stay. In the end, she would do what she wished, but some part of her wanted to know his preference. He was still such a mystery, and she was curious by nature.

Most of the time to her own detriment.

Lord Sterling gave his head the smallest shake, and then waited, clearly wondering what she would do.

Turning to Lord Westhouse, she gave a slight bow of her head. "Thank you for the dance. I'll return to the ballroom shortly."

Lord Westhouse frowned, his arm remaining extended as if expecting her to change her mind.

"I'm sure I'll see you soon," she added, wanting to give him some sort of assurance of her regard.

He merely blinked, turned to Lord Sterling with a cold expression, and then tugged on his coat and departed without a backward glance.

Or a good-bye.

Grace was irritated at his lack of good-bye, but she had larger problems to deal with.

Lord Sterling being number one.

There was no way through it but merely through it, so she turned to Lord Sterling and waited for whatever lecture on proper behavior was brewing behind his stormy gaze.

He leaned from the doorframe and walked toward her. Not one to back down from a challenge, she took a step toward him, meeting him halfway. She was no wilting flower; if he had something to say he could say it without fear she'd become a watering pot.

Squaring her shoulders, she tipped her chin up defiantly.

Was it wrong that she was looking forward to a bit of a verbal sparring match?

His gaze met hers with an intensity that gave her a slight shiver.

Apparently she wasn't the only one with a temper.

The garden was about to experience fireworks, just of a different variety.

Vauxhall was about to get some competition.

Chapter Sixteen

Ramsey wasn't the violent sort. He had seen his father's temper too often so he tended to avoid the more confrontational discussions.

Working at Temptations had taught him to conceal his emotions well. While he wasn't charming like Heathcliff, he was able to school his reactions just as smoothly, if not more so. Which was why he offered to go after Miss Grace when the viscount learned that she and Lord Westhouse had disappeared into the hall that led to the gardens. After all, he could easily claim his upcoming waltz and not make a scene. If Heathcliff went after her, there would most certainly be talk as to why a guardian had to chase down his missing ward. Her reputation could be questioned.

And with the gentleman in question being Lord Westhouse, that was certainly an avoidable outcome.

So he'd quickly traveled down the hall, toward the open door that led to the garden. But with each step, his chest grew tighter with dread. It didn't appear as if anyone else were in the garden; in fact, couples seemed to be vacating the premise.

He'd arrived just as Westhouse was going in for the kill.

Ramsey had seen red.

How many maids had to be sent off from the Westhouse estate because they were carrying by-blows? How many ladies had been ruined by his careless dealings with their hearts and bodies? Glenwood Manor bordered the lands of Westhouse's estate, and word traveled quickly within the region. He was a scoundrel of the worst sort.

More than anything, he wanted to grab Westhouse's shoulder, wrench him back onto his ass, and bloody him up with a right hook. But a stronger impulse stayed him.

He wanted to see if she'd follow through.

Would she kiss him?

Would she allow him the liberty? Had she fallen for the snake in the grass? He was charming, to be sure, and a good liar, but that didn't mean that she had bought it.

He watched her pink tongue dart out and lick her full lower lip. Her lips parted and she drew in a breath.

He couldn't wait longer, he had to prevent the damage before it happened. Clearly, she wasn't about to tell him to go to hell, not with those inviting movements. So he spoke up, something mundane like the weather, or moon, something benign. Her gasp rent the air.

And now that Lord Westhouse had stomped away like a spoiled child, he was faced with the very real threat of losing his temper.

With a lady, no less.

One that was not about to back down, not if the expression in her emerald eyes were any indication.

No. If he were a betting man, which, ironically, he was not, he would bet at least a thousand pounds that she was hoping for a fight.

"That was interesting." He spoke through his teeth, his jaw tense as he regarded her. He didn't remember her being quite so beautiful. It was bloody distracting and he forced the unhelpful realization away.

"Depends on your perspective. Some might have called it rude," she returned, arching one light brow.

"Or scandalous," he countered.

"Adventurous." Her lips broke into a smile. "If I were more daring, but I'll have you know that your intervention wasn't necessary."

He couldn't help the sarcastic laugh that escaped his lips. "I'm sure. You looked as if you had everything well in hand. Reputation be damned. Do you have any idea what that would have done to your guardians? How you would have broken all the faith they have in you, clearly unwarranted." He closed his eyes, hating how much he sounded like his father in that last statement. He was about to apologize when a finger poked him in the chest. He blinked down at the offending appendage.

"Don't," she bit out.

"Why not?" he asked in the same tone.

She sighed and removed her finger from his person, leaving a slight achy spot where she poked. "I was about to say no. I'm aware that Samantha and the viscount wouldn't approve, though I can't for the life of me understand why, but I wouldn't harm their faith in me this way." She sighed.

He wasn't buying it. "You're almost as skilled a liar as he is. Maybe you do deserve one another."

Her gaze shot up to meet his, anger burning beneath her green irises. "What did you just say?"

"I said—"

"I heard it, I just wanted to give you the opportunity to apologize for being such an ass," she replied.

He half expected her to cover her mouth at such a word, but she glared at him, brazen and bold and utterly beautiful. How was it that he was just as aroused as he was angry?

He swallowed down his reactions. "You were going to kiss him," he accused.

She had the audacity to roll her eyes. "I was not. I had considered it . . . but I wasn't going to."

"You can't convince me otherwise." He gave his head a slight shake.

"Why ever not?" She had the most offended expression on her face, as if shocked her word carried so little weight.

He was about to reply, and then glanced to the open door. So far no one had come out into the garden to see their argument, but his luck would only last so long.

Luck never stayed.

He frowned, then closed the open door, knowing that he was playing a dangerous game but he wanted—no, he needed—to make a point.

When he turned back to her, she was watching him with a very dubious and irritated expression.

He stomped back to her, angry with her for not being honest. Was it so difficult to admit her weak moment?

"You wouldn't have denied him, you would have ruined yourself, and in that, sealed your future! Why would you risk such a thing?" he asked, his tone accusing.

"I wasn't going to!" she shouted. He half expected her to stomp her foot.

He scoffed, absently placing his hands on his hips.

She let out a low growl of frustration and closed the distance between them, her finger poking him in the chest.

Again.

"I was tempted, but I was *not going to kiss him.*"

He narrowed his eyes. "You licked your lips," he stated accusingly.

She reared her head back, her expression fierce. "*That* is your evidence against my word?" She gave a humorless laugh and pulled her finger back. "People lick their lips all the time *when they are about to speak.*"

"Or, when they are about to kiss," he added triumphantly.

"I've never kissed anyone before so I wouldn't know!" she retorted hotly. "So if that is your only evidence against me—"

"You parted your lips next," he interrupted.

She gave him the most irritated expression. "You just parted your lips as well, *to speak!*" she replied hotly.

He had to admit, his argument wasn't gaining traction, not when she didn't understand the mechanics. Individually, licking one's lips and parting them was normal, but . . . in a kiss it was . . . telling. How did he explain that? Wasn't this something a mother or a governess explained?

He was out of his element.

But he was also unwilling to give up. No. The gauntlet had been thrown and he wasn't about to back down.

"You simply don't understand," he said.

"Clearly! Since I'm licking my lips and opening my mouth during this conversation and not *once* have you accused me of trying to kiss *you!*" she argued.

And damn it all, she had a point.

But what she didn't know was that it was damned hard *not* to want to kiss her.

As if pushing the temptation further, she licked her lips.

And he had the stupidest, most ill-advised, and reckless impulse ever.

He tipped his head, quickly assessing the distance between them. It wasn't much; she was nearly stepping on his toes. He met her gaze, then studied her features, resting his study on her full lips. After he'd looked his fill, he met her curious but not unaccepting expression.

He licked his lips.

She mirrored the movement, her lips parting just a fraction of in inch as she took in a shaky breath.

"I'm . . . that is . . ." she trailed off, swallowing. "Talking."

"You indeed are," he murmured softly, then lowered his head to trace the line of her cheek with the edge of his nose, inhaling deeply the faint and inviting fragrance of lavender.

She released a shaking breath. "Oh."

"Still talking," he whispered against her skin.

"That's what . . ." She let out a tight breath, then breathed in again. "What happens when we open our . . . mouths?" she finished.

He reached up and traced the length of her arms with his fingers, tickling her skin softly till he reached her shoulders, then grasped them warmly, holding her in place.

He trailed several kisses from her cheek, along her

jaw to the base of her neck. Her pulse pounded against his lips, her heart feverishly pumping. He smiled at the reaction she was experiencing from his attentions.

Though, truth be told, his heart was pounding just as fast.

His mind kept telling him that he was riding a dangerous line.

He kept telling his mind to shut up as he feathered kisses up her neck to the base of her ear. She tipped her neck just enough to grant him further access as she let out a soft sigh.

"You aren't talking anymore," he whispered into her ear, then nipped the earlobe teasingly.

"I . . ." she murmured, then didn't finish.

He wasn't ready yet; he wanted every coherent thought from her mind, he wanted to drive her so mad with need that she couldn't whisper even one word.

He trailed his fingers along her shoulders, to the base of her neck and down the lines of her back as he kissed down to the hollow of her throat, lingering there as his tongue swirled against her skin.

"Anything else you wish to add to the conversation?" he asked, proud of himself that he was able to trail together any words at all. His body hummed with need.

When she didn't answer, he knew he'd won.

But victory wasn't complete, not without the prize.

He leaned back to meet her closed eyes. When they opened, they were unfocused and hungry.

He lowered his head.

She licked her lips.

He was a breath away.

She parted her mouth.

And he claimed the prize.

Her kiss was warm, untutored, and inviting all at once. Like a cool, refreshing lake in the middle of a hot summer day, the sensation was as electrifying as it was delightful. Her lips were soft, her scent intoxicating, and she willingly leaned into him with the smallest invitation from his hand on her back. He released her from the kiss, but only to tip his head in the other direction and claim her lips again. He wanted to taste her from every direction, in every way. Like taking a drink of cool water only to realize you were parched with thirst, one kiss wasn't enough, two wouldn't be enough. He drank her in, reminding himself that she was innocent, that she was learning to accept and return a kiss, when what he wanted to do was ravage her utterly.

He knew his control was wavering, and whatever honorable shred of his dignity remained gave him the strength to slow the kiss and end it.

Yet, as she opened her eyes, a sobering realization tickled the back of his mind.

Rather than simply collecting the prize of her kiss, he might have forfeited something more important.

His heart.

God save him.

Heathcliff was going to kill him.

Chapter Seventeen

Grace's lips still tingled from Lord Sterling's kiss more than half an hour after it happened. She still couldn't quite fathom that it had occurred, or even how.

Well, she knew *how.* She wasn't an idiot, but well . . . one moment he was arguing with her, the next moment she was melting in his arms.

Like a wanton woman.

Wasn't she half in love with Lord Westhouse? How could she accept another's attentions easily? Was she a strumpet in ladies clothing? How had she never even suspected such a nature lurking within!

Her mind kept spinning like the dancers in the middle of the room as she stayed rooted to her place beside Samantha.

Lord Sterling had returned her to Samantha's side as soon as the kiss ended, not saying one word about it.

Damn the man.

As soon as she could think coherently, she was going to have plenty of words to say regarding it.

First of all, why?

He didn't love her.

She was quite certain he didn't even particularly like her, but he'd kissed her.

And it wasn't an innocent-type kiss.

Granted, she wasn't exactly an authority on the subject, but she was quite certain her assumption was correct.

It was a kiss that spoke of passion, desire, and all those other words she had heard but never experienced.

Till now.

It made her want more.

To experience it all.

Yes, if she needed any further confirmation, the last thought sealed the truth. Clearly she was a strumpet at heart. That was the only explanation.

Good Lord, what was she to do?

She'd studiously avoided glancing about the ballroom, half terrified to meet the gaze of either gentleman; rather she kept her gaze ahead as her mind continued to process all the mixed emotions of the evening. Lord Greywick had collected her for the first waltz shortly after she'd returned to Samantha's side. The dance had progressed well enough, she hadn't stepped on his toes more than twice, but she was too distracted to be much of a conversationalist.

When the waltz ended, she had remained in her place, and remained there still, uncertain on how to continue. What did one do after experiencing a kiss like that?

"Are you well?" Samantha asked, breaking into her swirling thoughts.

Grace turned to her, nodding once. "Yes."

Samantha tipped her chin. "You're certain?" Her hazel eyes were concerned as she narrowed her gaze slightly.

Grace took a silent breath. "Yes. I'm merely . . . thoughtful," she answered, staying as close to the truth as possible to keep from a lie, but still not revealing the entire truth.

"About?" Samantha inquired softly, her gaze shifting to the surrounding area as if making sure they didn't have eavesdroppers on their private conversation.

As if there was any privacy to be had in a London ballroom.

Grace gave her head a slight shake, hoping that Samantha would drop the subject, at least till later.

"Very well," Samantha remarked, but her tone indicated that she was simply biding her time till she'd ferret out the truth.

Grace didn't begrudge her intrusion; rather, she practically welcomed it. If she ever needed any assistance in life, it was now. Though, Grace was not particularly sure if she would mention the kiss with Lord Sterling. Perhaps she would just ask some questions in generalities that would hopefully be enough.

The current dance ended and another took its place, all while Grace's thoughts continued to pour through her like water. Who knew that a kiss could be so confusing?

She'd always assumed that a kiss would be telling, would indicate a decision, something that clarified.

Not something that utterly confounded her, made

the situation even cloudier rather than bring it into focus.

Apparently, she had much more to learn about love other than just the tingling feeling.

And was a kiss an indication of love? She had always assumed it was, but that assumption was on its ear now since she was certain Lord Sterling didn't love her.

And she was equally certain that she didn't love him.

Attraction, however, was an entirely different story.

And again, she was back to square one, just as confused, without any progress toward an answer to even one of her millions of questions.

And the one person who could answer her inquiries was the very person she wasn't exactly wanting to speak to, at least not yet.

But life didn't wait till you were prepared, that she *was* certain of, and it was proven true once more as a familiar voice greeted Samantha from the other side of Grace.

"Lady Kilpatrick."

Grace held her breath, her heart speeding faster like a horse galloping. She released the tense breath only to trade it for another, waiting for his address of her.

Or would he not?

Did she want him to?

Good Lord, would the questions never end?

It was then that she realized that rather than wait, she could take some initiative.

Why hadn't she thought of it before?

She turned to face Lord Sterling, regarding him as coolly as she could with her face burning with a blush she couldn't suppress.

Well, so be it.

"Miss Grace," he greeted her politely.

As if they were having perfectly proper tea.

Not as if he'd kissed her senseless no more than an hour before.

Well, if he wasn't going to act as if anything happened, she could follow suit. "Lord Sterling," she replied coolly.

"Ah, perfect timing," the viscount commented as he walked up to their small, somewhat tense party.

As if on cue, the strains of a waltz began, and to both her delight and her horror, Lord Sterling offered his hand for the dance.

She'd forgotten he'd already requested it through the viscount earlier.

And she was thrilled to accept the opportunity perhaps to ease a bit of her curiosity.

Trepidation replaced the horror at the knowledge that she'd surely step on his toes, probably more than she would have normally, simply because she would be under stress.

She accepted his hand, and swallowed her tension as they made their way to the center of the dance floor.

He placed his hand at the side of her waist; the warmth seeped through her, heating her very soul in a way she'd never experienced. It was different when Lord Westhouse held her in the frame of the waltz. Her whole body reacted to the heat of Lord Sterling's hand, causing her already pounding heart to take flight.

She forced her reactions to the back of her mind as she held her chin high and placed her hand on his shoulder, and the other hand within his. Even through her glove his hand was warm, and so much larger than hers that it nearly swallowed it whole. And good Lord, the man was tall. She'd noticed it before, and again when he'd kissed her. But that kiss was so sudden that she hadn't truly taken the time to consider any other nuances present. But now, she desperately needed a distraction and that was the perfect one. Her head was just to the height of his shoulder in such close proximity, but even in his height, he wasn't slight. She'd always thought that tall men were merely more stretched out, so they were smaller, leaner in other ways.

Not so with Lord Sterling.

He was . . . oh, what was the word? Proportionate. Yes. And she was thrilled to have such a perfect distraction from the way he led her around the dance floor, keeping her mind occupied.

"You're unusually quiet," he remarked, a twinkle of mischief in his eyes. They were a lovely color, bright and cheerful. How had she not noticed before?

Drat, she was losing her footing. She felt the telltale bump under her slipper that meant she had stepped halfway on his boot rather than the floor.

To his credit, he didn't wince.

Not too much.

Grace found herself in the odd position of not knowing what to say. Speechlessness wasn't a malady she suffered often, if ever. However, she was having a rather difficult time coming up with an answer to his comment.

"Oh?" was all she could reply, then kicked herself mentally for such a stupid answer.

"Yes. You're usually rather . . . chatty."

She blinked. *Chatty?* "Perhaps I have nothing to say," she replied tersely.

"I find that hard to believe."

"Apparently believing me is not something you're

able to do this evening. I can't imagine why," she bit out, trying to keep her face from betraying her irritation.

He smirked, the cad! "You're rather hard to believe when your words say one thing, and your actions say another."

"I already told you—"

"Yes, and how did that end?" he interrupted, an arch to his brow.

She twisted her lips and glanced to the side. Drat! He had a point, miserable man that he was.

All her trepidation melted in the heat of her anger at the realization that the kiss had been given in order to make a point.

And she'd fallen for it.

Her nostrils flared; she could feel them as she breathed in the realization that she'd been taken in, fooled, and made a fool of in the process!

"How dare you—"

"Shhh, you'll make a scene." He gave his head a little shake and gave a meaningful glance around the ballroom.

Grace stepped on his toe, hard.

"That was on purpose," he accused with a small grin, as if her efforts were merely amusing.

"I was making a point. Like you did earlier this evening." She arched a brow, stiffening her spine.

His brow furrowed, and he regarded her as if studying a specimen. She wanted to do more than simply step on his foot. How dare he even pretend he didn't fully understand!

"Do you think so little of my intelligence that you didn't imagine I'd figure it out? You were simply pushing your point, and I conceded. You won. But I'm a fast learner, and I won't make the same mistake twice." Her face was hot with perturbation as she regarded him, daring him to deny it.

"Pity, that."

Grace frowned. That was not the reaction she was expecting.

"Pardon?" she asked, not certain how to continue.

"Pity. It was a rather delightful point to communicate. And I thought I articulated it well," he answered benignly, as if discussing the weather. Not a soul-moving kiss that wasn't supposed to happen.

At least, wasn't supposed to happen with him.

"And for the record, I do not have any misgivings about your intelligence. You're probably one of the quickest wits I've met, and your mind is just as sharp. You're a formidable counterpart in repartee; however, I would make one suggestion."

Grace arched a disbelieving brow.

"Stick to subject matter with which you have experience," he added with a slow grin.

"You're insufferable," she accused, her face heating, but this time with a tinge of shame.

"Perhaps. But I also saved your reputation."

"You also tried to ruin it."

"I did nothing of the sort. You were perfectly safe from ruination. If I had wanted to ruin you . . ." He paused, leaning forward as they made the corner. "You'd know by now," he answered softly, as if the word were a promise rather than a threat.

She couldn't think of a proper response to such a statement, so she held her peace, narrowing her eyes instead.

"Ah, speechless for the second time tonight. I must say, I'm quite impressed with myself."

"At least one of us is impressed. I find I'm rather disappointed."

"You didn't act disappointed." He alluded to their kiss.

"I don't have much to compare it with, as you mentioned regarding my lack of experience. To take my reaction as favorable when I have so little to compare it with would be the most arrogant assumption you've made this evening," she finished, proud to have put together such a statement as she fought the temper that was rising within.

"Ah, so maybe not so speechless," he remarked. "You know, Miss Grace, I think I like you."

Grace blinked; apparently that was her favorite reaction of the evening. Along with not being to follow the man who kissed her one moment and then engaged in verbal sparring the next. She was never quite certain what he would say, or do.

It was an oddly exhilarating combination.

"Is that a compliment?" she asked as the music came to an end.

"It's certainly not an insult," he replied.

Apparently, he wasn't going to explain his answer further because he led her to the viscount's side, bowed, and then departed. She watched his back as he wound through the scene of people, and then through the doors that led to the foyer, leaving the ballroom entirely.

"Why is Lord Sterling leaving?" Grace heard Samantha ask the viscount. She turned so she could better hear the answer.

The viscount shrugged. "Probably to work. He's overly diligent. I'm surprised he stayed as long as he has."

Grace turned back to where Lord Sterling had left, her curiosity concerning the man ever growing.

Who was the man who kissed ladies one moment, insulted them the next, then disappeared to work at a nameless place she wasn't allowed to know about, let alone visit?

One thing was for certain.

She wanted to find out.

Chapter Eighteen

Ramsey stood up beside his study desk at Temptations the moment the knock sounded at the door. He had been waiting.

It was only a matter of time, and honestly, he was shocked it had taken as long as it had.

Sure enough, like an executioner headed for duty, Heathcliff walked into the room, his expression unreadable.

Ramsey took a breath, already knowing that he wouldn't fight back. No. He'd taken the past few hours to resign himself to the fate that awaited him.

He'd do the honorable thing. He'd marry the girl; he would have to do it. Honor demanded it, and more importantly, he'd done the stupidest thing in his life—well, almost the stupidest thing in his life—and kissed his best friend's ward when he was supposed to be protecting her from the other rogue.

Well, he'd made his bed, and it was his turn to lie in

it. Hopefully, Heathcliff would not bloody him up too much; if he were to suffer through a wedding, he didn't want to wear two black eyes for the occasion. He lifted his chin just slightly, waiting, bracing for the blow that was surely only moments away.

Heathcliff approached the desk and frowned. "What the hell is wrong with you?"

Ramsey was about to answer, even though he couldn't find the most articulate response. He wasn't sure what had come over him in that forbidden moment when he'd kissed Miss Grace. What excuse did he have? Insanity? Desire? Need? All were true, and all were bloody worthless as far as excuses.

"Are you well? You look as if you're about to be violently ill." Heathcliff took a step back as if expecting Ramsey to cast up his accounts that very moment.

It was Ramsey's turn to be confused. "Pardon?"

"I told cook to stop making the tattie scones with those green potatoes. Makes me sick every time too. Sit down, it'll pass." Heathcliff gestured to Ramsey's chair and then took a seat as well on the opposite side.

Ramsey sat dubiously, wondering when the thunder would take place.

"So, what did you find out about Grace and West-house?" Heathcliff asked casually, crossing his ankles as he leaned back in the chair.

But was it too casually? Ramsey couldn't figure it out. Didn't he know? Didn't Miss Grace tell him what had transpired between them? He was certain she'd at least confide in Heathcliff's wife, but . . . maybe he had assumed incorrectly.

It wouldn't be the first time. But it would certainly be surprising.

Curious.

Heathcliff arched his brows, encouraging Ramsey to answer.

Ramsey cleared his throat and relaxed his rigid posture. "He was moving in for the kill when I arrived, bloody bastard. Needless to say, my intrusion broke up the tender moment." Ramsey's chest felt tight. He wasn't lying to his friend, but he damned well wasn't telling the truth either.

"Bastard," Heathcliff swore under his breath.

Ramsey also left out the portion that would implicate Miss Grace in accepting Westhouse's attentions. No need to draw attention to that portion of the conversation; it would only lead to more questions.

Ones that he really didn't want to answer, especially if Heathcliff wasn't aware.

The last thing he wanted was another wife. And that's certainly what he would end up with if Heathcliff knew the truth.

Or at least, the whole story.

"What do you suggest we do now? Do you think he'll stop his attentions or do you think you just encouraged him to fight harder?" Heathcliff asked, sitting up and leaning over his knees, tenting his fingers as he leaned against his hands in query.

"He's not going to just walk away. There's a reason for his intrusion; we just don't know it yet. Have you found anything on your end? Has John uncovered any leads?" Ramsey frowned as he concentrated on Heathcliff's words.

"Just confirmation of what we already knew. He's not suspected to be after a wife, and he's not deep enough into debt to be a fortune hunter. He's financially stable, but reckless in his personal life. The rumors are that the women on staff at his London home are more courtesan than parlor maid. At least that part of his character is already well known to us."

"Not shocking," Ramsey remarked, agreeing.

"Indeed. So, if he has so many other women to feed his fantasies, why turn to my ward?"

"That is exactly what we need to find out." Ramsey leaned forward. "Could it have to do with Miss Grace's family? Her parents? Her past? Any sort of correlation that we could potentially uncover?"

Heathcliff gave his head a decisive shake. "They—Grace's parents—were hardly in the country at all; they roamed about. It would be hard to make any correlation between them and Lord Westhouse. He's never been one to travel."

"Then we can assume that it has nothing to do with her history, so that leaves . . ." Ramsey leaned back in his chair slowly.

"You." Heathcliff spoke the word simply, but it carried a weight that settled over Ramsey's shoulders.

"How in heaven's name, though? I'm not connected with her in the slightest! There's no reason for him to single her out with me in mind!" Ramsey reacted angrily.

"I haven't a clue. But you're the only common denominator in the whole complicated problem."

Ramsey sighed. "What a bloody mess."

"Indeed. I'm half tempted to just sequester her from attending any events till we can be certain what he's about."

"That's not a bad idea, but I have doubts about your being able to achieve it."

Heathcliff let out a beleaguered sigh. "She is rather stubborn."

Ramsey scoffed.

Heathcliff narrowed his eyes slightly, his gaze questioning.

Ramsey sobered immediately, no need to raise suspicion.

Heathcliff's gaze shifted, and Ramsey was immediately on edge at the adjustment. "You're not . . . interested in her, are you?" He articulated the words carefully.

Interested? No. *Attracted*, yes. Dangerously so. However, to Ramsey's great benefit, Heathcliff had asked the first question, not the second. So it was with a mostly clear conscience that he said, "No."

Heathcliff shrugged. "Well, until we figure this out, would you mind keeping one of her waltzes in reserve if we are in attendance at a party? Keep talk down, and try to manage the situation while we figure things out."

"Of course, raise suspicion about my designs on her as well."

"At least it will be speculation about you, rather than he."

"You mean, in addition to his."

"At least the speculation won't be entirely about him." Heathcliff all but rolled his eyes in exasperation. "Besides, I trust you. You're not going to do something stupid. He, however, I do not trust."

Ramsey's chest tightened, his breathing grew shallow and he nearly vomited the truth out at his friend's statement of faith in him, but he barely restrained himself.

There was no need to reveal what happened.

Because it would never happen again.

That was how he would make penance. If he wouldn't be honest, at least he would be honorable and keep his distance. He'd dance the damn waltz with her to keep her from Westhouse, but nothing more.

As Heathcliff gave his leave and quit the room, Ramsey nodded, vowing to be worthy of his friend's trust.

Yet as the door closed, leaving him with his traitorous thoughts, he wondered if perhaps this was one of those times where the spirit was willing, but the body was weak.

Because even as he swore he'd never do it again . . . her kiss haunted him.

And he didn't want to be rid of that ghost.

It was with that same trepidation that Ramsey accepted the invitation to the Martins' rout that evening. It was a popular party and would be well attended, no doubt attracting half the ton, including Lord Westhouse.

While Ramsey wasn't proud of his lack of self-control, he also knew that his nature was far more honorable than that of Lord Westhouse. If Miss Grace had to be at one of their mercies, it would be his.

But Ramsey was resolved to be distant, aloof, and above temptation. So it was with a false sense of security he attended the party that evening.

He tugged on his shirt cuffs, straightening his shoulders and tipping his chin up ever so slightly as he walked into the already well-attended ballroom. The music filtered through the air, muted by the buzzing of a hundred conversations while footmen wound around people offering refreshment. He'd seen it all a thousand times, and it had never taken on any shine in his opinion. It was a mystery why so many people lived for these events, when he'd rather avoid them all together.

A lady caught his eye, her fan slowly moving in front of her face as she gave the signal for him to come closer.

He walked in the other direction.

That was another thing he'd never understand. Why flirt with a fan? Bloody useless if you asked him. No. He was on a mission. Find Heathcliff, locate Westhouse, keep Miss Grace occupied for a waltz, then leave.

It sounded simple.

But, seeing as it involved Miss Grace, he had the nagging suspicion it wouldn't be as easily executed as it sounded.

She was a menace in every sense of the word, especially to his peace of mind. He'd tried in vain to force all thoughts of their kiss to the furthest reaches of his mind. But the memories always flooded back.

It was one bloody kiss.

It shouldn't have meant anything.

It shouldn't have affected him so.

Yet, it did.

Which was why it had him so concerned. It didn't make sense. And he couldn't abide things that stood against reason.

Irritated, he turned and scanned the room for Heathcliff once more, his gaze meeting that of a pair of startling green eyes.

She was not more than a few yards away, close enough for him to see the small arch of her brow as she studied him, unabashedly.

There was nothing coy about her.

Nothing flirtatious.

Just brazen, bold, and beautiful.

His heart started to pound harder, deeper, as if it were performing in a race.

All his grand deceptions about his immovability emotionally came crashing down, and Ramsey was forced to reconcile himself with the truth.

He was in trouble.

And once again, it defied reason.

He should turn and quit the room.

He should hightail it back to his study at Temptations.

Instead, he put one foot in front of the other, meeting her inquiring gaze.

She tipped her head, as if curious as to his intentions. It was an honest question, one he didn't have an honest answer to. He wasn't sure about anything at the moment, except that he would be damned if Westhouse connived his way into her life.

Not without a fight.

A swift movement caught his gaze and he flickered his gaze away from Miss Grace to watching the swiftly approaching figure of Lord Westhouse.

Apparently, the fight was about to happen sooner rather than later.

Pity it wasn't in a place less civil. Ramsey squeezed his hands into hard fists, fantasizing about the pleasant crunch Westhouse's nose would make under a solid swing of his fist.

But in society, fighting had to take on a more cloak-and-dagger camouflage.

It was a good thing Ramsey had learned the art well.

Because judging from the expression on Westhouse's face, they were in for a long night.

Round one, Ramsey thought, watching as Heathcliff turned from beside Miss Grace, noting the approach of each gentleman.

He stiffened at the sight of Lord Westhouse, and as his gaze shifted to Ramsey, he gave the slightest nod.

Ramsey almost felt pity for Westhouse, almost. With two against one, it was hardly a fair fight.

Even if it would never actually come to physical blows.

"Ah, Lord Westhouse," Miss Grace greeted, causing Ramsey's hackles to rise.

He should have known.

Miss Grace wouldn't make this easy on them. No.

He took a deep breath, and closed the distance. "Westhouse," he all but clipped.

Let the gauntlet be thrown.

"Ah, Sterling," Westhouse replied in a polite tone that was overlaid with venom, but only those who knew him would have noticed its presence. "Good evening. I'm just collecting Miss Grace for our first dance." He turned to Grace and offered his hand.

And damn the woman, she took it, turned her back, and walked with him onto the dance floor.

Leaving Ramsey standing beside Heathcliff with a disapproving frown.

"That was unfortunate timing," Ramsey remarked.

"At least it wasn't a bloody waltz."

"That's mine," Ramsey replied with a possessive tone. He shook his head.

If Heathcliff noted the tone of his voice, he didn't offer a response to it.

"In my mind, I saw this scene playing out differently," Ramsey spoke after a moment.

"Was blood involved?" Heathcliff asked quietly, but with a smile in his voice."

"A great amount."

"We were thinking the same thing," Heathcliff replied. "I need you to come by tomorrow. There was some news that John uncovered and I need to discuss it with you."

Ramsey nodded, his gaze never leaving the two dancers that had escaped.

"I'll be there midafternoon."

"Very well." Heathcliff paused. "At least he's getting his dance over with. He can't ask for more without causing talk and I do think I at least have Grace's help in that department. She promised that only one dance would be accepted."

"How did you wrestle such a promise?" Ramsey asked with a little irony in his tone.

"In return, if she cooperated, I promised to tell her about Temptations." Heathcliff sighed.

Ramsey almost choked. "Dear Lord, what were you thinking?"

"She's been inquiring, relentlessly I might add, and it seemed like a good idea at the time. At least it gave me what I needed most. Cooperation."

"No, my friend that is called blackmail." Ramsey shook his head. "She's more of a menace than I gave her credit for, which is saying a lot."

"She's a good girl," Heathcliff added in her defense. "She's not a wilting English flower, and I don't wish to break her spirit. It's her defense, and while I could press the issue—I am her guardian—I don't wish to destroy her free will and strong spirit."

Ramsey turned to his friend. "Growing soft in your old age?"

"Apparently." He shrugged.

"Well . . . at least you have her cooperation."

"I'll take the victories I can win without much fighting. I'll save that for Westhouse when I can finally give him the facer he deserves."

"Me first," Ramsey remarked, then turned his attention back to the dancers.

Me first.

Chapter Nineteen

When Grace had lived in India, there was a house on the corner that had a beautiful front garden. In the lush garden was a small flock of peacocks. The females were lovely, but nowhere near the magnificence of the males with their long feathery tails that would spread wide to display their colors. The males would strut about the lawn, showing off to all who would take a moment to watch. They were proud of their feathers, and would often fight other males to show dominance.

As the dance ended with Lord Westhouse and he led her back to her guardian, she had the same sensation from long ago when watching the male peacocks.

Lord Westhouse's shoulders were broad and straight, his chest slightly puffed up as he all but strutted with her at his side to where the viscount and Lord Sterling waited.

The viscount didn't appear as combative as Lord Sterling. Rather than puff his chest up like Lord Westhouse, Lord Sterling's height made him tower over them all, as if a king surveying his subjects. It was a different display, but just as evident.

At once she decided that peacocks were overrated. All this display, for what? What was the prize? Her? Unlikely. It was about ego, attitude, and dominance. With a beleaguered sigh, she stepped from Lord Westhouse at the earliest opportunity and stood by Samantha, mentioning the need for some lemonade.

Let them *peacock* for each other; *she* had no use for it.

But at least one good thing came from the whole mess with Lord Westhouse and the viscount. She would finally learn what the viscount did when he left the residence for the evening. The mystery had been eating her alive, and with everyone so close-lipped about it, it nearly drove her mad! What delicious secret was she finally ferreting out? It was heady to know that she'd finally learn what had been concealed for so long. She was, however, loathe to give up any further dancing opportunities with Lord Westhouse, but she also saw the wisdom of her guardian's request. There was, after all, no reason to cause talk. And truth be told, she was rather put out with Lord Westhouse's behavior when he'd stormed off from Lord Sterling's intrusion.

And she was rather frustrated with Lord Sterling as well! Who kissed a woman like that and then didn't call on her? Or at least request a dance? It was irritating to say the least, and at first opportunity she was going to give him a piece of her mind.

Thankfully her mind was working quite well now that the fog of confusion, and—dare she say it?—pleasure, had finally dissipated. Now, all that remained was anger.

And if she were honest, a little bit of a wound to her pride.

Had she not kissed well? Was she somehow wanting in some area? No doubt he had scads more experience than she, but . . . well, she wanted a kiss to mean something! Was that too much to ask? Her first kiss, no less!

Her opportunity to give that piece of her mind to Lord Sterling came about far quicker than she was expecting.

When they returned to their party, Lord Westhouse had departed and as the first bars of the waltz music were played, Lord Sterling offered his hand. "Would you honor me with the pleasure?"

She almost said no.

Then remembered all that she had to say.

Perhaps she needed more than one dance to speak it all. So, she accepted and bit back a satisfied grin when she stepped on his toe the very first turn.

Served him right.

"Could you have been more condescending?" she asked from the gate, earning a startled and then mutinous expression from her dance partner.

"Pardon?"

"Your expressions are clear as day, Lord Sterling. You think yourself above Lord Westhouse—"

"I am, in rank and in every other possible way," he interrupted in an irritated manner.

She sighed, "Be that as it may, regarding rank that is, but there is no need to parade about and look down upon the rest of humanity as if they were below you."

His expression was offended, his lips drawn into a thin line. "How so?"

She bit her lip as the fleeting picture of a peacock flitted through her mind again. "You were—honestly, you both were strutting about like peacocks. It was amusing as much as it was irritating. Tell me, what color are your feathers if you're so interested in displaying them?" she teased, unable to keep her anger in full force. She was far too amused by the bewildered and stunned expression on his face.

"Peacocks?" he repeated.

"Yes." She nodded once and he turned her.

His brows drew together and he looked as if he wished to say something but still hadn't pulled together an appropriate reply to such an odd statement.

"I do believe I have rendered *you* speechless." She turned the tables, remembering when he had mentioned the same to her. It didn't matter that such a bold statement alluded directly to their kiss; she had much to say on *that* topic as well!

He narrowed his eyes as his lips pursed as if trying to suppress a twinge of a smile. Grace had to wonder, how often did he actually release his tension and grin without constraint? All at once she wanted to provoke that type of grin, to draw it from him. It was a challenge, with a worthy prize.

When he didn't reply readily, she continued. "Although I must say it's less of a challenge for me since you are less disposed to conversation than I. In that way, I must forfeit that your ability to render *me* speechless is a greater feat."

"Yes, since you rarely give me the opportunity to get a word in edgewise," he interrupted. "But I must defend myself."

"Oh? From what have I accused you that wasn't founded in some truth?"

He grinned, adding a mischievous light to his expression and rendering her with a fast heartbeat in response. She had the satisfaction of achieving the goal of provoking a smile, and it was a worthy endeavor, one she decided needed to be repeated as often as possible.

"A great many things, but for the sake of time, I'll merely address one."

"It seems I have many sins to atone for," she added.

"And a great many more I'm sure you'll commit," he replied, with a slight exasperation to his tone. "But I digress. You accused me of putting on airs to appear as if I'm of higher importance than those around me, specifically Lord Westhouse." He said the name with a venom in his tone before continuing. "To add insult, you compared me with a useless bird."

"A peacock, specifically," she couldn't stop herself from adding.

"Yes." He arched a brow. "I have no use for the man, and I know my admittance of this truth will not shock you as you are already fully aware. He's a wastrel and has abused far too many women to be called a gentleman, even in the loosest terms. I don't make a habit of disparaging a peer of the realm, but my acquaintance with him is far too long lasting and his character is deeply rooted in neglect of the most basic principles of morality."

"And you're such a paragon of morality yourself? That makes you a proper judge?" she asked, raising a brow.

He paused. "No. I'm not in any position to point a moral finger in one direction that doesn't also point in mine; however, you would be wise to listen to my words."

"But, my lord." She released a tight breath, weary of the tide of conversation. Yet she was far more willing to give such accusations merit coming from Lord Sterling. With his aversion to scandal and his proper behavior, he would be overly sensitive to weaknesses in moral fabric, not that the viscount would not, but somehow the words coming from Lord Sterling affected her differently. She shoved the thoughts aside to address the current thought that must be voiced. "My lord, you are addressing the character of a man no longer present. You've yet to answer for yourself in defense of the original reason you found offense."

He frowned. "Not so easily deterred, are you?"

"I've been called worse than persistent."

At this he chuckled, and the dance came to an end. "So have I, Miss Grace. A peacock being one," he added as he led her back to the viscount. After a quick bow he took his leave.

Her gaze lingered on his back, and an anticipation welled within her.

It was one thing to be attracted to a man.

But to find a worthy opponent in dialogue? It was priceless.

And she was quite certain that Lord Sterling was such a treasure.

But she was equally certain he hadn't a clue.

It would be fun to enlighten him . . . and hopefully she'd earn another shocked expression.

As the evening ended, and she finally found herself in bed, her thoughts lingered not on Lord Westhouse, but on Lord Sterling.

And if she had the energy, she would have asked herself why. But exhausted, all she could do was willingly fall asleep thinking of the next time she'd be able to test his wit.

Chapter Twenty

"You've lost your bloody mind," Ramsey remarked, again, for Heathcliff's benefit.

"A promise is a promise," Heathcliff replied, his tone impatient and beleaguered. "It won't take long, but I just wanted you to know in case you saw her about."

"I won't be seeing her because you have no business bringing her here! Do you know what she'll do? She'll find it fascinating, devour each scandalous idea and then sneak here just like Lucas's wife and we'll have a bloody mess all over again!" Ramsey threw up his hands as he paced about Heathcliff's office at Temptations.

Ramsey paused his pacing to cast a glare at his friend, who didn't remotely look as concerned as he should. "You mark my words."

"They are marked." Heathcliff sighed. "Would you rather her spend more of her time with Lord Westhouse? Is this truly such an ill trade?" Heathcliff asked, arching a brow as he watched his friend.

Ramsey didn't have a proper response to such a logical question. He was feeling rather illogical at the moment. Everything about Miss Grace had him in knots, all rationality was tossed out the window, and he simply reacted.

It all had been a domino effect from that first kiss.

And it had been tumbling down around his ears ever since.

Especially since he kept restarting the whole damned effect by thinking, dwelling, and reliving the bloody kiss.

He cast a glance to Heathcliff, thankful that he couldn't read minds. That would be a holy disaster on top of another. "I still think it's a terrible idea," Ramsey added, just because it bore saying again.

"You've mentioned that," Heathcliff reminded him.

"When are you bringing her?" Ramsey asked the question but it came out more of a growl than an actual query. He ran his fingers through his hair and tensed as he listened to the answer.

"This afternoon. It will be deserted and she can answer a little of her curiosity and move on," Heathcliff answered, his expression clearly indicating that he didn't see what all the fuss was about.

Ramsey studied him. How was it that he was so dense? It truly was a mystery. The moment that Miss Grace stepped into Temptations her curiosity would not be satisfied, but would be roused to a whole new level of irritating and insatiable. She wouldn't stop after seeing it for a few moments in broad daylight. No. She'd simply create more questions, which would lead to deeper questions, which would mean she would

not get the answers she sought, because while Heathcliff was inexcusably dense, he wasn't a fool, and so
she'd simply decide to find a way to uncover the answers herself. It was a bloody mess and it hadn't even
happened yet! How did Heathcliff not see the ruin that
waited? The disaster?

"You look quite deranged," Heathcliff remarked as
if commenting on the color of his coat.

"I'm feeling it," Ramsey told him. "No thanks to
you."

Heathcliff tipped his chin to the side, evaluating
Ramsey. "Need I remind you that she is *my* ward? Not
yours."

"Thank God," he replied with more feeling than
necessary for such a statement.

Heathcliff rolled his eyes.

Ramsey released a breath. So far he had dodged suspicion.

But he knew his luck would last only so long.

Just another thing to cause him to be frustratingly
tense.

All for a woman.

But wasn't it always about a woman? Empires could
rise and fall over one woman. Mighty men would fight
wars. As much as mankind had become more civilized,
much had remained the same.

Women created mayhem.

In mind, body, and country.

"Anything else to add before I go and collect her?"
Heathcliff asked as he headed toward the door.

Ramsey was tempted to say a great many things, but
in the end, he knew nothing would matter or change
his friend's mind. Might as well just be done with the
whole sordid mess and then he would have the satis-

faction of telling his friend that he had warned him, just before all hell broke loose. It wasn't a soothing idea, but it did validate Ramsey enough to simply shake his head and watch his friend depart.

After about a quarter hour, Ramsey had the miserable feeling of indecision overtake him. Should he go? Should he stay? He wasn't quite certain since every option had different negative potential. If he left, then he wouldn't be tempted by Miss Grace, and he would simply avoid the whole mess altogether. But . . . if he left and she got into some scrape, or dodged Heathcliff—he wouldn't put it past her to evade her guardian in efforts to explore—then his presence would be necessary to avoid greater peril. Heathcliff was to bring her in the afternoon and it was creeping dangerously closer every moment. But afternoon was only a few hours away from evening, and that was when all the . . . activity . . . began. Heaven help them if Heathcliff couldn't get her off the premises before preparations for the evening began in earnest.

There would be no end to the questions or curiosity. Not that he could blame her.

Gently bred ladies were not accustomed to such a situation. And with their luck—rather, his luck—Miss Grace wouldn't be scandalized, but simply intrigued and insist on remaining.

It was decided then. He would stay.

He would watch the carriage wreck about to happen and hold his ground. It was the right thing to do, to support his friend in his time of great need—and chaperoning an inquiring lady in a gamble hell certainly qualified as a time of need.

So it was with great trepidation that he watched the

hours tick by as he finished calculating the ledgers in his office. By three in the afternoon Ramsey had already taken tea, paced about the floor a while, and contemplated sending a servant after Heathcliff. He'd asked for a servant to notify him the moment the Viscount Kilpatrick arrived, but he was sorely tempted simply to be on the lookout himself. It was growing dangerously close to evening, and if Miss Grace didn't arrive and depart within an hour's time, it would be dangerous.

For his nerves.

In the end, the servant wasn't necessary. Thank the lord.

A knock sounded at the door and he strode to answer it, expecting the servant, but instead was face to face with the minx in question.

"Good afternoon, Lord Sterling." Miss Grace curtsied prettily while her guardian stood beside her.

"Afternoon," Ramsey replied, casting a glance at Heathcliff.

"I told her that you were reluctant about her paying a visit, and suggested that we inform you when we arrive. No doubt you had servants watching." Heathcliff tsked his tongue while shaking his head.

"How gracious of you," Ramsey replied through almost clenched teeth. He didn't want to simply underline Heathcliff's accusation with his reaction, but he did so regardless, unwillingly.

"Is this your office?" Miss Grace asked, leaning forward slightly to peek inside. The movement brought her close enough that the now familiar scent of lavender surrounded him, teasing his senses. He swallowed against the desire that welled within him so uninvited and he nodded. "Yes."

"May I come in?" she asked, turning to him, then as if realizing how close they were, her cheeks flushed pink and she stepped back.

"I'm sure there are more important venues you wish to see," he said, casting a dubious glance at Heathcliff. They truly must be on with the tour if they were to get her off the premises in time.

"Oh." Her brow puckered slightly in disappointment. "I suppose. Will you be joining us?"

He nodded, ignoring the smirk on Heathcliff's face as he gestured down the hall. "If you'll follow me this way, I'll give a tour of the main floor," Heathcliff announced.

And Ramsey followed, his nerves tense, and his mind ticking like a clock with the minutes escaping faster than he liked. Each moment ticking past reminded him that they were walking a dangerous line.

And he was the only one concerned about the danger, while the other two seemed willingly to run headlong into it. Bloody hell, it was going to be a long night.

Chapter Twenty-one

Grace wasn't sure why her nerves were taut. Perhaps she was simply reacting to the tension radiating from Lord Sterling. She cast a sidelong glance at him, noting the tight frame of his shoulders, the thin line of his lips, and the way his tone was ever so clipped.

The man was a bundle of nerves, and she was still irritated with him to the point of enjoyment of his discomfort. In fact, she was sorely tempted to compound it if possible.

Lord Sterling picked up his pace, his body language clearly indicating that he was anxious to be rid of her, so, with a mischievous grin she tried desperately to suppress, she slowed her steps.

Her guardian slowed as well, and she waited eagerly for Lord Sterling to notice how they lagged behind.

She cast a glance to the viscount, who had just finished explaining some sort of historical aspect of the room, and he shared a grin with her as he turned his gaze toward Lord Sterling. He arched a brow, indicating that he was fully aware of her mischief, but did nothing to temper it; if anything, she noted that the viscount's steps slowed even more than hers!

It was a lovely thing to have an ally.

She returned her attention to Lord Sterling's back a moment before he paused, then turned. His brows were knit over his expressive eyes, frustration and impatience stamped in his expression as he released a sigh. "Woolgathering?"

"Indeed," Grace answered, halting her progress entirely while she spoke. "The viscount was just relaying some interesting information about the historical relevance of this hall." She prayed that Lord Sterling wouldn't ask the particulars, since she hadn't the slightest clue as to what they were.

"I see," Lord Sterling replied tightly. "If you are interested in the historical aspects, then I might suggest we see the ballroom first. It's rather antique in many aspects." He gestured to the left.

Heathcliff chimed in. "An excellent idea."

As she resumed following Lord Sterling, he continued the conversation. "Besides, there is not much more to see besides the ballroom. That is the main location of all the events, and then you can still have time to yourself this afternoon. I'm sure a walk through Hyde Park would be just the thing."

Grace bit her lip to keep from grinning. Ah, the true motives were revealed. *Hurry up, see it, and then leave, quickly.*

"It's raining, Ramsey. I highly doubt Miss Grace wishes to parade through the park in such a downpour as we had as we arrived."

Grace caught a wink from the viscount and she restrained a giggle as she turned her attention to Lord

Sterling's back. There was a slight hitch in his shoulders. "It's London, it's always raining. Besides, I'm quite certain that Miss Grace is more than resilient enough to endure a little rain."

"It was quite the downpour," Grace felt the need to add, just to be contrary.

"Downpours seldom last long," Lord Sterling replied, glancing over his shoulder to them.

The viscount took a breath as if to say something, but they had reached a wide double door that was firmly shut. Lord Sterling paused, then opened one of the doors, revealing a dimly lit room. All Grace's other questions melted as she struggled to see into the semi-darkness. The shape of tables littered the room, and she took a step forward, and to her surprise, Lord Sterling stepped out of her way, allowing her passage.

The room had a distinct odor, not unpleasant, but also not quite like anything she'd ever smelled before. It was an odd mix of old cigar smoke, brandy, and some sort of stale perfume. The room was masculine in its style and tenor. The wood tables were far more substantial than what she had expected, along with the chairs. Each table was labeled with a particular purpose or game, and as she walked further into the room, she noted a long wooden table along the back of the ballroom, with several other doors leading out. There was a smaller area cleared for what she assumed to be dancing, and all around them were polished glassware and silver, all awaiting a footman's tray and some sort of drink to fill it.

"Well?" The viscount's voice pulled her from her musings and she turned to face him. He was grinning, clearly amused by her immediate exploration.

She glanced at Lord Sterling, who seemed ready to

haul her out by force if she didn't hurry up and get her interest satisfied.

Little did he know that was an impossible feat. Her inquisitiveness could never be satisfied once she learned the truth. When her guardian had, in very polite terms, let her know what his night escapades included, along with the location and names of his associates, her curiously grew to mammoth proportions and it was still expanding.

But the viscount was awaiting her response, so she addressed him. "It's far different than I had in mind."

"Because you had some sort of frame of reference?" Lord Sterling replied with a hint of sarcasm.

She gave him an arch look before continuing. "I've never been in one, mind you, but there were quite a few gambling establishments in India. They were mad about cricket, so I'm certain that there wasn't a game played that didn't have an unholy number of bets placed." She gave a shake of her head. "It was quite obsessive. My mother was set against it, but my father bet once. He lost, of course, but it was only a trivial amount of money so my mother never found out. It was a lovely little secret we kept between us," Grace mused, a wave of mourning dampening her excitement.

"Cricket." The viscount nodded. "Good sport."

"You'd certainly think so," Lord Sterling replied.

The viscount turned to his friend, a grin spreading across his face. "Just because you could never play well."

Grace glanced to Lord Sterling, eager for his reply. "I nearly have to fold myself in half just to use the bloody bat."

The viscount rolled his eyes. "You're not much taller than I."

"Apparently even small amounts matter in the game of cricket," he muttered.

Grace grinned.

He glared at her, as if just realizing that they had gotten far off subject. "I suppose you have questions?"

The viscount turned to her as well, awaiting her leisure.

"What is your most popular game?" she asked.

"Whist." They both answered in conjunction, then glanced at each other. Lord Sterling continued, "The next is Hazard and Faro."

"I see. And how many people do you have attend each evening that you're open?" She glanced to the tables, counting them mentally while she waited.

"That is not information that we can share," the viscount replied kindly.

Grace calculated the math quickly in her head. There were twelve tables, all seating around eight to ten men. That would equal from ninety-six to one hundred twenty men just at the tables, assuming they were all full. That didn't include men dancing or milling about. . . . It was indeed a large club. She was fascinated.

"I can see the wheels turning in your mind, Miss Grace. What else do you wish to know?" Lord Sterling asked. But his tone implied the rest of the statement: *what else do you wish to know so we can move on and get you out of here.*

She held back a glare. Why was he so impatient? She frowned as she considered the possible answers. Then it struck her, and she couldn't restrain her grin. "There's a party tonight, isn't there?"

Lord Sterling turned to the viscount, his expression mutinous.

The viscount simply shrugged. "I cannot answer that question either."

"Can I stay?" she asked, stepping forward.

"No!" Lord Sterling practically roared while the viscount said, "That's not a good idea."

"Why ever not? I'll stay out of the way. Oh! I can dress up and—"

This time both gentlemen roared. "No!" The viscount was holding back a grin of amusement, while Lord Sterling had an expression of panic on his face.

"You cannot dress up! Dear Lord, I told you this would be Lady Heightfield all over again!" Ramsey practically growled, and in the vacant room the sound vibrated all over the walls.

Grace watched with interest as the two men argued.

"She's not going to dress up as a courtesan—"

"Bloody hell, man! Don't give her ideas!"

"I would never—" she started to interrupt, but was given dubious looks by both gentleman that clearly indicated that they didn't believe her.

"I wouldn't! I have morals," Grace felt the need to affirm.

"You would simply dress as a servant girl, but with your fiery hair and temper to match we'd have more than a few men interested and problems aplenty with the lot of you. Don't even think of it," Lord Sterling remarked.

"She does remind me ever so much of Liliah," Heathcliff mused, chuckling.

"Damn both of you," Lord Sterling swore but without heat.

Grace was immediately aware of the name, and then

connected the previous mention of Lady Heightfield. "Are you saying that Samantha's sister—"

"I don't think that is something we should discuss here," the viscount interrupted. "You can ask Samantha later . . . it's quite a story and we do not have time to do it sufficient justice here."

"Nor do I wish to relive it," Lord Sterling added.

"You're quite uptight," Grace remarked, tipping her head as she studied him.

He glared at her.

The viscount laughed.

Lord Sterling glared at them both.

"Why?" Grace asked. "I'm fully aware you wish my swift departure, but you're being unpardonably rude."

"You're being unpardonably impertinent."

The viscount chuckled. "You sound like her grandfather, Ramsey."

"You do," Grace felt the need to add.

Lord Sterling didn't reply, simply sighed. "If the both of you are done casting stones at my character, I'll leave you to your tour." He gave a swift bow and then, without waiting for their answer, departed.

The viscount approached her after he left. "He isn't angry, just uptight. One day he will learn to release that tension, but today is, apparently, not that day. What else do you wish to see?"

Grace had a long list of things she had thought she wished to explore, but after the departure of Lord Sterling, they held little interest. It was far more fun with him to pester, and some of the polish of the evening was now gone with him. All she wished to do now was see the interior of his office, since that was where she was certain he had retreated. "Where do you suggest?"

The viscount suggested the kitchens for a spot of tea, and they left the ballroom.

As she followed along the hall toward the kitchen, she wondered just how terrible and reprehensible it would be to sneak away and find Lord Sterling. Surely she owed him an apology for pushing him so far, and it really wasn't well done of her to accuse him of being grandfatherly.

She glanced backward, making a quick map of the area. Certainly the viscount wouldn't mind if she explored a little on her own.

At least not mind too much.

Chapter Twenty-two

Ramsey had been called many things in his life, all of which revolved around either his inability to perform up to the standard of his father, or being too proper and prudish in his own standards and expectations.

Words never feel good when delivered in such a way, but they hadn't quite stung like the word spoken over him.

Grandfatherly.

Dear lord, she truly knew how to emasculate a man, even if she hadn't come up with the word herself, she had agreed. It was more than enough.

It wasn't that he had anything against an older gentleman, but he didn't associate them with lovely, vibrant, and ardent young women. Or if he did, it wasn't in a good way. And after such a passionate exchange as they had experienced only a short time ago, it was a little frustrating and irritating to think she considered him on that level.

His nerves were still tight from knowing she was somewhere on the premise, but it was a different tension than he had anticipated. It was a constant push and pull with her, an equal balance of desire and irritation that had his body and mind spinning in opposition. Everything about her tempted him, teased him, yet she was equally talented at provoking him in the most frustrating ways, so that he never really knew if he wished to gag her or kiss her senseless.

Too bad doing both at the same time wasn't an option.

But either option led to her mouth, which, he had admitted, he had an utter fascination with. Her lips were the perfect pink and constantly moving, whether in words or a smile, or some sort of twitch that gave away her thoughts just as much as her expressive eyes. It was bewitching, and he was under the spell.

And hopeless to explore it.

Because temptation wasn't an excuse to act rashly, and compromising his best friend's ward certainly would be acting rashly.

And he wasn't quite certain that his self-control would extend to simply allowing a chaste kiss.

No.

He wouldn't be able to temper his need, and it would consume them both.

And they would both wind up burned.

It wasn't an option. He knew it in his mind, but his body was constantly rejecting the truth.

Bloody traitorous thing.

He buried himself in his ledgers, preparing for the betting that was to take place that evening. About a half hour into his work, his body had started to cool and his mind had begun to unwind from the tension.

Certainly, by this point she had departed with Heathcliff and they were no longer on the property. It was a heady release as he crossed a "t" in the ledger.

A knock sounded at the door, and he called for whomever it was to come in, neglecting even to glance up from his book while the door opened.

When no further communication was made by the person entering, he glanced up, then nearly swallowed his tongue.

The pen fell from his hand as he blinked, not quite certain if he should believe his eyes or if he had maybe had some brandy that had gone sideways earlier, causing him to see things.

"It's larger than I expected," Miss Grace commented and then closed the bloody door.

He blinked, unable to formulate any thoughts that could come out as words at the moment.

"Hmm . . . and brighter too. You have a lovely study. Is that the park?" She strode forward, completely uninvited, and moved aside the heavy drapery that concealed part of the window. "Oh, no. Not the park, but it is a charming view. The rain stopped, I'm glad." She turned to face him, her expression angelic, utterly unconcerned that she was in an unmarried gentleman's office, with the door closed, in a gambling hell, with a man who was trying to convince himself that he couldn't act on his distinct desire for her. No. She was oblivious and commenting on the weather. *The bloody weather*.

Good Lord. This was a disaster. It was worse than when Liliah came to the club and tried to seduce Lucas. This was of greater danger because Heathcliff knew Grace was in the club, and there would be no clandestine affair where she could slip away unnoticed . . . no.

She would be ruined.

Hell, she was already ruined just being here with him.

And all he could do was restrain himself from making it a thorough ruining indeed.

But that wasn't going to happen.

She wasn't interested in him.

No.

She had likened him to a grandfather.

Not that he was old; heavens, he was maybe eight years older than she was.

But his heart was ancient. Maybe it was because she had a way to see further inside, to the soul, and recognized his was decades older than his body.

Which somehow made the idea worse.

"You're probably wondering why I'm here," she said, approaching his desk.

He nodded. "The thought had crossed my mind."

"Yes, you look quite confused," she remarked, hitching a shoulder. "I tend to have that effect on people, especially you."

"You do indeed," he answered, watching her like she was a snake about to strike.

"Well . . . I owe you an apology and I rather thought that you owed me one as well."

This surprised him even more than her unchaperoned visit to his office. Why did he owe her an apology? For the kiss? That was all he could think of. And it might be true, but he rather thought she was a willing rather than a reluctant participant.

"I see," he replied, waiting for her to continue. She took measured steps around the chairs in front of the desk, her hand grazing the back of one. The trailing of her fingers along the wood was surprisingly erotic, and a faint shiver of need trailed down his back.

"May I sit?" she asked, arching a brow, again. Apparently, she was of the expectation that she would be here for some time.

Ramsey motioned to the chair with his hand, making a grand sweeping motion that was a bit dramatic. Hell, everything felt dramatic in this insane situation. He leaned back in his chair, increasing the distance between them, even small as it was. Every little bit helped.

"As I was saying." Grace smoothed her skirt as she sat. It was a prim and proper movement, completely at odds with the improper situation she had run headlong into. The irony was delicious and he found himself grinning in spite of it all.

"What do you find amusing?" She frowned. Damn, she was easily distracted. At this rate he would never find out the rest of her initial statement.

"Nothing, continue," he replied quickly, eager to somehow move the process along and get her safely away.

Yet even as his mind thought it, his body revolted against such an idea. His entire being was at odds once more because of this woman. His mind and morals wanted her absence, while the rest of his body wanted to pull her closer.

"I apologize for intentionally provoking your irritation and anger earlier."

"Just earlier?" he replied before he could give his words a proper thought as to how they would be interpreted.

Her eyes narrowed, and she glanced away, heaving a delicate sigh. "At least for today, all the other irritations I've caused I must inform you that I feel no regret over."

"Honesty is not as becoming as many think," he replied. "But your apology is accepted." He stood, gesturing to the door, his morals silently applauding his actions.

"Why the devil are you always trying to get rid of me?" she asked, her tone irritated. A smile tugged his lips at her rather indelicate word usage. It was his turn to arch a brow.

She turned a slight pink. "You're just as irritating as I'm accused of being."

"The accuser being yourself, in this situation. Because I have never called you irritating to your face," he remarked.

"Your actions sure imply it implicitly," she returned. "And, as they say, actions speak louder than words."

That was a truth if he'd ever heard one. And a solid point, one for which he didn't have a ready reply. "Regardless, your apology is accepted. What more do you need?" he asked, trying to keep his tone from sounding desperate.

"Usually, one apology encourages another."

Ah, yes. The other apology. The one for which he didn't know what trespass he'd committed. "What am I to apologize for?"

She frowned. "You truly don't know?"

He shook his head, and then, rather reluctantly, took his seat again. Apparently, she wasn't inclined to leave just yet.

Her cheeks grew pink once more, and she glanced down to her lap, toying with her gloves as she took a silent breath. "Because, that is, in the garden, you . . ." She didn't continue.

And he was delighted to discover that she did have an Achilles heel. She mercilessly toyed with his weakness; it was quite diverting to discover that she had one, which he could easily prey upon as well. The temptation was overwhelming, and even as his more gentlemanly side was persuaded against it, he found himself leaning forward to provoke her further. "In the garden . . ." he encouraged, his face aching from keeping the grin in check.

"Yes." She glanced up, nodding firmly, her lips in a fine line as if forcing composure she didn't feel. "You kissed me."

"I did." He nodded.

She waited.

He waited as well.

Miss Grace glanced away, her shoulders heaving a rather heavy sigh, and she turned back to him. "You kissed me and then said nothing. Pretended as if it never happened. It's rather infuriating."

Ah, so that was the truth of it. Her pride was wounded, and she wanted retribution for the offense. It made sense now; she would have a streak of pride down the length of her back just as she had the stripe of stubbornness. "I wounded your pride."

Her gaze flared to life and she studied him, not speaking. "You did nothing of the sort."

"That is what you implied," he returned.

"That was not intentional. I was offended because you . . ." She trailed off, and seemed to be unable to finish the sentence. "You can't kiss a lady like that and expect her to . . ."

"Not expect something?" he finished, knowing they were wading into very dangerous waters. Certainly she didn't expect him to offer for her after one kiss?

She might have the right to expect something, but certainly she knew better than to expect it from him.

"No!" She rose, moving to stand behind the chair as if it were a barrier between them. "I don't expect . . . that." She blushed again. "I just rather thought that you regretted it, and didn't mean for it to happen, so you'd wish to apologize." She cast her gaze to the chair below her, her face flaming with a rather fetching blush.

Ramsey swallowed against the intense desire to kiss her once more, to feel the heat of her blush under his hand, to tell her that he didn't regret the kiss at all, not even a little bit. And it was intentional, every part. But he couldn't; rather, he wouldn't. "I see. Why did you not say that in the first place?" he asked, keeping his tone gentle, not wishing to offend her further. There were limits, after all, and he was quite certain she had hit hers.

"Because I was giving you the opportunity to be a gentleman," she said with a little heat, enough to remind him that she wasn't about to back down from any challenge.

It was endearing, it was infuriating, and he respected her strength. Admired it, even. "Well, now that we've established that I have not acted like a gentleman, and that I am perpetuating that behavior by not realizing that I needed to apologize, I do believe that we are finished here." He spoke cautiously, keeping his tone even. It was for the best, to excuse her, to get her away from him.

"I never said you weren't a gentleman," she countered. "I said that I was giving you the opportunity to be one. That's . . . different."

"Very well," he replied.

"Well?" she asked, her tone impatient.

"Well, what?" he replied, not quite following her thought trail.

"Are you going to apologize?" she asked, her expression adorably bewildered with just a hint of indignation.

"I thought we just established that I had nothing to apologize for?" he returned.

"No. You surmised that, I did not. And I'm not under your jurisdiction, my lord."

At this, he chuckled. "Oh, of that I'm completely aware." He shook his head. "And the answer is no."

She frowned, and studied him.

He glanced away, realizing belatedly that he had made a fatal mistake. She wouldn't leave it at that. She would simply ask why, and then he'd be in the position to either lie or tell her the truth, and he hated liars.

Which only left the truth.

Damn it all. He was doomed.

"Why?" she asked, just as he had predicted, and he felt a slight edge of panic seize him. He shook his head. "It is of no importance."

"It is to me."

"It is not to me," he returned a little too quickly.

He could feel her gaze on his face; he could practically hear the gears working in her mind as she waited.

"Unless . . ." she added breathlessly.

He couldn't resist glancing up to see what was written in her expression, in the form of her lips. They were like a book he would love to read every day, telling of her every emotion, every nuance of her perception. It was delirious, it was delicious, it was utterly damning to his self-control.

"Unless?" he said, desperately trying to keep his features neutral.

She stepped from behind the chair and moved toward him with cautious motions, as if she were afraid of spooking a wild horse. He felt like a wild horse in that moment, unpredictable and wild and utterly fool-hardy because he didn't back away, he didn't laugh and shrug it off. He watched her, studied her, burned for her.

"After all, you are a great many things, Lord Sterling. But a liar, you are not. So, if you did not find the need to apologize, then that only leaves one option." She moved closer, her steps not as brave as her words, and his heart ached with the realization that she was braver than he. A vow echoed deep in his soul that it wouldn't be the truth, that he would rise to the occasion as damnable as the occasion may be, that she wouldn't need to be the brave one.

It should be him.

She was awaiting his response. "And that option is?" he asked, walking the line of both not wanting to push her into a compromising situation, but wanting it so desperately he could taste it. But not unless she wanted it, wanted him.

Dear Lord, let her want him.

"Unless you didn't regret it at all," she finished, her eyes alight with understanding.

"And what if I didn't?" He found himself asking, turning to face her fully, evaluating the small distance between them.

"Then you're right." She hitched a shoulder and stopped her steps.

This brought him up a little short. It wasn't the response he was expecting, though, to be honest, he wasn't sure what exactly he had been expecting. But not that. Though, it was nice to hear the words, validating even. Oddly enough.

"If I'm going to be so brave, the least you can do is meet me halfway."

He came up short at such a statement, confused and afraid to interpret the meaning incorrectly, and then all the fear melted away as her pink tongue darted out to lick her bottom lip.

The memory of their kiss hit him full force, the ironic conversation about how a kiss starts with licking one's lips that turned from a conversation to an exploration, and he was undone.

He stepped toward her, his hand instinctively wrapping around her waist and pulling her in close. Her eyes widened, and he indulged in the fantasy of touching the blush upon her cheek, the warmth seeping into his very soul, feeding it. Her eyes fluttered closed and he did more than meet her halfway; he went the entire distance and seared her lips with his, immediately wondering why he had taken so damn long to kiss her again.

It was the feeling of home, the sensation of peace and the fire of need all wrapped into one perfect present.

And this time, he wasn't about to leave the present wrapped.

Chapter Twenty-three

Grace had never experienced such a delirious sensation in all her life as when she melted into Lord Sterling's arms. Dear Lord, it was everything. Her greatest fear was that it would end with her waking up, realizing it was nothing but a dream, and she should be dreaming because she was certain that Lord Sterling, proper and strict Lord Sterling, did not kiss women in his office. Rather, he did not kiss debutantes in his office, his office at the gambling hell, that is.

Good Lord, what was she doing?

Yet, as soon as the thought entered her mind, it flew away like a frightened bird, and all that was left was the melting sensation of being in Lord Sterling's very warm, amazingly strong arms. Her hands trailed upward, and some corner of her mind realized how firm his limbs were, and the strength within. As she gently wound her hands around his shoulders, she arched her fingers into his back, feeling the solid strength of it, of him. Her heart pounded, her lips tingled, and her mind was utterly spinning with pleasure. His kiss was hot and demanding, yet gentle enough that she was left wanting something more, as if she instinctively knew he was holding back some part of himself, of his kiss. She was greedy for it, for every part of him, for every part of the pleasure he was giving her. The room faded away, and all that remained was the acutely blissful feeling of being held and kissed very well.

His lips tutored hers, and she mimicked the way he nibbled on her lower lip, her body surging with delight when he let out a small groan. That she could offer him any sort of pleasure in her innocent experience was a heady realization, and she gloried in it. She ached to be closer, as if some part of her mind knew instinctively what it needed, even if she didn't understand it. His arms tightened around her, and she became aware of the hard length of him pressing against her hip bone. Intrigued, she pressed into him more, breathing in his moan of pleasure.

"Miss Grac—"

She cut off his words with a kiss, her lips bending into a smile. Ever proper, her Lord Sterling. Only, at the moment he was behaving anything but properly.

And she was guilty of the same sin. The same delicious sin.

"Don't you think," she kissed him again firmly, this time allowing her tongue to slip along the seam of his lips, much like he had done earlier. Then she withdrew just enough to finish her sentence, "that you should call me Grace?"

He chuckled against her lips, then nipped them playfully, his arms like a band of strength holding her close, yet tenderly at the same time as he ravaged her senses. "Perhaps."

Passion had not diminished her sense of humor, and she leaned back to give him an arch look. But rather than receive the teasing scolding, his gaze roamed her features, cataloguing them like a scientist would study a new species. He was memorizing her, and she had never before been seen so fully. It was humbling, it was terrifying, it spoke of passion and need with a slight sprinkling of adoration to make it complete. "Yes?" Grace mouthed the word, unable to quite make it voiced.

He gave his head a shake, as if breaking his own spell, and rather than speak, he leaned down to kiss her once more.

This kiss was different, more deliberate. Though how it was possible for her to know, she wasn't sure. There was purpose to the kiss, and she was happy to discover it, breath by breath.

The room grew warm as his hands began slowly to roam. Everywhere he touched sent a shot of heat through her body, feeding an addiction to his kiss. After trailing down the spine of her back with a featherlike touch, he spanned her hips with his hands, cupping her bottom in the most delicious and scandalous way. He pressed her tightly against him, reminding her of his own state of arousal before breaking the seal of her kiss only to trail playful nips and teasing kisses along her jawline down to her neck.

It was difficult to breathe, or at least breathe enough. Heart pounding, she lost herself in the pleasure of it all. "Good Lord," she murmured, nonsensical.

Lord Sterling let out a low chuckle of approval as he nipped the bone along her shoulder, his other hand scandalously close to her breast. All she could think was, *closer.* She wanted to arch her body: she didn't know exactly what she needed, but she wanted it. Oh, how desperately did she want it!

As if reading her mind, or at the very least, her body language, his hand brushed against the swell of her breast, his fingers tracing over the tip and even through her dress, it was acutely pleasurable. Her breath caught, her body tensed, and even as his hand swept away, she felt his touch like a brand, still searing through her skin. His lips were hot against her neck as he kissed her, his hands slowly circling around the collar of her dress, and then his hand touched her sensitive skin. If she had thought the sensations of his touch through her dress were almost too much to bear, it was nothing like the feeling of flesh on flesh. Heart hammering, her blood rushed through her body, sounding in her ears as she fought for breath. How in the world could one small part of her body be so fantastically sensitive? It was glorious, it was wicked, it was not enough, she decided.

Oh, she was wanton! Never before would she have imagined such pleasure at a simple, yet scandalous, touch!

"Do you like that?" he murmured against the skin of her neck as he caressed his fingertips around her sensitive flesh, teasing, tickling, and pinching playfully.

She could hardly catch her breath to answer, but some semblance of a squeak came out in a "yes."

"Good Lord, you're perfect."

Before she could process the overly appreciative compliment, his mouth replaced his fingertips, and she lost her footing, only to be swept up into his arms. His mouth left her breast only long enough to carry her to the small chaise longue in the study's small sitting area. If she had any sense of propriety, she would have spoken up, but before she could have found her breath, his mouth was on her breast again, his hand slipping up the hem of her skirt, tickling in the most delicious way as he moved up her calf.

She should stop.

She should want to stop.

She should do something before she wasn't just ruined, she was ruined completely.

But . . . she found she didn't have the strength to do anything but arch into him, gasp for breath, and simply glory in the new delicious sensations her body continued to explore at his touch.

"Tell me you want me," he whispered against the flesh of her breast, then nipped her playfully, almost punishingly, as if warning against a refusal.

Not that she had any inclination of refusing him. No, she was past that point, she was past any point except quenching the fire-hot need surging through her body, needing some sort of completion.

And instinctively she knew he could give it.

"Tell me you burn for me," he whispered, his hand tiptoeing up her thigh.

"Y-yes," she whispered, her thoughts scrambled; it was all light and color.

"Tell me you want me to do this." His tongue did wicked things to her breast, and she forgot to breathe.

He paused, but only long enough to turn his attention to her other breast. "Tell me you want more."

"More." The word never left her lips, but she was certain it formed there as all the breath left her at the hot, needy sensation humming through her at his touch.

He let out a low groan; it was primal, it was hungry,

and her body caught fire at just the sound. "Tell me you want me to touch you here."

His hand slid along her most private area, the area she never even named out loud, and instinctively she spread her legs just slightly, arching her hips into his touch, her body shivering with need.

"Do you want this?" He nipped her breast, his breath hot and demanding.

"Yes," she whispered.

"Say my name," he demanded, sliding his fingers inside of her, teasing her core, making her body sing like a siren call.

"I—I—"

"Say it," he demanded, suckling her breast and sliding his fingers deeper.

"Lor—"

"No. My name, damn it. I want to hear it on your lips. I want to hear you say it with the breathless passion that's slowly killing me with need. I want to hear you cry my name when you experience your first pleasure. My. Name." His whisper was urgent, hot, unrelenting, and nearly mad with desire.

"Ramsey," she murmured, then said it again, just because it tasted so good on her lips.

Ramsey's mouth was demanding on her breast, his fingers urgent as he called, "Come for me."

His fingers surged forward, and her body snapped with the pleasure, a thousand fragments of light splintering from within her as her body came alive, pulsating from within.

"Dear Lord." She whispered the prayer, because surely she was somewhere suspended between heaven and earth, floating downward like a feather.

First, she was aware of her breathing, the pounding of her heart as if she had run a great distance. Then she noted the tingling sensation in her limbs, as if they had been thoroughly relaxed and were almost waking up from a deep sleep. She was completely sated, completely and delightfully happy.

Second, she noted the labored breathing of Ramsey as he pressed his head against her heart, listening. His body was tight, and she realized he had not experienced the same . . . release, as she had. It was a pity, but she was also aware that she might not have survived the experience if there was *more* than what they had just shared. At least not for her first time, perhaps.

And then it hit her.

Her first time . . . did that mean there *would* be more?

Good Lord, she hoped so. She wanted more. And soon, please. Would it be terrible to ask? She was a lady after all, even if she didn't behave as such.

Then another though hit her, *was* she still a lady?

She had given herself to him in the way only a wife should give herself to her husband. And they were most certainly not married.

They weren't even courting.

He'd kissed her, but that didn't signify . . .

Her body started to tighten up as she thought about it more.

"Stop."

She blinked and then waited for Ramsey to continue the rest of his statement.

"Stop worrying. I didn't completely ruin you."

At this, she felt her eyebrow arch in an incredulous expression. If it wasn't a complete ruin, it was only by an infinitesimal amount.

"Well, at least it wasn't a thorough ruining. It was

about as damnably close as I can get without procuring an heir," he murmured, almost to himself. The tone was almost wistful, as if he wished he had done a more thorough job of it.

Was she wicked to wish he had too?

"I see," she remarked, because, well, she wasn't sure what else to say.

He didn't reply readily, and she closed her eyes to try and return to the blissful state that had somehow faded away with her thoughts.

Ramsey slowly slid away and then stood. She opened her eyes to watch him. His eyes were cloudy with unfulfilled need, and his cravat was hopelessly ruined. Clothing rumpled, he looked well loved, or at least well ravished, but he was none of those.

Was he?

Could she love him? She could certainly want him, even need him. But did that mean love? She had always thought that love would come first, and . . .

"Stop," he commanded again.

"You're quite bossy," she told him, not able to help the smile that tipped her lips.

"You are as well," he returned, a bit of a grin teasing his lips. Good Lord, she loved his lips. They were so soft and wicked, her body tingled in all the sensitive areas those lips had touched.

His gaze roamed her features, then sobered, and his brows frowned as he took in the rest of her state. His gaze took on a hungry glint as they traveled down her neck and settled to where her breasts were. She glanced down and then blushed, she was utterly exposed. With a quick adjustment, she was at least more presentable than a moment ago.

"Pity," he remarked.

She gave him an arch look.

"You have lovely breasts. They are perfect in every way."

She blinked, not quite sure what to say to that. She had never had a compliment about her breasts. She was quite sure that it wasn't a proper compliment, but at the same time, it made her feel beautiful and wanted. So she simply replied, "thank you."

He offered her a hand, and she grasped it. His strength gently pulled her up from the chaise and she proceeded to tidy up her dress, realizing it was hopeless, as rumpled as it had become.

"Allow me to assist," Ramsey whispered, then stood behind her. His hands swept over her bodice, tucking, smoothing and aligning things as he moved down her body. His hands were warm, and the contrast made her skin goose bump.

"It's not perfect, but at least it won't be overly suspicious."

"Thank you."

"Heathcliff will be searching for you," he said after a long pause.

His breath was warm at her neck, and she shivered as he placed a lingering kiss there. His hands wrapped round her waist, pulling her back into the strength of his body.

"I'm quite reluctant to let you go."

"Oh?" She found her voice.

"Indeed." He kissed her again softly, his tongue flickering against her skin. "I'm afraid you're addictive. And I've never been addicted to anything in my life. Which is saying a lot, since I run a gambling hell."

She breathed out unevenly. "I've heard gambling is terribly addictive."

"Yet I've remained unscathed for this whole time," he murmured, his hands spanning her hips and gripping.

Her breath caught. "That's most admirable."

"Is it? I must admit I've not been acting admirably. And I can't find it within the strength of my morals to remedy that." He pressed his hard length into her backside. "But there's always tomorrow."

"Is there?" she asked breathlessly, not caring that she sounded wanton. Good Lord, that ship had sailed when she'd entered his office alone.

"Are you going to the Rymans' ball tonight?" he asked, his voice almost a groan as he kissed her neck once more.

"Yes."

"I'll find you." The words were a promise as he reluctantly released her, as was apparent by the expression in his eyes as she turned to meet his gaze.

"I'll be waiting," she replied, giving herself over to the truth of it; she would be waiting, she would be wanting, and she would be a very willing participant.

"Until this evening." He lifted her hand and kissed it, then stepped back, as if needing the distance to simply allow her to leave.

She felt the space between them immediately, like a chilling breeze when you were expecting warmth. And as she forced herself to walk to the door, the sensation of the increased distance grew more acute.

And it was then that Grace realized, she was in love.

And it wasn't anything like she expected. No, it was so much more.

So much dangerously more.

Chapter Twenty-four

Ramsey called himself a great many things after Grace departed. In fact, he was still calling himself more colorful versions of those things that evening as he readied himself for the Ryman ball.

But even the greatest scolding he could deliver to himself couldn't deter him from seeing her again, or at least trying. He was honest when he had said that he'd never experienced addiction, but he was quite certain he was a victim now. Before, she had haunted his thoughts, teased his curiosity, and provoked his frustration. Now, she was a siren that fed his need for her, and he wasn't going to be satisfied till he had every part.

Which only meant one thing.

He'd have to marry her.

He wasn't against it, which was shocking enough, but the current deterrent was finding a way to approach the conversation with Heathcliff.

No. He could think of a million other things he'd

rather do. In fact, as his valet tied his cravat for his evening kit, he compiled a list of things he'd rather do than approach Heathcliff about Grace.

Have malaria.

Drink cold tea for the rest of his life.

Have a doctor give him leeches.

Drink that horrible confection Mrs. White gave him when he was sick as a lad.

Swim the Thames in winter.

Yes. There were a great many things he'd rather do, but unfortunately, he had no other option. He had quite completely ruined Grace that afternoon—even if he had said otherwise—and he was quite certain that only the slight possibility of Heathcliff knocking on the door had stopped him from making it a thorough ruining indeed.

His body flared to life with the memory of it.

He cleared his throat, and his valet stepped back to behold his handiwork. With a quick bow, and Ramsey's nod of approval, the valet quit the room, leaving Ramsey with his thoughts.

Immediately those thoughts turned back to Grace. Dear Lord, he loved even thinking her name. She had been a siren in his arms.

Only two aspects could have made the experience more complete.

For her flaming red hair to be down and splayed across his pillow.

And for no damn clothes on either of them.

His body had pulsed with need, and he'd nearly lost himself when she had tightened around his fingers. It was only sheer determination that had kept him from taking her completely, spilling himself within her and taking every part of her delicious body.

He burned with it now, the desperate need. It was overpowering, and he doubted his self-control to be content with anything less than complete satisfaction. And the Ryman ball wasn't the place to ruin innocent ladies.

But, he grinned in spite of himself, she wasn't *completely* innocent anymore.

And it was at his hand, his kiss, his touch that she'd experienced her first pleasure. He loved that, damn, he loved her. Even if it was a lustful love, he was quite certain it had a deeper root, one that was as insane as his need for her. He only hoped she would be open to his courtship . . . his advances.

Good Lord, let her be a willing participant.

He had seen the light of awareness come into her expression as she came back from her surge of pleasure. She hadn't gone into hysterics; no, she'd taken it all with aplomb, but she'd also had several hours to herself to think, and there was no guessing what had transpired between then and now.

Well, he would know soon.

The time was approaching to depart, and with a good long moment of thinking about less desirable things, he was able to be presentable in polite company.

So it was with a determined stride that he entered his carriage, and set forth to the Ryman ball. The bays sprang forward as soon as he rapped on the side of the carriage, and he leaned back into his seat, expectation his companion.

As they started down the familiar streets of Mayfair, he allowed his mind to wander ahead to the ball. He was slightly late, which only meant that Grace would likely already be in attendance. It was a calculation he'd intentionally made in order to alleviate some of the pressure on his patience. It was in short supply, and he rather thought he should keep his patience in reserve for the time he needed to act the gentleman when the woman in question made him lose all sense of reason.

They rounded a corner, and he leaned slightly to the left with the motion, but the carriage squeaked in a fashion that wasn't usual, and his ears perked at the sound. The carriage continued on, and Ramsey had almost dismissed the noise when a snapping sound reverberated through the carriage. Instinctively, he gripped the window, anchoring himself as the carriage swayed, slowed, and then came to a complete halt about five blocks from the Ryman residence. Ramsey's breath was tight as he took account of the situation, then as the footman opened the door for him, he carefully stepped from the carriage into the waning evening light.

"Are you well, milord?" the footman asked, just as the coachman came around from the front.

"Well enough," Ramsey replied, tugging on the cuff of his coat, evaluating the carriage wheels in the dim light.

"'Twas a loud crack, milord. We thought it best to stop," the coachman said, bending down to get a better view of the carriage. "I don't think we've broken a wheel, but the axle may be damaged."

Ramsey simply nodded.

"If it was the axle, it's a good thing we didn't snap it. 'Twould have been disastrous," the coachman mumbled, then stood. "My apologies, my lord. But we cannot continue till we've fixed the problem."

"I understand." Ramsey nodded, then took in his surroundings more fully. He wasn't more than a block away from Heathcliff's residence, and he could send for a hack from there. "I believe I'll head toward the viscount's residence and hire a conveyance from there. I'll send word back to the stables and have some assistance sent to you as well."

"Thank you, milord." The coachman bowed.

"I'll accompany you, milord." The footman stepped forward, and soon they were making their way to Heathcliff's residence. As Ramsey had suspected, they had already left for the ball nearly an hour before, but John was more than accommodating, allowing them entrance into the house immediately. After showing them into one of the parlors, John immediately dispatched a missive to request a hack coach. Ramsey conveyed his thanks, but didn't dismiss John. There was a slightly anxious edge to his demeanor, and he kept casting assessing gazes at the footman who had accompanied Ramsey. After a moment, Ramsey dismissed the footman and instructed John to stay.

The footman obeyed and closed the door, and no sooner had he left than John strode forward. "My lord, I can only assume that you have not seen the viscount this eve."

John's demeanor had Ramsey immediately on alert. "No. I have not."

"Then may I speak plainly, my lord?" John asked, his tone eager.

Ramsey nodded, frowning as he did so. John was beyond trustworthy, and loyal to a fault. If he was requesting to speak in such a way, it was something that needed to be heard.

"The viscount requested that I do some checking on Lord Westhouse. It has taken me longer than I anticipated, since he's quite good at covering his tracks."

At this, Ramsey snorted. He was well aware of that fact.

John continued after giving an agreeing expression. "But it would seem that there is some circulation of a possible connection between Lord Westhouse and your father," John finished, his tone hesitant.

"Continue." Ramsey tipped his head, a slight edge of dread spreading like ink through his blood.

"It would seem that Lord Westhouse is . . . that is to say . . . there are rumors that—"

"Plain speaking, John," Ramsey almost ground out.

"He's quite possibly your half-brother."

Ramsey wasn't quite sure what he had been expecting, but most certainly not that.

John continued. "That is all the information I have now, but I'm not certain that there aren't more implications to be uncovered, so I would be on my guard, my lord. I'll let Mrs. Marilla know that I'll be taking my leave to evaluate your carriage myself. I want to rule out some sort of foul play. It would be a stretch, but I've learned never to underestimate a man."

Ramsey nodded; that was all he was bloody able to do at the moment. He was still processing the emotional roundhouse punch John's words had delivered. "Thank you, John," he was able to say after a moment.

There was a knock at the door, and Ramsey found the presence of mind to call for the person to enter. Mrs. Marilla opened the door. "The hack is here, my lord. And your footman is already with it." She curtsied.

Ramsey nodded, taking in the slight blush on her cheeks when she mentioned the footman. It would be good for her to find a companion; she'd been dealt a severe blow in life, and as such, deserved some happiness.

He pushed these thoughts away and nodded. "Very good." He gave a curt nod to John, who bowed back, his expression a promise that he would not miss any detail, and with that, Ramsey quit the room.

The hack swayed slightly as he stepped inside. The faint scent of pipe smoke spiced the air and he immediately missed the more luxurious furnishing of his own carriage, but it wasn't of import.

No.

What was of import was figuring out how the hell Westhouse could be his half-brother.

Their lands bordered each other, that was true enough. It was possible as far as distance, but they were nearly the same age. No. That wasn't true. Westhouse was about six months older. Ramsey thought back over his childhood, scouring his mind for any recollection of his father mentioning Lord or Lady Westhouse. He hadn't.

Which, as he thought about it, was rather odd.

His father had no scruples in mentioning other noblemen, or their wives. No, he would often berate them or make sport of them whenever possible. But Ramsey couldn't remember the mentioning of their names even once.

The carriage lurched forward from a stop at a crossroads, then continued, and Ramsey's thoughts slipped back in time. Lord Westhouse had died before he was born—his mind tickled with awareness that this piece of information was a clue, but he had no idea where it fit in the grand scheme of things. The carriage came to a halt just before the Ryman residence, and Ramsey took a fleeting moment to collect his wits. He wasn't feeling in the mood to be in polite society, any society, really. But he needed to speak with Heathcliff about the information from John. And there was Grace.

Thinking her name snapped his attention back into place, and he alighted from the carriage. The ball was in full swing, and had been for quite some time based on the din of music and voices that carried out into the foyer. He nodded to several gentlemen who were speaking by the front door and then proceeded down the hall toward the ballroom. The air was more humid than usual, and he had the urge to tug on his cravat. As he walked into the crowded ballroom, he started scanning the sea of faces for Heathcliff, Lady Kilpatrick, or Grace.

"Evening, Lord Ramsey." Lady Whipplemen nodded her head, fanning herself quite enthusiastically.

"Good evening," he returned, then continued along, nodding to Lord and Lady Ryman, who were in conversation with Lord Pennwood. It was at times like these when he was thankful for his height. He could easily see over most of the gentry's heads, unless they were wearing those dreadful ostrich feathers. Those were the bane of a tall man's existence. Always in the way, and always tickling his nose. Bloody awful things. He made a wide arc around a few dowagers who were sporting the dreadful things, and scanned the faces for those he sought.

He was halfway through the crowd when he spotted Heathcliff. Not more than twenty yards away, he was beside his wife and next to her—his breath caught.

Grace.

Her hair was nearly glowing fire in the bright candlelight, and her emerald dress merely drew the eye to her creamy shoulders with just the barest hint of the curve of her breasts. Like the most delicious dessert wrapped in gold foil, she was tempting even from a distance. He took a deep breath to pull his thoughts into line, and started toward them. Belatedly, he noted the ending of the music as the first strains of a waltz began.

Grace turned slightly, her face no longer visible. Foreboding tickled his senses. A moment later, he knew why. Lord Westhouse had approached their small party and was extending his hand expectantly to Grace.

Foreboding quickly shifted to rage.

"No, refuse him," Ramsey muttered, increasing his pace.

Grace turned her head slightly as if furtively searching for him nearby.

"I'm here, turn around," he commanded softly, turning slightly to slip through a narrow space between two ladies with their backs turned.

"Don't do it," he muttered a little louder.

He noted the way her shoulders sagged slightly. No. They didn't sag, they merely rounded, as if disappointed, and she followed his lead onto the dance floor.

Ramsey paused, watching her back disappear into the swirling dancers before he caught a glimpse of her face, but she didn't see him. Her eyes were on her partner, and her expression was alight with amusement, as if Lord Westhouse had said something witty.

Ramsey took in a deep breath of frustration, releasing it slightly. Creating a scene in the middle of the Rymans' ballroom wouldn't be good for either him or Grace. Plus, there was something else afoot, he just didn't know what.

When Ramsey forced his gaze away from Grace, he turned back to Heathcliff, only it wasn't Heathcliff's gaze that met his, it was Lucas's.

And Lucas, eighth Earl of Heightfield and third partner in Temptations, was clearly back in town, clearly
aware of what had just happened, and clearly amused
that Ramsey was in hot pursuit of Heathcliff's ward.

Good Lord. The evening just kept getting better.

He meant that in the most sarcastic way possible.

Lucas arched his dark brows, a knowing smile teasing his blue eyes. He took a step back as Ramsey approached, as if thrilled to be able to watch whatever
happened, but not be necessarily close enough to accidentally get hit should it come to fisticuffs.

"About bloody time you got here," Heathcliff said
by way of greeting.

"Good evening to you, too," Ramsey remarked
dryly.

"What in the hell took you so long? I've been fend-
ing off Westhouse for nearly an hour and I ran out of
excuses. But I must say that at least Grace acted less
interested. Thank the good Lord for that small boon.
No thanks to you."

Ramsey thought her lack of interest was rather in direct thanks to him, but he didn't think it was the time to
mention that fact. Rather, his attention was shifted to
the mention of Lord Westhouse's name, and his blood
boiled.

He cast a cautious glance to Lucas, who merely
grinned and glanced away.

What a bloody useless friend, Ramsey decided. "Finally in town?" He directed the statement to Lucas.

"I figured you needed me. I was correct." He
shrugged. "My lovely wife did not accompany me,
due to her delicate condition."

"Samantha is still frustrated with that piece of information, though she understands. I'm sure you'll have a visitor quite early."

"My lovely sister-in-law is always welcome." Lucas gave a slight bow, grinning in the direction of Samantha, who was in conversation with Lady Greywick.

"Now, back to the issue at hand. Why are you so bloody late?" Heathcliff turned to Ramsey.

Ramsey had focused his gaze back on the dance floor and was searching for Grace. He could only catch a glimpse of her back, but his eyes greedily trailed down the length of her spine, his hands tingling with the memory of her curves within his grasp.

"Ramsey?" Heathcliff's voice interrupted his rather scandalous thoughts.

"Pardon?" Ramsey turned to Heathcliff.

Lucas snickered.

Ramsey shot him a glare that silently commanded him to shut up.

Lucas chuckled louder.

Bloody brilliant.

"So?" Heathcliff asked rather impatiently.

"So, what?" Ramsey asked, tugging on his coat sleeves; damn it was hot in there.

Heathcliff tipped his chin to the side and studied his friend. "Have you been into the brandy early?"

"What? No. It's bloody hot in here."

"I'm sure it is," Lucas murmured just over his glass of champagne.

"Where have you been? I ask again because clearly you didn't hear the first two inquiries."

"Oh, that. Interesting. I'd think you'd be wanting to convey some rather interesting information."

At this, Heathcliff stilled, his eyes narrowing with intelligence and he leaned forward. "You saw John."

Ramsey gave a curt nod.

"Before I ask how, the more important question is how you're dealing with the information," Heathcliff whispered.

Lucas moved into the close confederacy and his expression was one of understanding. Apparently, Heathcliff had communicated the knowledge to Lucas.

"I'm still processing it." Ramsey swallowed.

"Understandable," Lucas remarked. "What I don't understand is how we weren't aware of the possible connection. You'd think it would have been whispered about for ages."

"I think it was, but hushed. You know my father, the scandal—" Ramsey paused. That was it. It had to be.

"What?" Heathcliff asked impatiently. "You figured something out."

Ramsey nodded absentmindedly, realizing the music had ended. He turned expectantly, waiting for Lord Westhouse to return Grace to her guardian.

But amongst the sea of faces, he didn't see Grace's.

"Where is she?" Ramsey whispered, turning to Heathcliff and then immediately scanning the room.

"Who?" Heathcliff asked.

"Grace, damn it! She should be done by now. The music . . ." He trailed off and started to turn around to scan the people behind him.

"Damn," Heathcliff remarked.

Ramsey searched, coming up empty. His mind had merely one goal: find her. He turned to Heathcliff. "When did you see them last?"

"Same as you, on the bloody dance floor."

"I'd wager Ramsey saw her more readily than you," Lucas replied, arching a brow, but his expression was sober as he searched Ramsey's gaze. "We'll find her."

"What could he mean by taking her from the room?" Ramsey asked, then his heart chilled with fear. He couldn't possibly, he wouldn't suspect that—

"Let's split up. Ramsey, you take the gardens. Heathcliff, take the halls, and I'll take the ballroom." With a curt nod, the gentlemen all went their separate ways, and Ramsey made a direct line to the nearest exit to the garden.

He wasn't sure Westhouse would go that direction. It would be too obvious.

Unless . . .

Unless he was waiting to be found.

Chapter Twenty-five

Grace rubbed the sore area of her arm that Lord Westhouse had just released. Anger burning, she spun to face him, ready to give him a large piece of her mind when she noted the way he held his fingers to his lips. She wouldn't have heeded him, but the whole situation was so absurd, she paused just long enough for him to whisper. "I'd watch that devil's tongue you've got, Miss Grace. If you make too much noise, people will hear and if they find you here, alone with me, you'll be ruined." He paused for effect. "You don't want that, do you?"

She wanted to let him know that she was already quite ruined. Or at least ruined enough, but she thought better of it. Her heart pinched at the idea, because Lord Sterling, Ramsey, hadn't come to the ball. At least he wasn't there *yet*. Hope sprang eternal and all.

But he wouldn't be looking for her in the garden.

And she suddenly felt quite alone. She rubbed her arms, trying to think clearly through her rather undesirable situation. The horrible man had a point, and if people found them alone in the garden, she would be forced to marry him. It would be a scandal, and she didn't want that type of attention. No. She simply wanted to get away from Lord Westhouse and sneak back into the ball without anyone the wiser.

How had she thought she loved him? Or at least was falling in love with him? It was so obvious now that she wasn't in love with him. She studied him in the flickering torchlight and moonlight of the garden. He was still handsome, that was undeniable, but there was something hard in his eyes, in his expression. Gone was that tenderness that she'd thought he had for her. Did that mean it was an act? Had his intentions toward her been a ruse? If so, why?

And why in the *hell* did she not notice it? How had she been so blind? It was infuriating, frustrating, and she blamed herself.

When she knew she should be blaming him.

But guilt was never rational.

She gave her head a slight shake and took a small step back.

"Is that an answer?" he asked, tipping his head just slightly.

"To what question?" She responded softly, glancing about to make sure they were alone.

"Your glancing about is answer enough. You don't wish to be caught with me. And one has to wonder . . ." He took a step to the side, then snapped a flower from its stem. It was a sprig of lavender, and he lifted the fragrant purple buds to his nose and inhaled, sighing softly. "Why."

She watched him offer her the flower, and she took it, thankful to have something to occupy her hands. Or else she would certainly do something foolish, like slap him. But that would only create a bigger problem. No, she needed simply to escape, not get into a fistfight, one she would certainly lose, in more ways than one.

She twisted the flower in her fingers, the rich scent of lavender a comfort in the middle of the terrible situation. "I'm afraid you'll have to rephrase your question."

He let out a low chuckle and glanced toward the garden entrance. He turned back to her and answered. "The question was quite simple. A week ago, you were quite eager for my attention; tonight you are not. I can only surmise that some sort of catalyst has caused so elemental a change. Unless you are like the other debutantes with shifting fancies. But I rather thought you were different."

An urge to defend herself bubbled to her lips, and she spoke without thinking through her words. "I am different. Whether that is a good or bad thing is left to be decided. However, I must say that a week ago I would never have imagined that you'd behave in such an ungentlemanly manner as this," she scolded, hoping that her remarks would hit some chivalrous mark.

His chuckle proved otherwise. "Is that so?"

Well, that didn't work, she mused. "Do you have some purpose in mind to keep me out here against my will?" she asked plainly, resisting the urge to place her hands on her hips.

"I do, indeed," he answered, his brows raised as if surprised by her frank question.

"So, then you're saying I'm not free to leave," she tested, quite certain he would say no, but wanting the confirmation.

"You're free to leave, but it will be at a price."

"That's not freedom."

He shrugged as if such a detail was of little consequence.

She took a step toward the path.

He moved to block her.

"What is the price?" she asked softly, not wanting to hear the answer, but a lack of knowledge wouldn't help either.

"Marry me."

She blinked, tipped her head, and then waited for him to add to the small but profound phrase. He stepped closer, and she took an answering step back. "Pardon?"

"Marry me." He shrugged. As if he had commented about the traffic on Bond Street, or the amount of boat traffic on the Thames. Not as if he'd asked the single most important question in her life.

"No," she replied, her tone half surprised, half incredulous.

"Then I'm afraid you cannot leave." He flicked an invisible piece of lint from his coat. "You see, I have a goal and I will see it through."

"And I'm part of this, how?" she asked, growing more frustrated, less cautious, and feeling an edge of fear leak through her mind.

"That's a very good question."

Grace turned toward the path just out of view, her heart pinching with a desperate hope that, rationally, she knew had to be impossible. Yet she would recognize that voice anywhere.

"Ah, just in time." Lord Westhouse turned to greet Lord Sterling, an expectant expression on his face.

"I rather think I'm quite late, actually," he remarked, closing the distance with a relaxed air about him, but his gaze was acutely aware, in strict contrast to his stride. "Are you well, Grace?" he asked, not glancing to her, but keeping his gaze trained on Lord West-house.

"Ah, a first name acquaintance, is she? I rather thought it might be that way," Lord Westhouse replied in a jovial manner.

"Yes, annoyed but well," Grace answered, curious as to why Lord Westhouse looked so bloody pleased with the situation.

Ramsey paused about a half yard from Lord West-house, who turned to meet him. Grace watched as the gentlemen faced off, their expressions calculating. Ramsey was much taller than Lord Westhouse, and equally as broad, but there was an edge to Lord West-house's stance that implied that he wasn't one to back down from a fight. Good Lord, she hoped it wouldn't come to blows. *That* would certainly lead to a disaster.

"I learned something interesting tonight," Lord Sterling started, easing his posture from the rigid stance he had a moment before and taking a step toward Lord Westhouse, but slightly to the side.

Lord Westhouse frowned, but listened.

"I wait with bated breath," Lord Westhouse remarked, then moved to stand between Lord Sterling and herself, blocking Lord Sterling's path.

"I suspect it's something you've known for a while," Ramsey remarked.

"I suspect I know a great many things that you do not. Take your pick," Lord Westhouse said rather testily.

Ramsey chuckled; the sound wasn't the warm one she expected. No, it was cold, hard, and had an edge. She couldn't see his face—Lord Westhouse's back blocked the view—but she could hear his voice, and it was silk over a sword, smooth and deadly. For the first time, she suspected that Lord Ramsey was a dangerous man to cross.

When provoked enough.

And apparently, she was enough.

The knowledge comforted her.

But she wasn't simply going to be a damsel in distress; she could save herself too, thank you very much.

She noted the way that Lord Westhouse had all but given her his back, and she slowly edged away, her focus on just moving around him enough to make it to the path and run inside. If she were to get inside, she could send out the viscount and Lord Heightfield to assist Ramsey. There was something going on, and as much as it seemed to involve her, she suspected that the root went much deeper.

Ramsey's gaze never left Lord Westhouse's, and she suspected it was on purpose. If he shifted his gaze, Lord Westhouse would follow it, and see her moving slowly along the edge of the path.

"You know, my father never had a problem disparaging the other gentry around our estate," Ramsey continued.

Grace took another step.

"Why do I not find that surprising?" Lord Westhouse asked in a bored tone, but his posture was rigid as if expecting some verbal blow.

"But he never mentioned your family."

It was almost imperceptible, but Grace was watching Lord Westhouse so closely that she noticed how his shoulders froze, and his fists clenched.

"Never?" he asked, as if surprised and caught off guard.

"Never," Ramsey remarked, a slight edge of triumph in his tone. "Which was curious, and helped me confirm some news."

"What is that?" Westhouse barked.

Grace was only a few feet from being able to run to freedom, but it was the most visible part. If Lord Westhouse wasn't completely distracted, he could easily see her, seize her, and then she'd be back to square one. She breathed out slowly, and waited.

"That after years of wishing for a younger brother, I discovered I had an older one."

Grace nearly gasped, but caught herself, and sprung forward the last steps and then ran.

To her surprise, she made it to the garden door, and was down the hall before she realized that Lord Westhouse hadn't even tried to pursue her.

And all of a sudden, she had the chilling thought that maybe she wasn't whom he was after.

Maybe she had just been the bait.

Chapter Twenty-six

Ramsey watched as Grace fled the scene, and his body relaxed slightly. Now that she was safe, he could focus on dispatching Lord Westhouse, or Julian, which was his first name. He'd always hated that name, or rather he'd hated Westhouse and associated the name with him, so it all went together. But as he studied him, he saw afresh all the details that should have made the truth come to light sooner.

He was shorter, that much was true, but the height had come from his mother's side, not his father's. But Westhouse had their father's nose, the same shade of walnut hair, and the same severe streak in temperament that made him a total ass.

No wonder he'd hated Westhouse from the beginning. He'd been a copy of his father.

Good Lord, the world didn't need a replica, that was certain.

"I can't believe it took you so bloody long to figure

that out. Here I was anticipating some great secret, and it seems the only one who didn't know was you."

Westhouse hitched a shoulder as if it didn't matter, but Ramsey knew it did. It had to matter. Or else why would he have taken always to seeking out Ramsey for ridicule, why would he have targeted him in school? The question was, why?

And what bloody part did Grace play in all this? She didn't fit anywhere in the equation.

"As I said, my father never mentioned you. Or your mother," Ramsey replied, repeating the earlier statement. It seemed to have met a mark earlier, and he wanted to push it further now that Grace was safely away.

"I don't believe you."

At this, Ramsey laughed. It wasn't a joyful sound, rather a cynical, hard noise that was a result of years of dealing with his father's silence as well.

"What have I to hide? He's dead; your family is as well . . . what will lies get us? Nothing."

"He may have never mentioned me to you, but he said plenty to me regarding the disappointment that you were to him," Westhouse remarked with venom.

At this, Ramsey felt a punch to the gut. He'd always known it, his father had often said it, but hearing it again, it broke open the still-healing wounds from earlier.

Not who I was . . .

Ramsey repeated the words in his mind, for once the pain not festering, but instead, it disappeared and the next words didn't hit the same mark.

"He always said it was a pity that he couldn't allow me to inherit." Westhouse shook his head as if he pitied Ramsey. "But with my father dead, and the world, mostly, believing that I was his heir, I couldn't rightly be heir to both men."

"So your mother was a whore," Ramsey remarked, watching as Westhouse's face turned bright red. Perhaps it was a low blow, but since Westhouse wasn't holding back anything, neither would he. "But my father hated scandal so he would have paid her well to keep silent. That probably paid for your education at Eton." He took a step closer to Westhouse, murmuring. "I heard that the coffers were somewhat low. Perhaps you were after an heiress?"

Ramsey angled his words to try and ferret out the truth regarding his interest in Grace. He was growing less concerned about whatever forsaken situation he had in familial ties with Westhouse, and found it more important to keep Grace free and clear of him.

"The coffers are quite full, thank you. Though I'm sure you are fully aware and simply trying to bait me. You and your spy, what's his name, John? Sniffing about my business. Are you not man enough to simply inquire yourself?

Ramsey didn't even reply to such a baiting statement. "Miss Grace was easy prey, is that it?"

"Ah, yes, *Miss* Grace. Odd how now you use her proper name. I suspect you've had rather improper moments with her, however." He grinned wolfishly, tauntingly, and all the control that Ramsey had been tightly reining in snapped. His fist tingled, his arm flexed, and before he could even understand the temptation, he was shaking his hand from the solid roundhouse he'd delivered to Lord Westhouse's right eye.

Westhouse stumbled back, swearing epithets at Ramsey and wiping the blood from a cut near his eye. "Bastard."

"Actually, that would be you," Ramsey remarked heartlessly.

Westhouse swore, then flexed his fists. "You just can't stop creating scandal, can you?"

Ramsey's blood chilled at the words. It was as if his father were speaking to him from the grave. Those very words had been hurled at him constantly after the holy wreck that was his marriage, and the resulting fallout. His father had spoken them over him like a curse, like a prophecy, and the weight of it settled back on his chest.

"You can't deny it," Westhouse spat, taking a step toward him. "Your disaster of a marriage that made your father a laughingstock in front of his peers, and tarnished your title forever. He told me, you know. I may not have carried his name, but he treated me like the son he never had . . . even though he had you. He never wanted you, but he needed you. You were a tool for him, and one that never performed the basic function he wanted you to accomplish. You failed him in every way," Westhouse continued, hurling the words like arrows.

Ramsey replayed a thousand conversations with his father, all sounding the same, all a repetition of every word that Westhouse said. "You think you're saying something that I never knew?" he remarked after a moment, regaining himself a little.

"I don't doubt it, but I just wanted you to remember. And when I walk into the ballroom, everyone will see me, and know."

Ramsey was about to ask how, but Westhouse reared back to punch him. Ramsey dodged the blow, but only nearly. Holding up his hands, he waited for the second attempt. He blocked the majority of the blow but it grazed his lip, and he tasted the salty flavor of blood. Watching his opponent, he waited for another blow, but Westhouse just stepped back. "That should be enough."

Ramsey was curious at his quick retreat and was immediately on edge.

"For?"

"To implicate you when they see my eye. They'll know it was you, it was me . . . it was her."

Ramsey saw red at the mention of Grace in the middle of their personal drama. "Why her?"

Westhouse continued like he hadn't heard the question." And with your reputation versus mine . . . I must say, the ton will certainly look on me with more favor and assume that I was protecting her honor from the likes of you . . ."

"She'll be ruined."

Westhouse chuckled. "I'm quite certain that she's ruined already, but yes, it will create enough scandal that no one will want her. A pity that, but quite helpful."

Ramsey frowned. "Why does it matter? What use is she to you? Clearly you don't have an interest in her—"

"No. But you do," Westhouse answered simply, as if it were obvious.

Ramsey waited, hoping he'd continue. In his experience, people only needed a little silence to be tempted to fill it, and they start talking, or in this case, continue speaking.

And he rather thought that Westhouse wanted him to know, wanted to use it in some fashion to make him suffer more.

"She was a venue to you, at first. Your friends are so bloody protective, it's quite frustrating, but she was an easy pathway to gain your attention. It was an added delight to discover you were interested in the chit. I must say I wasn't expecting that boon."

"So she was a—"

"Means to an end, but delightful in conversation, I have to admit. She must be a hellion in bed though," he said with some insinuation.

Ramsey delivered another blow to Westhouse's midsection, but this time he didn't stop. When Westhouse bent over form the blow, Ramsey lifted his knee to collide with his head, rendering him a bloody nose that spewed red over his white shirt, and splashed onto Ramsey's. Westhouse spat blood, then roared, charging Ramsey, who was waiting with anticipation for the fight.

"Good Lord." Lucas charged into the middle of the battle and held back Westhouse, while Heathcliff stood between the two men, acting like a buffer.

"What in the hell?" Lucas asked, or rather demanded.

As if unable to resist one final blow, Westhouse spat blood to the side and then met Ramsey's gaze with a hateful gaze. He then shifted his gaze to Heathcliff, and grinned. "I suspect you don't know, but you might want to restrain your friend rather than me. I'm merely trying to save your ward's honor from that rakehell."

The blood drained from Ramsey's face. No. Not like this. This wasn't how he was going to tell his friend.

Heathcliff swore and moved to deliver a blow to Westhouse, but Ramsey said one word. "Stop."

Westhouse's expression was one of triumph.

Ramsey touched Heathcliff on the shoulder, waiting for him to turn. "I was going to ask you tonight . . ."

Lucas swore under his breath. "Is now really the time, Ramsey?" he asked, then growled.

Heathcliff held up a hand. "Did you compromise her?"

Ramsey opened his mouth, his damn honor and honesty being rather obnoxiously insistent on the truth, "not entirely."

"Damn it," Heathcliff swore, his expression full of frustration and something much more painful: disappointment.

"I love her." Ramsey added quickly. "And I wish to marry her, should you give me your permission."

Lucas whistled.

Westhouse gave a snort of derision.

Heathcliff paused.

"Please," Ramsey remarked, his heart in his words as he humbled himself, bloody, broken and utterly a disaster waiting to happen, before his greatest friend, asking, quite frankly, for the world.

"How?"

Ramsey swallowed, not certain he felt comfortable going into all the details of how he had "not entirely" compromised Grace.

"No, bloody hell, not that. How do you know you love her? I swore to my wife that I'd not let Grace go to someone who merely felt she was a prize, or, in your case, some misbegotten sensation of guilt."

"Can we please carry on this conversation later?" Lucas asked, still restraining Lord Westhouse, who wasn't fighting the restraint, but Lucas didn't look as if he wished to test his compliance.

Ramsey ignored him. "Because." He grinned in spite of himself, in spite of the absurd situation he found himself in, in spite of the craziness of the situation and the improbability of it. "Because her mind fascinates me, her laugh heals me, and in her utter imperfection, she's perfection to me."

Lucas gave a low chuckle.

Heathcliff blinked.

Westhouse snorted, again. This time Lucas booted him. "Shut up. I'll deal with you later."

"Well then, I guess it's decided. That is, if she'll have you," Heathcliff added.

"I will be most persuasive," Ramsey remarked, then realized just how his words could be interpreted.

Heathcliff arched his brow, looking every inch the disparaging father. No one could fault his affection for his ward.

"Now that this is all settled, how do you suggest we get from the garden to the carriages without making the gossip papers tomorrow morning? Not that I'm against it, but I rather thought we were trying to be respectable for our wives and all," Lucas remarked dryly.

"No, first I need to know why." Ramsey turned to Westhouse.

Heathcliff gave a curious glance and turned as well.

"Why, why come after me, why all the effort?" Ramsey asked again.

Westhouse glared. "Because it should have been me. The title, the name, everything should have belonged to me, never to you. I kept my name clear of scandal, your name is a byword for it," he ground out lowly, his words an epithet.

Ramsey started to ask something, but Lucas shook his head, suggesting him to stop.

"Jealousy gets you nowhere, haven't you learned that yet, Westhouse?" Lucas remarked. "You hit on one very real truth, however. And that's regarding your name. So far, there are no black marks against it, which is admirable, though wholly unknown as to how you've done it with the terrible temperament you possess." Lucas sighed as if bored. "However, if we walk into the room, all of us mind you, with you in tow, that good name will be no longer, and you'll be subject to several weeks of speculation as to why you got such a thrashing. And we're more than happy to circulate some fresh fodder for the gossipmongers every few days or so. . . ." He let the open threat hang in the air for a moment. "Unless you want to merely walk away."

Ramsey arched his brow. It was quite lovely, having diabolical friends. They had learned several tricks of the trade, since it was a survival skill in managing Temptations.

There was a long pause, and Ramsey watched the steely resolve in Westhouse's expression harden a moment before he spoke. "I'll walk," Westhouse ground out.

"See that the walk takes you out of London for a while," Lucas added.

"As if that won't cause talk—"

"Don't you have an estate that needs your attention?" Ramsey asked, giving him a way out. It wasn't necessary, he didn't deserve any sort of aid, but he gave it, regardless. He was, after all, his half-brother. Good Lord, what a scandal . . . and several other details clicked into place. He pushed them aside for the moment as he awaited Westhouse's final agreement.

Westhouse met his gaze, then nodded slowly. "Very well."

"I'll just escort you to your carriage, make sure you get there safely," Lucas remarked, slowly releasing him.

Westhouse gave him a disbelieving glare, but didn't fight it. He dusted off his coat, straightened his shoulders slightly, as if adjusting his dignity, and then left the gardens with Lucas following close behind as they wound around the house, avoiding the ballroom.

"Well, that was interesting."

"You don't know the half of it," Ramsey remarked, then proceeded to tell Heathcliff all he had missed.

After he was finished, Heathcliff nodded, then tipped his head. "I guess only one question remains."

"And which one is that?" Ramsey asked.

Heathcliff grinned, raising a hand to set it on Ramsey's shoulder approvingly. "When are we having a wedding?"

Chapter Twenty-seven

Grace was quite certain that she was going to thrash them all soundly the moment they finally showed their faces back in the ballroom. As it was, she couldn't very well run into the fray; it would be not only unnecessary, but she could easily create a larger problem than solve any of the issues at hand. She wasn't foolish enough to try such a move, but she was dreadfully curious, and that curiosity seemed quite corrosive to her mood.

Not that Samantha was faring any better.

"And you're quite certain you sent them in the right direction?" Samantha watched the entrance to the ballroom from the direction of the Garden with a trained focus.

"Yes." Grace bit out the word. Her patience was spent, but Samantha had asked that same question several times before. She wanted to remind her that she wasn't about to change her mind about the answer.

"We should not go after them," Samantha remarked, though the words had the slight lilt of a question.

"No," Grace replied, resolved yet utterly irritated in it.

"No. They are used to this type of thing, I imagine." Samantha sighed. "Wretched to be aware of it though. This has taught me a dear love for ignorance." She arched a chestnut brow and gave a rueful grin to Grace.

"Of that I am in complete agreement," Grace replied, nodding with emphasis.

"Pardon, my lady?" A footman addressed Samantha with a soft mummer.

Grace turned to fully face the man, waiting while he spoke in hushed tones to Samantha.

Unable to hear the words, Grace watched Samantha's expression. At first, her brows were furrowed as she focused on the words, then her eyes lighted with understanding as she gave a kind nod, and then turned to Grace.

"We are requested at the front where our carriage has been summoned. The viscount has fallen ill and needs to return home." She arched a brow, just enough for Grace to note her inflection, and then thanked the footman before they departed.

Grace resisted the urge to scoff at such a falsehood. *Ill.* The viscount was a paragon of health, yet it was as good a reason as any to avoid the ballroom and head back home.

She and Samantha walked as quickly as was polite. Grace's heart was pounding with anticipation; at least *now* she'd finally know what happened after she fled the scene. Just as the footman had said, the Kilpatrick carriage was waiting at the bottom of the steps, a footman holding the door open for the ladies.

Samantha stepped up first, taking a seat beside her husband. Grace grasped the hand of the footman and stepped up, ducking slightly as she entered into the dark carriage. She turned to the side opposite Samantha, but gasped when she noted that the bench seat was not vacant, but was occupied by no one other than Lord Sterling.

She inhaled softly, but recovered and took the seat beside him. Upon inspection, she noted the darker shadow under one eye, along with what seemed to be dried blood just below the corner of his mouth. "Does he look worse?" Grace asked, not thinking about her words.

Ramsey chuckled, the sound deep and surprised.

"Well, does he?" she asked, after he didn't readily respond. Bother with being polite, she wanted to know!

"Yes, he does, Miss Grace."

"Good. Though, now that I think of it, I'd hardly expect you to say anything else, pride and all," she mused.

"You may also ask your guardian's opinion of the matter if my word is not enough to satisfy your inquiry." He nodded toward the viscount.

Grace turned to him, noting the way he pinched his lips as if suppressing a smile.

"Ramsey has but one black eye, Westhouse has two."

"Amongst other things," Ramsey added, as if making certain there could be no confusion on who came out the victor.

"I see. Good," Grace replied.

"Will you finally tell us what happened? We've been out of our minds with worry!" Samantha directed her question to her husband, her hand resting upon his arm and clutching it slightly, giving her words emphasis.

"It's a rather long story."

Grace sighed in exasperation. "Of course it is. And I'm sure that this is not the place to speak of it, etc. Forgive my frankness—"

Ramsey snickered softly.

She turned an aggravated glance in his direction, then continued, "But what part of tonight has been proper, may I ask? And why must we suddenly be concerned about propriety now? Give me one good reason."

Samantha turned to her husband, her expression expectant.

"Because the secrets aren't mine to tell," the viscount replied.

"They are mine," Ramsey remarked. "And while Miss Grace has an excellent point"—he smiled at her, as if giving proper credit, and she lifted her chin a touch higher—"this is truly something that should be discussed in private. But, before you begin to petition the resolution, you will be happy to know that since I have no plans to leave Kilpatrick House before all is settled, your curiosity will not have long to wait."

Grace sighed, but gave a nod. It was acceptable, but just barely. Yet some part of his words carried a further interest. What else needed to be settled? What exactly had transpired? Was Westhouse blackmailing them? Were they blackmailing Westhouse? Good lord, never had she imagined such intrigue till she came to London.

Granted, she was also in the company of two of the three most notorious men in London, owners of the most notorious and secretive club in London, which certainly contributed to the situation.

She turned to the viscount, but he wasn't watching her, or Samantha; he was giving a very level gaze to Ramsey, conveying some intense meaning.

Her head hurt.

She blew out a rather unladylike sigh.

"Soon enough," Ramsey remarked softly, only for her to hear. It was intimate, it was private, and her tension fled and a new sort of anticipation flooded in.

And then she remembered.

He saved her.

She turned to him. "I don't believe I ever said thank you, my lord," she remarked softly.

His lips parted to say something, but he simply shook his head, leaving her to interpret the meaning.

Thankfully it was a short trip to Kilpatrick House, and after they arrived, it was decided that Ramsey be given some time to refresh himself and tend to his wounds.

Grace changed from her evening gown into a more comfortable day dress. She had the feeling it was going to be a rather long conversation and she wanted to be comfortable, or at least more comfortable than if she hadn't changed.

In less than half an hour, they all reconvened in the parlor, with tea and biscuits awaiting their leisure. Mrs. Marilla had closed the door with a soft click once they all arrived, and finally, they were in the privacy needed to divulge all the information Grace desperately wished to know.

The silence was thick, and though it only lasted perhaps a few seconds, to Grace it seemed to stretch for hours. Finally, the viscount cleared his throat and began.

"I'm sure that you are all aware than Lord Westhouse forcibly led Miss Grace from the ballroom this evening."

Samantha gave a sharp nod. She was seated beside her husband, and Grace was opposite them in a wingback chair. Samantha's gaze flickered to Grace, her expression tender and concerned.

"I'm quite well," Grace reminded her.

The viscount continued, "Once Ramsey noted that Grace was missing, we all searched for you." He directed these words to Grace, and then took a breath. "Ramsey took the gardens, where he found you with Lord Westhouse. Now, that should be an ample platform for the rest of the story." He nodded to Ramsey, who gave an agreeing nod.

"Now then, after you quite cleverly escaped—"

Grace interrupted, "You did do an excellent job of distracting him. Are you really his half-brother?" On the edge of her seat, she eagerly listened to Ramsey as he started his answer with a curt nod.

"Indeed. Which led to some further understandings that have quite colored what I knew as a child."

"Good Lord," Samantha murmured.

Ramsey twisted his lips, as if uncertain where exactly to begin. "Suffice to say that there is quite the history of jealousy and dishonesty, but I must lay the blame for most of it at my father's feet. It seems they carried quite a close confederacy as Westhouse grew, more so than my father's interest in me. As such, I must say it was very much like speaking to my father, when I was speaking with Westhouse. Not something I'd like to repeat, ever. I can't imagine how I didn't see it, there are so many similarities, it's rather absurd. Regardless, in the end his downfall was the same as my father's, his bloody pride. And after Lucas and Heathcliff asserted themselves in the situation, Westhouse was forced to walk away slowly, or be exposed to ruin. It was an easy choice for him to make since he loves his reputation and honor nearly as much as our father did."

Ramsey took a deep, slow breath and then took a seat to the left of Grace. He had been pacing about while speaking, his words as restless as his feet. Now, with the story told, it seemed he had lost the restless edge to his manners.

Grace thought over his words, comparing them with what she had experienced with Lord Westhouse. In the most basic ways, they didn't look related, but there was something in the eyes, in the posture, that was familiar. It wasn't of any consequence, but it was interesting.

"Will we be seeing any more of Lord Westhouse this season?" Samantha asked cautiously.

"No," the viscount answered. "His . . . estate needed some tending."

Ramsey snickered softly.

Grace raised an eyebrow, but said nothing.

"I see." Samantha nodded.

The viscount continued, "I imagine him to be much like your father, my dear. Once the waters have settled, he sees no need to rock the boat. After all, the one that would sustain damage would be him, and both your father and Lord Westhouse love their reputations far too much to put them in jeopardy when there is not a certain victory."

"Well said," Ramsey remarked.

Samantha tipped her head. "When did you get so astute?"

"Ach, I always have been. I just hide it well."

"Very well," Ramsey added, earning a glare from his friend.

Grace was still considering Ramsey's words from earlier, one part not quite adding up. "But . . . if he was acting in jealousy, why ever did he take me from the ballroom? What part do I play in any of this? It doesn't make sense." She furrowed her brows, as she tried to think through all the plausible answers.

The viscount shifted in her peripheral vision, and she turned to see him give a rather meaningful look to Ramsey.

She turned to Ramsey to see his response.

"That is a very good question," Ramsey replied.

Grace waited for the answer to the "very good question," and when none seemed forthcoming, she turned to the viscount, who had just finished whispering to his wife.

"We're going to give Ramsey a moment to speak to you, Grace." The viscount and Samantha stood. Samantha gave a surprised and somewhat concerned smile to Grace, then followed her husband from the room, making a slight show of opening the door full wide and arching a brow before stepping into the hall.

"Curious." Grace mumbled, then turned to Ramsey. "I'm expectantly awaiting your response, especially since it apparently needed the evacuation of the room to be heard."

Ramsey chuckled softly, then turned in his chair to face her fully. "It seems Westhouse was far more astute than I gave him credit for."

Grace nodded, her brow still furrowed.

"And was rather determined to continue to be a thorn in my side, and the only way to get to me was through my friends. He understood this, as it had been that way since our days at Eton. There is a strength in numbers, and I have quite loyal friends."

"Indeed," Grace agreed.

"He'd been waiting for an opportunity, and when Heathcliff presented you to society, it was like an open door. If Westhouse could get to you, then he knew I'd not stand by idly, but I'd help Heathcliff in anyway necessary."

"That makes sense." Grace twisted her lips. So, Westhouse's interest in her was merely a tool to be used somehow to get to Ramsey. That had to be some deep-rooted resentment to go to such lengths. She said as much to him.

"It is indeed deeply rooted, and this is why." Ramsey took a tight breath, and his expressive eyes held her captive in their gaze. "My mother died giving birth to me, so as I grew up all I had was my father. But he was a harsh, difficult, and exacting man. Perfection was the only acceptable way to live and I fell short time and time again. But the one thing my father hated most of all was scandal."

Grace nodded, her heartbeat pounding fiercely, her intuition telling her that a deep truth was about to be revealed.

"So, growing up, I avoided scandal like the black plague, only to fail in an epic, Greek-tragedy-type of way with my first marriage. The scandal was monumental, and my father never forgave me for it. He simply reminded me that I'd always been a failure. You can imagine how that affected me." He fell silent for a moment, as if reliving the blow.

"But what I didn't realize, or at least piece together, was why my father hated scandal so much. Why he expected such perfection from me."

Grace waited expectantly.

"Because I was to be his redemption."

Grace frowned. How did a person become another's redemption? It wasn't possible.

"I can tell by your expression that you see the absurdity of it."

"Yes," Grace replied, watching his face, the way his slight smile illuminated his gaze.

"It is absurd, but since when has humanity been utterly rational? Regardless, what I discovered was that my father had created quite the scandal of his own. I'm writing to my housekeeper to confirm the details, but I'm quite certain that it's well known that Westhouse's heir—the current Lord Westhouse—is simply a by-blow of my father's. The scandal at the time would have been monumental. When you factor in my birth, effectively putting an end to the need for my father to have an heir, you can see the tension."

"But, Lord Westhouse would never have been in line for your father's title," Grace argued. "So why have any attachment to it?"

"Because my father had quite the protégé in Westhouse, and cultivated it. Apparently, he lamented my incapability as a son, and it only fed the animosity. When my father died, Westhouse felt the need to pick up the torch, so to speak."

"Good Lord," Grace replied. "What a waste."

"Indeed."

"And so, in the end, it was always about you," Grace replied after a moment's reflection.

"Yes."

She nodded, feeling a cheap pawn. "I see. Forgive me if I sound a petulant child." She shook her head.

"What you've endured is much more than can ever be atoned."

"Oddly enough, while I was to be my father's re- demption, the true heir, the one born rightly into the title—I was also the one he resented most. So rather than live in a way that was atoning for his sins, I rather re-created them in many ways."

"No," Grace replied fiercely.

He tipped his head.

"No, you are nothing like the selfish man you've men- tioned. You're fiercely loyal to your friends, you give of yourself far more than necessary, and you defend those who cannot defend themselves. You saved me."

"I'm not nearly the paragon you describe, but I am thankful that you see me as such," he replied.

"It's the truth," Grace asserted. "But your agree- ment on it or not doesn't affect my convictions."

At this, Ramsey chuckled. "I don't think I will ever grow tired of your wit, Grace. And I don't think it's fair to say I saved you. You did a rather brilliant job of sav- ing yourself. And with that, I have another confes- sion."

Grace was about to make another remark, but stilled and waited for him to continue.

"Westhouse saw me arrive at the ball. Your back was turned to me, and I dare not think how fierce my expression appeared when he took your hand to lead you to the dance floor. I committed the biggest crime of gambling, I gave away my tell. In that moment, he knew he had me. And you were the bait."

Grace breathed in the words. "I waited for you," she whispered, her tone hesitant.

"I was rather unforgivably late," he remarked. "There

was an issue with my carriage so I'm not without some excuse, but . . . you still should not have been so long expectant of me, not when there was much that needed to be said, to be . . . discussed." He moved from his chair and stood. Taking the few steps to close the distance between them, he offered his hand to her to help her to stand.

Grace grasped his hand, the warmth going through her, and it was as if a crashing wave of emotion soaked her and she realized how desperately she had needed to touch him, to know he was well, to just be in his arms. Her body ached with the need for it.

He tipped her chin up slightly, and before he continued, he bent down and placed a kind, warm, reassuring kiss on her waiting lips. Then, as if one would never be enough, he kissed her again, equally as soft, and then once more before leaning away, a soft and satisfied smile on his face, reflecting in his eyes.

"How could I miss you so much when I was only apart from you for a few hours?"

Grace gave her head a slight shake. "I know not, but I do know it's entirely accurate."

He grinned and allowed his gaze to roam her features. "I was furious when I saw you take Westhouse's hand. But not furious with you—with myself. Do you have any idea how long I have fought my affection for you?" he mused.

She smiled, glancing down for a moment. "Truly?"

He didn't answer readily, but placed a tender kiss on her forehead. "I shall never forget how you asked what height of footstool you'd need to equal me in height." He chuckled against her skin, the warmth sending goose bumps across her flesh as the words seeped into her head.

"Dear me, my mouth often runs without my mind's permission."

"It's one of my favorite traits."

At this, she giggled. "Amongst my ability to constantly give you frustration."

"You provoke me in every way, Grace," he whispered meaningfully. "Every, single, way." He trailed gentle kisses down her temple, along the line of her jaw and then lingered at her lips.

"You make it sound like a good thing," she whispered, her voice catching as she took in a gulp of air. Her heart pounded, her body tingled, she wanted him closer.

"I rather think it is," he murmured against her lips.

"You are exceedingly easy to tease." She collected her thoughts and spoke them, leaning back to meet his warm gaze. "And I rather delight in frustrating you. It is one of my greatest faults."

"You keep me from remaining as I am, but push me to be better, to think differently, to . . . love." He spoke the word with reverence, as if it were a litany in church.

Her heart leapt at the word, daring to hope for what it could imply.

"I am rather loveable," she whispered breathlessly, but without the twist of humor she intended.

"Indeed you are." He then took her lips, coaxing them to open to his attentions. His hands grasped her fingers, tugging her in closer to his body, his heat melting through her with delightful power. Once he released her fingers, she reached up, winding her hands through his hair and pulling him more securely against her lips, nipping gently before kissing him fully.

He leaned back, even as she tried to pull him closer.

"Demanding little thing, aren't you?" he teased, his gaze alight with desire.

Her breath was hot and fast as she nodded, not caring that she basically admitted to a physical desire for him.

"As tempting as you are, I wish to live longer than this night. I do believe I've had enough bodily harm for the day, and I'd rather not have more at the hand of my friend, who will soundly thrash me, and rightly, if I compromise you in his parlor."

A heated blush seared her cheeks and she glanced away, then back to his lip. Carefully she reached up and touched the corner where she could see a cut. "Does it hurt?"

"Not nearly enough to tempt me to stop kissing you," he answered frankly.

At this, Grace smiled. Noticing the rather purple shade of skin along his eye, she refrained from touching it, knowing it had to hurt.

"Stop worrying about me. This is not the worst I've had, love. And I dare say it won't be the last black eye I'll have either."

At this, Grace rolled her eyes. "Men."

"You're quite fond of me, is that it?" Ramsey asked, his gaze taking on a dancing lilt.

"Yes. I rather am. I hope you don't think me willing to hand out my kisses to just anyone," she added with a bit of cheek.

"If you have, don't tell me. I'd be honor bound to

thrash them all and I would rather spend my time doing other things. . . ." He met her lips meaningfully.

She giggled, shaking her head. "Good thing I've only kissed one person."

His expression sobered, then grew fierce. "Me."

She nodded.

He kissed her then, deep and searchingly, as if making sure he had staked his claim.

When he released her, he leaned back, then bent down on one knee. "Since I'm rather fond of being the first and only, I'd like to make that completely and irrevocably official." His gaze met hers with a powerful determination as he took a slow breath before continuing.

Grace could hear her heartbeat pounding in her ears. Her limbs were tingling and she couldn't control the smile that stretched across her face in expectation.

"Miss Iris Grace Morgan, will you do me the great pleasure of consenting to be my wife?" he asked, quite properly she thought.

Her eyes prickled with tears, and she was nodding before she could form the word "yes," though it came through in a garbled mess a moment later.

Tears burred her eyes so she felt rather than saw Ramsey's grin as he kissed her soundly, his arms banding around her and holding her firmly against his strong chest.

"I love you," she whispered against his lips between kisses, her arms tight around his neck as she leaned into him.

"That's a very assuring thing to hear," he replied, then slowly gentled the kiss, much against her will, before disentangling himself from her grasp.

"You'll be happy to know that your guardian has given his consent as well," Ramsey added, putting space between them.

Grace took a step toward him, unwilling for any distance to part them.

"I'm trying to be honorable," Ramsey replied, grinning wildly as he arched a brow and took another step back.

Grace arched a brow, then daringly took another step toward him.

"You're making it exceedingly difficult."

"Good."

He put a chair between them, arching a brow and chuckling.

Grace stepped on top of the seat of the chair.

He smiled, then chuckled, which turned into a broad laugh as he shook his head. "Well, I believe that solves one question."

Grace frowned, looked down, and then back to her fiancé. "What is that?"

He glanced meaningfully down at the chair cushion she was standing upon, and then back to her, meeting her gaze directly. "You don't need a footstool to be my height, my love. You need a chair."

A smile teased her lips before a giggle bubbled out. Drat the man, he was right. She was finally seeing him eye to eye.

And it was all thanks to the chair between them.

Leave it to him to find the one thing that could distract her from her mission. With a twist of her lips, she leaned forward and kissed him. "All the better to kiss you."

When she released him, he met her gaze with one of warm affection. "Shall we tell the others?"

Grace nodded, reluctant to leave the cozy parlor, but knowing she needed especially to tell Samantha.

"After all, Heathcliff asked me an important question earlier tonight. And I finally have the answer."

"Oh? And what was that?" Grace asked as he took her hand and led them from the parlor.

"When were we having a wedding."

Chapter Twenty-eight

St. Georges was the most proper and most in-demand place to have a wedding amongst the ton.

St. Georges was *not* where Grace wanted her wedding.

No.

When she had dreamed of her wedding as a young girl, she dreamed of the outdoor weddings in India, the breeze blowing the canopy across the azure sky, and the colors, oh the beautiful colors.

And everything in London was in shades of pastel and gray.

It was her wedding, and she was going to have color, drat it all!

"Grace, dear, what do you think?" Samantha asked, pulling Grace's thoughts back to the present.

"About?" Grace asked, not caring that she was confirming that she wasn't paying proper attention. After all, she was quite deliriously happy, and as such, she found that she couldn't find the will to be sorry about anything. She was simply far too happy to feel anything but joy.

"We were asking about flowers," Samantha said, presumably again.

Grace twisted her lips, thinking. "I love flowers. Which are in season?"

Samantha glanced upward in thought. "It's too late for tulips, but I'm sure we could find roses, and maybe some other bulbs."

"Irises." She spoke the word before she could stop it, not that she would have, but regardless, her mind ran away with her mouth and as soon as the word left her lips, she knew it was the perfect idea.

And, judging by the smile spreading across Samantha's face, she agreed entirely. "I don't think we can do anything but irises, now that you mention it."

"And they should be in season."

"Indeed."

"And they come in a wide array of colors—"

"Which colors do you fancy most?" Samantha asked, leaning forward, clearly pleased to have some interest from the bride.

Grace considered the question, her thoughts parading a kaleidoscope of color through her mind's eye. "Must I choose one?"

At this Samantha paused, then tipped her head. "You know, it's normal to pick one or two, but I don't know why we must stick to convention in this area."

"I want as many colors as we can find. A medley, a rainbow of color." She smiled as she thought of it.

"Have you spoken regarding a date?" Samantha asked, making notes on her sheet of paper as she spoke.

Grace shook her head. It had happened quite fast after they'd left the parlor last night to share the news.

The viscount and Samantha had been waiting for them in the study, and upon Ramsey's arrival in the room, knowing grins spread across both people's faces.

"I was giving you thirty more seconds before I came to check on you. Propriety and all." The viscount grinned widely, standing to offer his friend a solid handshake.

"I take it she accepted you?" Samantha asked Ramsey, even as Grace gave her a hug.

"I used all my powers of persuasion," Ramsey remarked, turning to wink at Grace.

The viscount cleared his throat.

Ramsey sobered and Grace stifled a laugh.

They had accepted the congratulations and then, with a promise to return in the morning, Ramsey had kissed her hand and departed, his lingering gaze a memory that still made her skin erupt in gooseflesh.

She rubbed her arms absentmindedly.

"Grace? A date?" Samantha asked.

"No, we haven't discussed anything."

"Then we can only do so much planning. We need to know how much time we have to put everything in motion. First, we must have the banns read this Sunday—"

"I don't think that will be necessary."

The viscount strode into the sunny parlor. After giving a warm smile to Grace, he walked over to place a solid kiss on Samantha's head while he gave her shoulders a little squeeze.

"Oh? And why is that?" Samantha asked, looking up at him with affection.

"Because if I know Ramsey, and I do know him, he's planning a trip to Doctor's Commons."

"Oh." Samantha frowned. "That doesn't give us much time."

"Unless the bully of a guardian refuses the idea of a special license."

At this, Samantha batted his arm playfully, not once believing his bluff. "Sure, I'll believe that when I see it!"

"A special license?" Grace asked. She had heard of them, but never actually seen or known anyone to use one. Such a document came at a high cost, but precluded the interested parties from having to follow any normal protocol for a wedding.

With a special license, they could get married in a few days, rather than a few months.

"Well, that does change things," Grace remarked, tipping her head.

"We don't know for sure," Samantha replied. "But it is a good idea to have some contingency plans."

"When did Ramsey say he was arriving today?" the viscount asked, his gaze shifting to the door.

"I'm not entirely certain. He said morning," Grace replied, worrying her lip slightly.

"I wouldn't be concerned about it, Grace. I'm certain he has a full schedule this morning." The viscount clapped once, startling Grace. "Which leads me to my next question."

Grace smoothed her skirt and glanced up at him, her brow furrowed as she awaited the question.

"When did this all happen? I thought you were after Lord Westhouse's good opinion, and next thing I know, Lucas and I are breaking up fisticuffs and you wind up betrothed to my friend. It's been a rather busy day, I'd say."

"And this coming from a man who oversees a gambling hell," Samantha added dryly.

The viscount cut her an unamused glare.

She lifted her hands in surrender, her lips grinning.

"Be that as it may, I find that you have completely unsettled my preconceived notions, not that I object, I was just rather surprised."

"I take that as a compliment, that I can break convention and create a bit of havoc for you, in a good way of course," Grace amended

"In the best way. I say, at first I had teased Ramsey about offering for you. He had immediately refused such an idea, but I am rather delighted to have the opportunity to remind him of his earlier words," the viscount chuckled.

Grace hid a grin behind her hand as she giggled at the idea. She could quite imagine it. The viscount good naturedly teasing his friend, Ramsey taking it seriously and becoming offended; she could nearly see his expression in her mind's eye.

Just when had she grown to know him so well. How had it happened? It was a good and worthy question the viscount asked, regarding how it all came to be. And she was hard pressed to give a credible answer. The truth was, it just . . . did. It wasn't a slow feeling that crept over her, nor was it lightning that struck her heart. No, it was an awakening of sorts, only to find out she was in the middle of it before she realized she had begun.

It led to the question, how had Ramsey known? If he was so set against her earlier, as the viscount had said, when had that changed for him? A million questions swirled around in her mind, all demanding answers, yet she delighted in the fact that she would be able to answer them, rather than ask and uncover the answers like treasures.

Her lips were spreading into a grin before she even gave them permission.

"Ah, look who finally dragged himself in," the viscount commented as the door opened, revealing a very roguish-looking Ramsey.

"That expression terrifies me."

"It's about time I make you as terrified as you have made me so often over the years," the viscount countered, offering his friend a firm handshake as he rose to meet him.

Ramsey snorted at the viscount's statement, but shook his hand firmly, a warm smile on his face.

Then he turned and his gaze shifted into an intimate embrace as his eyes fixed on Grace. Her body tingled with the force of his gaze, and wherever his eyes roamed, her skin warmed like it had been touched. "Good morning," he said simply, but the words were much more than just a mere greeting; they were a promise.

A promise of many more mornings.

Together.

"Good morning," Grace returned, feeling the blood rush to her face in a blush.

A small sigh stole her attention and Grace turned to see Samantha's affectionate gaze on her, a slightly dreamy look in her eyes. "It's so delightful to see you in such a way, dear," she murmured, appearing abashed at being caught.

Grace wasn't exactly sure how to reply, so she nodded and then turned back to Ramsey.

"Have you considered a date? My wife has been pestering your betrothed for details so we can make plans." The viscount started the conversation.

Ramsey gave a nod, but before answering further, he walked over to Grace and offered his hand. She took it eagerly, and as he lifted her fingers to his mouth to place a warm kiss there, she let out a small sigh of her own.

"Careful, Ramsey, she'll swoon in the parlor and then where would we be?" the viscount teased.

Ramsey grinned wickedly.

Grace arched a brow and then cut a glare to her good-natured guardian.

"Did you go to Doctor's Commons?" Samantha asked, clearly not willing to wait patiently for the news.

Ramsey frowned and turned to face her. "Pardon?" Then he turned to the viscount. "Have you had John trailing me?" he asked with a slightly accusing tone.

"Heavens, no. Why, do I need to?" the viscount countered, taking a seat and chuckling at Ramsey's irritated grin.

"No. But it is odd that you'd know my whereabouts so quickly."

"You're not a difficult man to read, Ramsey. I'd wager I know you better than you know yourself. Which leads me to another topic of discourse." The viscount leaned forward, pausing a moment for effect.

Grace knew what was coming, and held her grin in check as she watched for Ramsey's reaction when the viscount reminded him that he'd once stated he had no interest in her.

Ramsey had the good grace to appear slightly abashed. "Let's just say I amended my ways and opened my eyes."

"What a diplomatic answer. Marriage will not be a hardship for you."

The viscount chuckled.

Samantha shot her husband a glare. "As if marriage is difficult for you."

"No. I'd never imagine thinking such a falsehood."

Ramsey gave him a curt nod of approval. "Very diplomatic."

Heathcliff raised a hand as if to say, *See? I know!*

"Are you quite done?" Samantha asked.

"No," both gentlemen replied in unison.

"Dear Lord, Grace, are you sure you want to put up with this?" Samantha asked.

"Mostly," Grace teased, earning a disbelieving glare from her future husband.

"I shall enjoy persuading you further," Ramsey remarked meaningfully.

"Not before you're married right and tight, mind you. Then it's none of my affair." The viscount held up his hands in surrender, as if hoping soon to wash his hands of the whole business.

"Of course." Ramsey replied, his tone a bit too innocent.

The viscount glared, but pushed on to the pressing inquiry. "So, by what type of license will you marry?"

"It was to be a surprise, but since that is no longer an option, I did in fact, acquire a special license today, and so the date now depends on your leisure."

Heathcliff grinned. "I like that, being in control. There is something delightfully sweet about being in control of a control mongrel."

"Tread carefully," Ramsey warned.

The viscount gave a wag of his brows. "A week? More? You know, since I am her guardian, you have yet to ask me if you can marry her without all the usual pomp and declaration—"

"Good lord, Heathcliff," Ramsey remarked. "Please," he asked, but it was less a request and more of a demand.

"Is there a reason?" the viscount asked.

Grace had been growing slightly uncomfortable during the conversation, but when her guardian asked that particular question, the blood flew to her face and she blushed painfully. Dear Lord, was he implying that they *needed* to marry? Could the moment grow more embarrassing?

"No," Ramsey replied quickly, putting an end to her embarrassment.

"Good."

"If I say yes will it speed things up?" Ramsey asked, his tone badgering.

"It might provoke me to give you another bruised eye," the viscount replied.

Grace studied Ramsey. His eye looked better than last night, but there was still a ring of purple around the outer edge. The cut on his lip looked better, but only just.

"Very well."

The viscount nodded. "Three days. Will that suffice?"

"Miss Grace?" Ramsey turned to her, not answering the viscount but directing the question to her.

He didn't have to, but he chose to include her in the timeline. Her heart grew more tender toward him, and she gave a decisive nod. "If I must wait that long, I suppose I shall endure it." She grinned.

Ramsey's answering smile was all the confirmation she needed that her words were well chosen.

"Dear Lord, you two are already driving me crazy," the viscount said. "Very well. Three days. There is much to do, so I suggest you get to it. In the meantime, I'll visit my solicitor and draft the documents," Heathcliff replied, then giving his wife one lingering kiss on her head, he quit the room.

"Now then, since we have a date, let us get down to business," Samantha told them, her eyes alight with enthusiasm.

All the details seemed unimportant, save one.

The groom.

Chapter Twenty-nine

Ramsey once again found sleep elusive. Since he'd returned from Glenwood Manor, he'd been able to sleep quite well, up until he'd begun fighting the internal war over his affection for Grace. Then it all went to hell. Add in that he was getting married on the morrow, and he was quite certain that he was going to watch both the sunset and the sunrise.

Everything, all the many details had come together beautifully; it wasn't the stress of it, but something more. A missing piece, something he couldn't name but knew was not in place.

Westhouse had made good on his word and vacated his London home to spend several months tending to "estate business," and the club was moving along without so much as a single brawl in the past few evenings.

Then it hit him what was wrong.

Nothing.

Not a bloody thing.

Rather, he was expecting something to happen, something to point to how it all was doomed from the beginning, something to fall apart at his feet, making him bend over backward to pick up the pieces.

But that was the strangest thing. Nothing was broken, or even breaking. It was . . . good.

Feelings of unworthiness flooded him, and as before when he was planning his visit back to Glenwood Manor, he felt the need to punish himself for being happy, or at least he felt guilt for being happy.

And not just happy—deliriously happy.

Overjoyed, really.

Old habits die hard, and this one was not willing to fade into the darkness yet.

He rolled over on his bed, thinking over the past few days. He'd been a complete and utter gentleman, and as much as it had cost him in self-control, he'd kept his hands from Grace's tempting body, and only allowed himself a few chaste kisses.

The planning had taken up most of her time, and it was a welcome distraction for him as well, anything to make the time go by faster so that he would no longer have to exercise such strenuous self-discipline. But tomorrow, all that control would be allowed to snap, and he'd freely enjoy the glorious pleasure of Grace as his wife.

Never in a hundred years would he have guessed he'd marry again after Rebecca's betrayal, but it went to prove the point that the right person can change everything.

And Grace had changed him.

But it started with him deciding to let go of the past, to grow from it. It started with going back to Glenwood Manor, and the truth that Mrs. White had infused into his life like tea into hot water. And that seed of truth had grown and flourished, allowing his heart to heal.

To learn to love.

And as if fate had one cruel final joke, the past had risen up to haunt him once more through Westhouse. He still couldn't quite believe the pain in the ass was his half-brother, but it had brought so much clarity to his childhood. It was like the shackles of his past were constantly fighting for control of him.

But no more.

No. He finally had a future ahead of him that was hopeful, glorious, and full of wonderful expectation.

He just couldn't wait for it to start.

Which only added to why, again, he couldn't sleep.

He closed his eyes, but every time he did, he saw her face, her smile, the way her lips quirked when she was about to say something with a dry wit.

The hours ticked by, and soon, but not nearly soon enough, it was an acceptable time to start preparing for the wedding.

His wedding.

The wedding breakfast would take place at Heathcliff's house, and the wedding . . . that was his surprise for Grace.

She thought it was at a small chapel.

He grinned wildly at the way he knew she would be utterly surprised. Lady Kilpatrick had whispered that Grace had mentioned something in passing, and Ramsey was only overly thrilled to try and make it happen for her.

By nine in the morning, Ramsey was on his way to Lucas's house down the street in Mayfair. It was his job to procure a vicar to perform the ceremony. Ramsey dearly hoped he had found a different one than the poor soul who had performed Lucas's wedding. The man looked hostile as he led the vows. Of course, that he was marrying a notorious rake to a duke's daughter, presumably without the permission of said duke, likely contributed to his sour disposition.

Belatedly, Ramsey wondered what dirt Lucas had over the vicar's head in order to provoke him to risk the wrath of a peer of the realm. He'd have to ask later, if he remembered.

But he had the suspicion that he wouldn't be remembering to do anything but lavish his attention over his new wife.

And could anyone fault him?

No.

And if they did, he had no use for them anyway.

As the carriage pulled up to Kilpatrick House, Ramsey felt a rush of anticipation mixed with a slight tinge of fear overwhelm him. A thousand what-ifs flooded his mind, but he pushed them all aside, straightened his coat, and alighted from the carriage.

John was already opening the door, an unusual smile on his normally stoic face. "Good morning, my lord." John nodded respectfully.

"It is indeed a good morning, John," Ramsey returned.

John chuckled. "Indeed it is. And I have some final good news for you, my lord. The carriage incident was simply wear and tear. Nothing nefarious as far as I can tell, and I can speak with great authority since I went over every inch of the carriage myself, sir."

Ramsey nodded. "There is no more thorough man than you, John. Thank you for investigating. It is good news that there was nothing to it."

"I thought you'd appreciate the information on such a celebratory day," John returned.

"You were correct."

"I'll not detain you longer, my lord. The viscount is awaiting your arrival in his study."

"Then I shall not keep him waiting," Ramsey replied, gave a wide grin to John, and started down the hall.

Once he reached the door to Heathcliff's study, he noted it was already open and so he strode in. "Good morning."

"Ach, look what the dog dragged in." Heathcliff grinned, standing from behind his desk.

"You really need to talk with your butler. He will let anyone through that door," Ramsey returned, grinning widely at the irrationality of the statement. John was the most vigilant and formidable butler in all of London; he'd put money on that bet, and win.

Heathcliff gave a chuckle at Ramsey's words and then approached him, giving him a firm handshake. "So, today's the day?"

"Today is the day," Ramsey returned.

"Never thought I'd see it." Heathcliff sighed. "It's a good day, Ramsey."

Ramsey gave a disbelieving shrug. "Miracles happen."

"Don't they, now?" Heathcliff shrugged. "Lucas and his wife will be here shortly. My wife has been in a dither all morning and I lay the blame squarely at your feet."

Ramsey tipped his head. "Why? What crime have I committed?"

Heathcliff leveled him with a square expression as he took a seat behind his desk. "You agreed to *her* harebrained idea. Never have I heard of such a wedding."

"Then perhaps you need to get out more," Ramsey said, grinning unrepentantly. "And I find I can't apologize for taking your wife's excellent advice."

"When you put it that way, I cannot fault you either. Damn it," Heathcliff said without heat.

"Does Grace suspect?" Ramsey asked, glancing furtively at the open door.

"No." Heathcliff gave a decisive shake to his head.

"Good."

"Indeed. Now, before we can start celebrating, let's finish the final details. I have all the documents from my solicitor regarding Grace's inheritance, her dowry, and settlement."

Ramsey couldn't care two figs about whatever dowry and such Grace added to the marriage. His coffers were quite full. Yet as he read through the documents, the realization struck him that he was marrying quite the properly dowered, properly English, and properly innocent—ish—lady that his father had always held on such a pedestal. It was ironic, how when he was looking for such a lady, he'd found the opposite. And now, when he couldn't care less about the "proper" nature of a wife, he'd found the perfect one. And none of those details mattered, because he was in love with who she was, not what defined her on paper.

When the final details were settled and the ink had dried, Heathcliff offered his hand in a final agreement.

Ramsey shook his hand firmly. It was done.

Almost.

The ink was dried on the paper, but like so much in life, the most important things lived and breathed.

Ink meant nothing until the words were whispered: I do.

Chapter Thirty

"What have I missed?" Lady Liliah Heightfield asked the moment she came through Grace's dressing room door. "Oh! You're lovely! We need to just adjust—"

Grace didn't have to offer a greeting before Lady Liliah was adjusting a seam in her bodice that her maid apparently hadn't had quite perfected.

"Good morning, my lady," Grace replied once Lady Liliah had stepped back to regard Grace's gown.

"Good morning! Are you in a fit of nerves? I was quite distracted on my wedding morning—"

"That might have had something to do with us fleeing our home and you marrying the earl in secret . . ." Samantha said in a dry tone, even as she grinned and came to stand by her sister.

"That may have contributed to the tension of the morning. But it was a glorious wedding, even if it was rather secretive. I've not regretted it one moment. I rather loved the intimate affair rather than the scads of people who would have attended otherwise."

Samantha nodded. "It was quite dashing." She turned to Grace then. "That was the first day I met your Lord Sterling."

Grace smiled, awaiting the rest of the story.

"Indeed. I was quite out of sorts, my big sister rushing us both off from our home, basically fleeing our father and her marrying the scandalous Lord Heightfield in secret, and there he was, attending the wedding and nothing but a picture of calm, or at least, feigned calm. I found out later he was just as tense as the rest of us."

"I imagine that most of the men were on alert lest Father make a surprise appearance at the wedding."

"I'm sure that was the general concern," Samantha replied.

"But it was utterly romantic."

Samantha smiled. "It was indeed. I'd only just met the earl, and it was clear to see he was a man violently in love."

"It's rather clear that both of us are blessed with a love match." Lady Liliah gave her sister's arm a squeeze, then she turned to Grace. "And you as well, that much is clear." She gave her head a little shake. "Lucas and I were quite taken with the change that has come over Ramsey. Never would I have imagined I'd see him in fisticuffs. Well, *I* didn't see him in fisticuffs, Lucas did, but you gather my meaning."

Grace blushed slightly and nodded. "It is rather unlike him."

"He finally found something stronger than his fear of scandal," Samantha added.

"Yes. You," Lady Liliah replied, then turned to Samantha. "That being said, we need to finish here and get you downstairs. What needs to be done next?"

Over the next quarter hour, the ladies assisted Grace in finishing the final touches for her attire. Grace had never had a sister, or a brother for that matter, but she imagined that the chattering, teasing, and advice from both Samantha and Lady Liliah was quite kindred to that of older sisters. The thought was a balm to her nerves all tight with anticipation. She had refused to evaluate her reflection in the mirror until everything was finished, and now that the time had come, she was hesitant to do so.

"Lovely," Samantha whispered, stepping back and grasping her sister's hand as they both smiled warmly at Grace.

Encouraged by their responses, Grace turned her gaze to the mirror and smiled at her reflection.

The gown was an amethyst purple, brighter than was the fashion, but the exact color of the irises she'd picked out. The bold color brought her creamy skin to life, accenting the darker highlights of her auburn hair, making it more coffee than the vibrant red tone it usually boasted. Her eyes were clear, highlighted by a hint of kohl, and her cheeks were tinted the faintest shade of pink. But what struck her most was the expression on her face.

Wonder.

Delight.

Expectation.

Love.

It was a combination she'd never seen on herself, and it became her quite beautifully.

She had started out the season convinced she'd fail, convinced that she wouldn't fit in, and somehow would have to fake being the lady everyone thought she was trained to be. But studying her reflection, she realized that she was that lady: graceful, poised, loved. Well, graceful when not in motion, she amended. Just because she looked utterly ravishing didn't mean she'd magically be able to waltz without stepping on toes.

It was a day of miracles.

Not a day of the impossible.

"Are you ready?" Samantha asked softly, almost reverently.

Grace gave her reflection one final glance as she memorized it, then turned to Samantha. "I can't wait."

Liliah giggled behind her gloved hand. "That's the spirit."

Samantha and Liliah advised Grace to wait a moment while they made sure it was the appropriate time for her arrival.

Grace's hands grew damp under her gloves as she grew nervous. What if Ramsey didn't arrive on time?

What if he didn't arrive at all? What if he changed his mind, or what if— Her mind spun in a million different directions, and it was only by sheer force of will that she pulled her thoughts back into line. "No. It will be just fine," she murmured to herself.

Just as her heartbeat slowed, Samantha and Liliah came down the hall, their lips pinched as if trying to hold back wide grins. It was at times like this that Grace could see the very distinct familial relationship between the sisters. Their expressions were nearly identical.

"Shall we?" Samantha asked, arching a playful brow.

"Let's," Grace replied, following the ladies down the hall, down the steps, and into the foyer.

They started toward the small chapel, but Samantha

and Liliah didn't open the doors, rather they kept walking.

"Samantha? I think—"

"Just follow me," Samantha interrupted.

Grace twisted her lips, but obeyed.

As they traveled down the hall, Grace's brow furrowed in confusion. They were passing the library, the study, and continuing back toward the end of the hall, but there was nothing there but a door that led to their small courtyard and garden area.

"I—"

"Shh." Samantha didn't even turn around, but issued the command efficiently.

Grace twisted her lips, and she increased her pace to walk just behind the ladies. As they reached the door, Samantha spun around with her finger on her lips. "Not a word. And don't you dare peek till I tell you, are we understood?" Samantha had used her governess voice, and Grace felt obligated to obey, even as her curiosity was piqued severely.

"She must have been a rather strict governess," Lady Liliah remarked, almost to herself.

"When she needed to be," Grace replied.

"Which was often," Samantha answered. "Now, close your eyes. I'm going to open the door and then, when I tell you, you may open your eyes and come out," Samantha explained.

"Very well." Grace sighed, her heartbeat picking its pace back up as she awaited the moment she could see what was going on. She closed her eyes. The sound of the door opening was punctuated by a spilling in of light. Samantha sighed, or maybe it was Lady Liliah, and then she heard the shuffling of feet followed by reverent silence.

"Now," Samantha whispered.

Grace's eyes flew open, and she blinked, allowing them to adjust to the bright light. As her eyes adjusted, she gasped with surprise at the transformation of the small area.

Brightly colored cloth hung in swags along the edge of the courtyard. The sun shone brightly from between two or three puffy clouds, and the colors, goodness, the colors!

Irises of every color lined the makeshift aisle that led toward a purple canopy where Ramsey waited, his eyes trained on her, cataloging every expression of wonder. Her heart pounded with an overwhelming sense of home, of belonging, and she was walking down the aisle toward him before she even gave her feet the command.

A vicar waited at the front, Heathcliff beside him, while Lucas stood just behind Ramsey, grinning at her with a knowing smile.

Heathcliff leaned over to Ramsey, speaking just loud enough for her to hear. "Aye, I think she likes it."

Ramsey's grin widened, and he reached out for her hand.

Grace nearly tripped on the small step, she wasn't paying mind to her path, just the end of it, but she righted herself quickly and placed her hand in his.

The warmth seeped through her, warming her soul, her heart, everything. It was the strangest thing, she had come to London, never feeling more out of place and out of her element, only to find that home was a person rather than a place.

"Hello," Ramsey greeted her, his grasp on her hand turning to a caress.

Grace's face heated with a blush from the force of his regard. "Good morning."

"If you're ready?" the viscount asked, and upon Ramsey's nod, the vicar stepped forward.

The older man was balding at the top of his head, and was about the same height as Grace, but much wider in stature. He cleared his throat, gave a somewhat toothless smile, and opened the Book of Common Prayer.

Grace turned to Ramsey, and noted a slightly relieved expression on his face. Fleetingly she wondered what it was about, but the vicar started reading:

DEARLY beloved, we are gathered together here in the sight of God, and in the face of this Congregation, to join together this man and this woman in holy Matrimony; which is an honourable estate, instituted of God in the time of man's innocency, signifying unto us the mystical union that is betwixt Christ and his Church; which holy estate Christ adorned and beautified with his presence.

Grace tried to listen to the liturgy, but Ramsey's slow caress of her hands was utterly distracting, and she wondered if it was a sin to ignore the vicar on one's wedding day. Certainly God would excuse her inattention when her focus was on her soon-to-be husband.

Thinking the word made her heart do a flip. It had only been a few days, and those days had been so full of planning that she hadn't had much time to really think about the reality of it. Well, now it was sinking in and it was a heady and delightful prospect.

"WILT thou have this woman to thy wedded
wife, to live together after God's ordinance in
the holy estate of Matrimony? Wilt thou love her,
comfort her, honour, and keep her, in sickness
and in health; and, forsaking all other, keep thee
only unto her, so long as ye both shall live?

Ramsey met her gaze, his expression severe with
the depth of emotion in his eyes. "I will." He said the
words like a vow, an oath, a promise.

A shiver ran down Grace's back, her flesh starting to
goose bump with the gravity of it.

The vicar repeated the words to her.

Never taking her gaze from Ramsey, she slowly
nodded and said, "I will."

His answering grin was nearly blinding in its beauty,
and she struggled to keep her emotions in check. She
wanted to close the distance between them and kiss him
soundly, feel the touch of his hands on her waist, be
near him and know the strength of his arms around her.

But the vicar wasn't finished yet. Soon they completed the rest of their promises and rings, and Grace
was bubbling with anticipation for the final words that
declared it finished.

FORASMUCH as you have consented
together in holy wedlock, and have witnessed the
same before God and this company, and thereto
have given and pledged their troth either to
other, and have declared the same by giving and
receiving of a ring, and by joining of hands; I
pronounce that they be man and wife together, In
the Name of the Father, and of the Son, and of
the Holy Ghost. Amen.

The vicar paused, and Grace turned to him, wondering why he was waiting. He gave her a grin, then a wink to Ramsey. "You may now kiss your bride."

Ramsey wasted no time. He swept her into his arms, binding his hands around her waist as he seared his vows upon her lips.

Grace returned the enthusiasm, answering his with her own as she leaned into the kiss, knowing she should act more properly but not caring enough to actually do it, she melted into his arms, lingering in his kiss even as he gentled his attentions to her mouth. She didn't want it to end.

Then she realized it wasn't going to end.

They were merely going to take a break . . .

And then, heaven help her, she wouldn't have to obey propriety any longer.

Ramsey slowly released her. Resting his forehead against hers, he whispered, "I love you."

Grace bit her lip, soaking in the delight of the moment.

"It is my great honor to announce Lord and Lady Sterling." The vicar spoke, and their small group erupted into applause. Ramsey released her from his embrace and grasped her hand. Lifting it to his lips he kissed it softly, then tucked it tenderly under his arm as they walked back down the aisle.

Grace trained her eyes on her husband, then back to the aisle, appreciating once again the hue of the irises, the lovely kaleidoscope of colors from the draped fabric, and then she noted the azure sky . . . so much of her biggest and best dreams all a reality.

Yet as she turned to her husband, all of it paled in comparison to the love he held in his eyes when looking at her.

Everything else faded, and all she could think of was having him alone, all to herself, exploring the delights of being in love.

Yet, there was the celebration of the wedding breakfast they still needed to attend.

If she thought she was impatient for the wedding, that was nothing compared to the impatience she felt now. It was going to be a long few hours, but she consoled herself with the idea that anticipation made things better.

Though, she blushed as she thought it, how things could be any better than what she'd already experienced, she had no clue, but she was more than happy to discover it all.

Every, last, part.

Chapter Thirty-one

Ramsey was quite certain of three things:
One: the wedding breakfast was another word for the Catholic's purgatory.

Two: If he had to wait more than an hour, he was going to make a spectacle of himself as he hightailed it out of the house with his wife.

Three: simply a repetition of number one, purgatory. Or hell, it might be hell.

In fact, as he thought of it, hell was a much better description. Because heaven was near, but out of reach.

For the moment.

Bloody hell, how long did it take to eat breakfast anyway?

He glanced over to Heathcliff, who was watching him with a knowing grin.

Bastard, he knew the torment.

Ramsey cut his gaze over to Lucas, who was watching him as well. Only the idiot lifted his glass of champagne in salute.

He needed better friends.

No. That wasn't true, but he did need to get out of the Kilpatrick House so that he might finally have some privacy with his wife.

Dear Lord, how he loved to say it. Never did he think he'd see the day, but here he was.

He turned to watch Grace. She was utterly beautiful, a siren if he ever saw one, and all his. Her eyes had been alight with wonder, delight, and emotion as she saw the garden all decorated with her "kaleidoscope of color," as Samantha had said. And he loved the touch of the irises, it was duly appropriate. And her gown, he was utterly undone the moment he saw it. It was bold, vibrant, colorful, and full of life, just like her. It was Grace's character, in color form and perfect.

The vicar wasn't even half bad. He'd been utterly grateful when he noted it wasn't the same as Lucas had used . . . thank the Lord for small favors.

All in all, the wedding was perfect. Now if he could just suffer through the wedding breakfast, the world would be damn near perfect as well.

At least his world.

They were finishing the last course when Heathcliff stood, raising his glass.

"Never thought I'd see the day, and I can't tell you how thankful I am to be wrong. I give you my sincerest blessing, and my greatest gift—" he winked, "—an early end to the wedding breakfast."

Ramsey chuckled.

Lucas lifted his glass. "Hear, hear!"

The ladies giggled and Ramsey lost no time standing and giving his thanks. "Have I mentioned you're my favorite friend, Heathcliff?" Ramsey teased, moving to pull out Grace's seat.

"It was my idea," Lucas replied dryly.

"It was a group effort," Heathcliff amended.

"Then I thank you both and you both have the deepest appreciation from the bottom of my heart." Ramsey gave a little bow as Grace waited beside him.

"Ach, be gone with you. Save your pretty words."

"And your strength," Lucas chimed in.

Ramsey was quite certain he heard Lady Liliah groan with embarrassment, but he didn't turn to see if he was accurate in his assessment. He was already heading out the door with Grace.

His carriage was already out front, waiting, and Ramsey decided that his friends needed some fantastic French brandy for their thoughtfulness, a detail he'd see to much later.

Much, much later.

He finally had Grace all to himself, and had no intention of wasting any of these precious moments.

"Well, that was generous of them," Grace said, giving him a shy smile from the other side of the carriage, which, Ramsey decided, was much too far away.

He stood up and took a seat beside her, and with a grin, lifted her legs under her knees and placed them over his, pulling her in tight. "Much better."

Grace had gasped slightly, but recovered with a pleased smile. "Much better," she agreed.

It was a sweet torture, having her so close. He allowed himself the pleasure of teasing a single finger along the line of her jaw, watching as her lips dropped open just enough for him to give her an inviting kiss, if he wished, but he restrained himself and simply gloried in the kind of tension that builds before you experience something you've anticipated for a long while.

Her breathing was short and her eyes took on a

glazed expression that made his body hungry, his soul hungry, his entire being desperately hungry.

The carriage hit a bump in the road, blessedly distracting him from the temptation of Grace. His finger burned where he touched her, and he noted the rosy hue her skin took on after his gentle caress. It was fascinating, deliriously erotic, how one touch could do so much, create so much need. It only took one match to light a fire, and the same was true for desire: it only took one touch, and sometimes just a look.

"Ramsey." Grace whispered his name.

Dear Lord, how he loved hearing his name on her lips. He wanted to taste it there, to tear it from her as she cried out in pleasure. But for now, he simply met her warm gaze and replied with a simple, "Yes?"

Her gaze searched his, her need for him written as clearly in her expression as if it were jotted down on a page. "How far away is your house?"

He chuckled at her transparency, adored her for it. She was his constant spring of refreshment; in a world that worked in secrets, shades of gray, and intrigue, there was Grace. She was artless, and utterly honest to a fault. It was her greatest strength and he was thankful anew for her.

"Not nearly close enough," he whispered, and then, because he couldn't resist any longer, he took her lips with his. It was a slow kiss, one meant to prolong and draw out the pleasure of it all. He tipped his head slightly, just enough to capture more of her lips as he kissed her again. One hand reached up to sweep along her shoulders, the other rested on the carriage seat, just to the side of her, while he held on to his sanity and control, tempering himself with an iron grip on the upholstery while he waited.

The idea of purgatory sifted through his mind once more.

Except this was more of heaven than anything else.

Grace leaned into his kiss, her hands trailing up the arms of his coat till they circled around the back of his neck, her fingers teasing his hair. He let out a groan, giving himself over to the pleasure of her touch.

He deepened the kiss; pressing back into her, he reached down with the hand not gripping onto the carriage seat and teased the hem of her skirt as it hung over her legs, which were, subsequently, resting upon his legs. With a wicked grin just before he kissed her again, he trailed his fingers up her stocking-covered ankles, the memories of their earlier encounter flooding through him, setting his body on fire.

As his hand reached up to her knee, he felt her gasp against his lips before leaning back into the kiss with a stronger urgency. He was about to graze the inside of her thigh when the carriage came to a stop.

He slowly released her from their passionate kiss, and watched as realization took hold in her expression. Forcing his body to calm, at least calm enough to make an entrance to their home and subsequently to make it to their bedchamber, he offered a roguish smile. "Welcome home."

Grace blinked. Her gaze dropped to his lips, and if he could hear her thoughts, he swore it would have been a strong request to continue kissing, but rather than engage in her more amorous nature, she slowly distanced herself and, blushing, said, "I love the way that sounds."

"As do I," Ramsey replied, then thinking about the icy cold pond near Glenwood Manor, he straightened his jacket and alighted from the carriage. The staff was waiting for their arrival, as was apparent by the already open door where several of the staff waited with restrained grins.

Grace took his hand, and he reminded himself that the staff only needed a brief presentation of his wife before he could retire to the bedroom. After the introductions were made, and the excuses given—much to the blush of his bride—Ramsey tugged on Grace's hand, leading her to the stairs. When her pace wasn't as quick as he judged was imperative, he turned around, lifted her into his arms, and took the stairs at a quicker pace.

In less than five minutes, they had gone from the carriage to the bedroom, and that was the end of their rushing. Now, it was time to slow down every moment, every thought, and every touch. Time would wait for them, inside this room. For once, Ramsey wasn't concerned about the world around him, their opinions, their thoughts, their whispers—his world was entirely in this room.

His world was smiling at him.

His world was a woman.

The only woman who mattered.

His wife.

Chapter Thirty-two

Thump, thump, thump . . .

A pounding rhythm pulsed through her body, echoing her heart. She was equal parts ready, and not. Half thrilled, half scared, glorying in the moment, and worrying over it, all at once. How she could divide herself so equally, and with such opposition, was unknown, but it was the truth.

It was folly, because as soon as Ramsey—*her husband*—how she loved the way it sounded—kissed her, everything but need vanished. But when he wasn't kissing her, fear crept in.

Because she had very little experience, and no real knowledge on how to go about . . . it.

And while she was quite certain he would make the experience fantastic for her, she wanted to be able to return the favor, and that is why she was hesitant, because what if she couldn't please him as he pleased her?

"Grace." He whispered her name, and she licked her

lips. A smile teased her face as she thought back over to how it all started with the same instinct. And how so much had changed since then.

"Grace." He whispered again, stepping toward her. Upon arrival in the bedroom he'd set her on her feet, then moved to lock the door. He was now closing that distance, one step at a time. His gaze was hungry, full of desire and unspoken promises of pleasure. Her body hummed with the want of it, the fear thawing slowly in the warmth of her desire. The way he looked at her, it was music, it was glory, it made her not only feel beautiful but it made her feel . . . enough.

How could such a common word mean so much, and carry so deep a resonation in her soul? *Enough.* It was all she had ever wanted to be. Ladylike enough that she wouldn't be a disgrace, clever enough not to fail her tutors, dance well enough not to be a disaster . . . enough. But when her husband's gaze lingered on her, as if cataloguing every nuance of her face, her expression, and her body, it was as if she was not only enough, but perfect, at least to him.

And she decided that all the time she thought she only wanted to be enough, she actually just wanted to be enough for someone, the right one. For him.

Ramsey.

"Your mind is spinning, isn't it?" he asked, reaching up and tucking a curl behind her ear.

"Maybe," Grace replied, sighing softly. Why was she always so easy to read?

"I love that I can gather your thoughts just by gazing at your face. Your expressions are my favorite book, and I cannot wait to spend the rest of my life reading it."

Grace blinked, her lips dropping open slightly. "That

is quite possibly the most romantic thing I've ever heard."

"It's only the truth, though I'm pleased you find it romantic." He lifted her hand and placed a lingering kiss there. Without a word, he lowered her hand and tugged on each finger of her glove, slowly removing it from her hand. The leather whispered as it was taken off, and he allowed it to fall to the ground. He repeated the same movements with her other hand, kissing it first, then removing the glove.

Her heart started pounding again; when it had slowed she hadn't noticed, but it was no longer slow, but pounding hard—not fast, just powerfully, as if starting to gear up her body for something . . . for someone.

"I love your hands," Ramsey whispered against her wrist, kissing it softly, his lips delicate on her skin. "You talk with them, did you know?"

"My father often said I did."

"He was a wise man."

"The best."

"Do you think . . ." Ramsey paused and met her gaze. "Would he have liked me? Approved of us?"

Grace smiled warmly. "If you love me, then my father would have needed no other grounds to approve of you. He only wanted me to be loved like he loved my mother."

"A love match," Ramsey whispered, grinning. "Is that what we are?" He flirted, tugging on her hand to pull her in close enough to kiss.

"Would you disagree?" Grace teased, tipping her chin upward, just enough to make it easier for him to bend down and take her lips.

He kissed her nose instead. "I would never imagine disagreeing with you."

"Why do I find that hard to believe?" Grace returned, dryly.

"Because it's a lie." Ramsey let out a low chuckle, and then finally lowered his lips to hers, lingering there just enough to send her blood to pounding. "But what is not a lie is that I love you." He kissed her again, deeper, searchingly, as if answering his own question with a kiss by pulling the love from her heart and tasting it in her kiss.

Grace returned the kiss, her hands winding around his neck, lacing through his hair as he deepened the exchange, her body singing in response to the firm lines of his frame pressing into her softer ones.

"I love you too," she murmured against his lips, without giving him a chance to respond as she pressed harder into him, needing him to be closer.

His hands trailed down her back, pausing here and there, but she was barely aware as she was utterly distracted by the pleasure of his kiss as his tongue swept across her lips, while his teeth nipped and played.

She returned the gesture, nibbling on his bottom lip, her hands trailing down his shoulders, arching into the frame of his back. Wanting to feel more, she trailed her hands over his chest, sliding under his coat and encouraging him to shrug it off.

She felt his grin against her lips as she kissed him. "One moment." He pulled away slightly, then releasing her fully, he stepped back far enough to remove his coat.

But in stepping back, his hands were no longer at her back, and Grace was startled to realize that the buttons to the back of her dress were all loose, and her bodice fell forward. She caught it, covering herself only slightly and noted the wolfish grin on her husband's face.

She twisted her lips, then couldn't fight her own grin. "I must say I'm impressed."

"You need to set your standards higher, love," he returned, tossing his coat to the side and then untucking his shirt and discarding it as well.

Appreciating the view, Grace stepped back as he started toward her, but he paused. Deciding that appreciating the view wasn't nearly as delightful as caressing the man before her, she reached her hands up the ripples of his stomach, noting the warm texture of his skin as she traveled up toward the planes of his chest into his broad shoulders. Her body hummed with appreciation, and she leaned forward to kiss along his collarbone, gratified when he sucked in a quick breath of pleasure. She continued teasing the skin along his shoulder when a warm hand grasped her shoulder, then flirted with the edge of her dress. She was still holding it in place with one hand. He tugged on the edge of her dress, encouraging her to release it.

After a moment's hesitation, she closed her eyes and let it go.

Breathing against his chest, she felt the gown slip down between them and pool on the floor. Now only her underthings remained, and they were of the softest and thinnest silk, and as such, didn't hide any secrets.

"Grace." He whispered her name, but she kept her eyes closed as she leaned against the warmth of his chest. He bent and kissed her head, lingering there, and then started to pull the pins out. Her hair slowly unwound, draping along her shoulders, covering her enough that she felt enough courage to step back.

When she dragged her gaze up to meet her husband's, she nearly gasped at the power of his regard. "So lovely," he whispered, emotion thick in his voice as he leaned down to rub a lock of hair between his fingers. "I swear you set me on fire, love," he murmured, then bent down to kiss her, but this kiss was different than all the others. She realized that he had been restraining himself before, but all that restraint was lost, and raw need pulsed through his kiss, filling her with the same urgency.

His warm hands slid down her hips, removing the underthings, pooling them at her feet. Arching his hands upward, he broke their kiss just long enough to remove her chemise, then captured her lips once more, the urgency creating a fog in all her senses, yet making them clearer all at once.

The world was in the fog, but Ramsey, he was perfectly clear. It was as if she could see him better than ever before, hear his heartbeat, feel it in her own chest, her body echoing every resounding impulse of his. "Grace," he whispered against her lips, encouraging her backward, and after a few steps, her knees hit something soft: the bed.

He guided her onto the soft mattress, but rather than join her, she felt the excruciating sensation of his absence. Her eyes fluttering open, she watched as he disrobed from all his remaining clothing, and before she could fully appreciate the view he presented, he was kneeling beside her, his hands at her shoulders, encouraging her to lie down. His kiss was all the incentive needed, and as he teased her lips, she pressed back against the urgency of his kiss, her hips moving, arching, reaching. Her hands traced up the spine of his back, then spread across the expanse of his broad shoulders. He groaned against her lips as she arched her fingers into his muscles, pulling him closer.

"You want me," he whispered, not asking, but stating the words as if he already knew them.

"Yes," Grace replied, her body arching as his hand cupped her breast. Good Lord, it was even better than she had remembered. Her body tightened, arched, and her lungs gasped for air. She could feel his smile of pleasure against her lips as he pinched her rosy tip playfully.

She bucked off the bed in response.

"I love your breasts," he told her, then moved his lips elsewhere, to the very spot he mentioned, adoring her breast lovingly with his lips. Grace gasped with pleasure, her body growing tight, her hips arching as her hands dug into his shoulders, his back, his hair, anywhere she could reach.

"Tell me—"

"More," she gasped, finishing his words.

He chuckled, obeying her command.

Moving slightly, he covered her with his body, the hard length of him pressing into her hip, then lower, testing, teasing, tempting her.

"Ramsey," she gasped, arching against him as he moved his attention to her other breast.

"Do you want me to do more?" he asked, his tongue swirling against her nipple.

"Yes." She arched into his arousal, needing him. Her body was a flurry of need, a bundle of desperation for him. It was as painful as it was pleasant as she waited for the release that she knew he would give her.

"How much more?" he asked, only his voice was

losing its caressing quality, replaced with raw need as he leaned back to watch her.

"All," she whispered hoarsely.

He looked down between them, his fingers trailing along her hip bone till they touched her most sensitive spot, teasing her opening. "Here."

"Yes." And Grace reached down to stroke the hard length of him, hoping her touch was as pleasurable to him as it was to her.

He gasped, shuddered, and leaned his head against her chest while he pressed into her hand.

Withdrawing slightly, he gave her a hungry gaze before slowly aligning their bodies. "You want me here?" he asked, pressing his tip into her just slightly.

It was pleasure that was almost too much to bear, but he retreated quickly, leaving her feeling empty. "Yes. More." She pressed her hands onto his back, trying to pull him in closer.

"Like this." His tone was rough, his shoulders tense as he slid in further, then retreated, but this time Grace reached down to grab his rounded buttocks, holding him there. "All of you." She spoke the words like a demand, like a need, as if they would save her.

Ramsey obeyed, and upon her wince, paused, but the pain was fleeting as he soon filled her, stroking her innermost parts.

"Are you well?" he asked, teasing her lips with a shuddering kiss.

"Y-yes," Grace replied, arching into him, pulling him in tighter. Now that the pain was gone, all that was left was the need, the red-hot desperate need.

Ramsey groaned at her reply, moving within her. His long strokes made her gasp in pleasure, her body coiling on top of itself as if about to spring forward.

"You want all of me?" he asked with a strained tone.

"Yes."

"Inside you?" he demanded, arching into her with a new desperation.

Grace answered with the cry of his name, her body releasing the tight spring that held her to the earth, exploding her outward as her body pounded with release from deep within. Still soaring on the crest of her release, a new sensation filled her as Ramsey called her name, filling her with everything he had to give. The new sensations sent her back into the pounding rhythm, and she grasped his back, arching into him, pulling him in tight as she gasped for air, as they both gasped in release.

Soon, as her body cooled, she blinked her eyes open to watch her husband fall back from the same heaven, and right into her arms.

His tender smile melted her heart anew, and with a gentle kiss to her nose, he slowly rolled to the side.

Which was the last thing Grace remembered before waking up in the same position.

Her favorite place, her husband's arms.

Epilogue

"That is utterly unfair," Grace asserted as she strode into the parlor of Kilmarin House. Perhaps waddled would be a better word for it. Ramsey was close behind, trying desperately to hide a smile. They had just celebrated their fourth wedding anniversary, and he still was constantly amused, and surprised, by his lovely wife, who was now expecting their first heir.

"What are we in uproar about now?" Samantha asked, handing a biscuit to Lochlan, the youngest of their two sons.

"Do I dare ask?" Lucas called from the other side of the room, pouring port into three snifters. It was the usual custom to have dinner once a week at one of their houses. This week it was Kilmarin House; last week it had been the Heightfields' residence.

Lucas handed a snifter to Heathcliff, who raised it as if offering a salute.

"We deserve to have a place as well." Grace answered Lucas's question.

"Oh?" Heathcliff asked, bending down to kiss Samantha on the head.

"Yes," Liliah answered after picking up a wayward
tot, the youngest of her three girls.

They all were quite amused that Lucas, the most notorious rake of them all, had three daughters to worry
over. Who said fate didn't have a sense of humor?

"So you're in on this too?" Lucas asked his wife,
arching a brow and winking at her.

"Always," Liliah replied.

"Should I be afraid?" Heathcliff asked, then took a
sip of port.

"We. Should *we* be afraid?" Ramsey amended, sipping his own port that Heathcliff had just delivered to
him.

"That depends," Grace replied.

"On if we ever hear what the bloody problem is,"
Heathcliff remarked with some irritation. "Pardon my
language." He apologized when his wife gave him a
direct glare.

"We've decided that since you have your club,"
Grace started, and Ramsey watched her with both trepidation and pride. She was his world, but also the one
able to work him into a lather quicker than any other. It
was the spice in his life; he knew he needed it, and
most of the time he welcomed it. He had the suspicion
that he knew where she was going with the comments.
Temptations had been growing steadily over the past
few years, and as such, had taken on more than before.
Thankfully, they hadn't had any more incidents with
Westhouse or with the Duke of Chatterwood—Liliah
and Samantha's father. In some cases, it was a boon to
deal with people so devoted to their reputation. It made
blackmail so much easier—not that they had to resort

to such measures, but if necessary, they were always prepared.

Grace continued. "We've decided that we need our own place too. We even have a name."

"What do you mean your own place?" Heathcliff asked, his tone suspicious.

"When you go to the club, we stay home without you, and sometimes you're not home till late. We understand that this is part of life, but we thought it would be brilliant if there was a place where we . . ." Liliah paused.

". . . The wives . . ." Samantha clarified.

"Could go and be with you, and have our own parties and such, while you have yours," Grace finished.

Ramsey's suspicions were affirmed.

Heathcliff looked resigned.

Lucas looked surprised.

"So?" Liliah asked.

"Are you sure that's what you want? I mean, none of you are regular visitors to the club—"

"Because there's no place for us. There's plenty of room and we could oversee it—"

"But the possibility of keeping your good reputations while attending . . ." Lucas spoke up.

"Will be easy because we'll do the same as you . . . keep it a secret. We'll start out as just the three of us, and if it works, we'll go from there."

Ramsey glanced about the room, then decided to address the most obvious question. "So, I suppose the question is, are you asking us or telling us?"

"Telling," Grace replied, with a grin.

"That's what I suspected," Ramsey said.

Heathcliff let out a slow sigh. "I suppose it was going to happen sooner or later."

Lucas took a long sip of his port. "Nothing is sacred anymore."

"Says the man who was complaining about how much he's away from home. Now you can see me more often," Liliah replied with a saucy grin.

"I hate it when she's right." Lucas finished the rest of his port.

"Well, I suppose the final question is simply, what is this name you've figured out for yourselves?" Heathcliff asked.

Ramsey waited.

Lucas seemed concerned.

The ladies all glanced to one another, their expression various digress of pride.

Grace answered. "The Ladies of Hades."

We hope you enjoyed
THE TEMPTATION OF GRACE
by
Kristin Vayden.

Find out how it all began with
FALLING FROM HIS GRACE,
the first book in the Gentlemen of Temptation series.

Turn the page for a peek!

Chapter One

Lady Liliah Durary urged her mare, Penny, into a rapid gallop as she flew through Hyde Park. A proper lady should have a care about the strolling couples about the park. A proper lady should not ride at such breakneck speed. A proper lady should obey her father in all things.

Liliah was *not* a proper lady.

And hell would have to freeze over before she'd ever even try.

Tears burned the corners of her eyes, blurring her vision as she urged Penny faster, not caring that she was in a miserable sidesaddle—or that her speed was indeed dangerous for her precarious position. She wanted to outrun her problems—rather, *problem*. Because aside from the one damning issue at hand, life was otherwise quite lovely.

Being the elder daughter of a duke had its distinct advantages.

Of course, it had its distinct disadvantages as well. Like your father demanding you marry your best friend.

Who so happened to be in love with your other best friend.

It was a miserable mess . . . and she was caught in the middle of it all. If only her father would see reason! Yet asking such a thing was like expecting her mare to sprout wings and fly: impossible.

She slowed Penny down to a moderate walk and sighed deeply, the light breeze teasing the strands of unruly blond hair, which came loose from her coiffure as a result of her quick pace. She blew a particularly irritating curl from her forehead, and tucked it behind her ear. Glancing about, she groaned, remembering that she hadn't taken a maid with her. Again.

Thankfully, the staff at Whitefield House was accustomed to her constant disregard of propriety. Maybe Sarah, her maid, would notice and make herself scarce, giving the impression she was with her mistress. Liliah bit her lip, turning her mare toward home—even if that was the last place she wished to be—simply for Sarah's sake. It wouldn't go well for her maid if her father discovered the way his staff allowed his unruly daughter far more freedom than he did, and should he discover it, such freedom would end abruptly—and badly.

Being attached to the staff—especially her maid Sarah—Liliah increased her pace. Besides, running from problems didn't solve them. As she swayed with the steady rhythm of Penny's trot, she considered the situation at hand once more.

It made no sense.

Yet when had one of her father's decisions required logic? Never.

Her best friend Rebecca was delightful and from a well-bred and heavily pursed family. There was no reason for the family of her other best friend Meyer, the Baron of Scoffield, to be opposed to such a match. Yet Meyer's father refused to see reason, just as Liliah's father refused. Only Meyer's father, the Earl of Greywick, had threatened to disinherit his son and grant the title to a cousin when Meyer had objected to the arrangement.

It was wretched, no matter how one looked at it. Love matches were rare amongst the ton, and here was a golden opportunity for each family—squandered.

It was true, Liliah was quite the match herself. The elder daughter of a duke, she understood she was quite the heiress and pedigree, yet was her breeding of more importance than Rebecca's? She doubted it.

Apparently, her father didn't agree.

Nor did Lord Greywick.

As she crossed the cobble street toward her home, she took a deep breath of the spring air, feeling her freedom slowly sifting through her fingers like dry sand. As Whitefield House came into view, she pulled up on the reins, halting Penny's progress toward home. The horse nickered softly, no doubt anticipating a thorough brush-down and sweet oats upon returning, yet Liliah lingered, studying the stone structure. One of the larger houses in Mayfair, Whitefield demanded attention with its large stone pillars and wide, welcoming balcony overlooking the drive. It fit her father's personality well, as if magnifying his overinflated sense of importance. Reluctantly, she urged Penny on, taking the side entrance to the stable in the back.

Upon her arrival, a stable boy rushed out to greet

her, helping her dismount. Penny jostled the lad with her head, and he chuckled softly, petting her velvet nose.

"I'll take care of Penny, my lady. You needn't worry." With a quick bow, the boy led the all too pampered horse into the stable, murmuring softly as they walked.

Carefully glancing around, once she was certain that no one lingered about, she rushed to the servants' entrance just to the side of the large manor. The heavy wooden door opened silently and she slipped inside, leaning against the door once it was closed. Her eyes adjusted to the dim light, and she took the stairs to the second floor, turning left down a small hall and turning the latch on the door that would lead to the gallery, just a short distance from her chambers. The metal was cool against her gloved hand as she twisted, then peered out into the sunlight-filled room. Breathing quietly, she listened intently for footsteps or voices. Just before she dared to step out, Sarah, her maid, bustled down the hall, a pinched frown on her face as she opened the door leading to Liliah's rooms.

After waiting one more moment, Liliah stepped from the servants' hall, rushing her steps till she approached her room, then slowed as if she weren't in a hurry at all, just in case someone noticed her presence.

Quickly, she opened the door to her room and swiftly shut it silently behind her, Sarah's relieved sigh welcoming her.

"My lady! You've not but a moment to lose! Your father is searching about for you! When he noticed me, he bid me find you, but I fear he is growing impatient. He was in the library."

"Quick, help me disrobe. I need an afternoon dress." Liliah started to tug off her gloves, exchanging them for ones that did not bear the marks from the leather reins, as Sarah made quick work of the buttons on her riding habit.

In only a few short minutes, Liliah was properly attired—all evidence of her earlier unchaperoned excursion tucked away. And with a quick grin to Sarah, who offered a relieved sigh, Liliah left her chambers and strode down the hall as if without a care in the world.

When in truth, the cares were heavy upon her indeed.

Because her father rarely spoke to her, unless demanding her obedience in some matter—and she knew exactly what he had on his mind.

Drat.

She clasped her hands, trying to calm the slight tremble as she took the stairs and walked toward the library. How she hated feeling weak, out of control in her own life! With a fortifying breath, she made the final steps to the library entrance, the delicate clink of china teacups drifting through the air.

"Your Grace." Liliah curtseyed to her father, taking in the furrow in his expression, drawing his bushy salt-and-pepper eyebrows like thunderclouds over his gray eyes.

"At last. I was about to begin a search," he replied tersely, setting down his teacup and gesturing to a chair.

"Forgive me, I was quite absorbed in my—"

"Book, I know. Your little maid said as much. And I'll remind you that you mustn't spend so much time engaging your mind. Fine-tune your other qualities. Your pianoforte could benefit a great deal from some practice." He sighed, as if already tired of the conversation with his daughter.

Liliah bit her tongue, not wishing to initiate a battle of wills just yet; she'd save the fight for a more worthy cause.

The only worthy cause of the moment.

"Now that you're here, I need to inform you that Lord Greywick and I have decided on a date—"

"But, Your Grace . . ."

His brows knit further over his eyes, and he glared, his expression frosty and furious. "Do not interrupt me."

Liliah swallowed, clenching her teeth as she nodded.

"As I was saying . . ." He paused, arching a brow, daring her to interfere again. "Lord Greywick and I are tired of waiting. We've been patient, and your progress with Greywick's heir is apathetic at best. Therefore, tonight, at the Langford rout, Meyer will be asking you for two waltzes. That should set up the perfect tone for the banns being read in two weeks' time. Hence, you shall be wed at St. George's in two months. That is beyond generous and I—"

"It is anything but generous and you well know it!" Liliah couldn't restrain herself any longer. Standing, she took position behind the chair, her fingers biting into the damask fabric as she prepared for battle.

One she knew was already lost.

"How dare you!" Her father's voice boomed.

"Father, Meyer has no interest in me! How long will you imagine something greater than friendship?"

"I care not if he gives a fig about you!" her father roared, standing as well.

"I refuse." Liliah spoke softly, like silk over steel as she clenched her teeth.

Her father took a menacing step forward. "There is no other way. And consider this: If this arrangement is not made, your friend will lose his title. Do you think that Lord and Lady Grace will allow their daughter to be married to a man with no means? No title?" He shook his head, his eyes calculating. "They will not. So cease your reluctance. There is no other option." He took a deep breath and met her gaze. "I suggest you prepare for tonight; you'll certainly be the center of attention and you should look the part. You're dismissed." With a quick wave of his fingers, he turned and went back to his tea, sitting down.

Tears burned the back of Liliah's eyes, yet she held them in till she spun on her heel and quit the room, just as the first streams of warm tears spilled down her cheeks.

Surely there had to be another way?

Perhaps there was, but time was running out.

For everyone.

The Langford rout was buzzing with activity from London society's most elite, the *bon ton*. The orchestra's sweet melody floated through the air, drowning out most of the buzzing hum of voices. The dancers swirled around, a kaleidoscope of pastel colors amidst the gentlemen's black evening kits. Ostrich and peacock feathers decorated the main banquet table, along with painted silver eggs. But the beauty of the ballroom was lost on Liliah; even the prospect of a treacle tart didn't boost her mood. She meandered through the crush of humanity, swiping a glass of champagne from a passing footman. Sipping the cool liquid, she savored the bubbles as her gaze sharpened on her target.

Lady Grace—Rebecca—danced gracefully as she took the practiced steps of the quadrille. Rebecca smiled at her partner, and Liliah watched as the poor sop all but melted with admiration. Stifling a giggle, she waited till the dance ended, and made her way toward her friend. As she drew near, Rebecca caught sight and raised a hand in a wave, her overly expressive eyes smiling as wide as her lips.

"Liliah! Did you only just arrive? I was searching for you earlier." Rebecca reached out and squeezed Liliah's hand.

"I stalled," Liliah confessed.

Rebecca's smile faded, her green eyes no longer bright. "Did it work?"

"No." Liliah glanced away, not knowing if she could handle the heartbreak that must be evident in Rebecca's gaze.

"We understood it was a small chance. We must now simply seize every opportunity." Rebecca spoke with far more control than Liliah expected. As she turned to her friend, she saw a depth of pain, yet a depth of strength in her gaze.

"There's always hope," Liliah affirmed, squeezing her friend's hand.

"Always. And that being said, I must now seize this present opportunity." Rebecca's face lit up as only one deeply in love could do, and curtseyed as Meyer approached.

The Baron of Scoffield approached, but Liliah ever knew him as simply Meyer. Their friendship had been immediate and long-standing. Ever since Liliah, Rebecca, and Meyer had snuck away during a fireworks display at Vauxhall Gardens, they had created a special bond of friendship. But over the years, that friendship had shifted into something deeper between Meyer and Rebecca, while Liliah was happy to watch their ro-

mance bloom. Meyer's gaze smoldered as he studied
Rebecca, a secretive smile in place. As Liliah turned
back to Rebecca, she saw the most delicate blush tint
her olive skin. Liliah blushed as well, feeling like an
intruder in their private moment. "I'll just leave you
two . . ." She trailed off, walking away as she heard
Meyer ask Rebecca for a dance.

Liliah sipped the remaining champagne, watching
her friends dance. Their eyes never left each other's;
even if they switched partners for the steps, they always came together, their love apparent for anyone
who cared to look.

It was beautiful, and it was for naught.

As the dance ended, the first strains of a waltz
soared through the air. What should have been beautiful was poisoned, and her heart felt increasingly heavy
as Meyer walked in her direction, his lips a grim line.

He didn't ask, simply held out his hand, and Liliah
placed hers within his grasp, reluctantly following as
they took the floor.

"By your expression, I can only assume you had as
much progress with your father as I've had with mine,"
Meyer said, his brown eyes sober as his gaze flickered
away—likely looking for Rebecca.

"Your assumption would be correct," Liliah replied.

Meyer took a deep breath, meeting her gaze. "We'll
figure something out."

"But Meyer—" Liliah started.

"We will. We just need to bide our time till the opportunity presents itself." He nodded with a brave confidence in his deep eyes.

"But what if we don't?" Liliah hated to give voice to
her deepest fears, watching as Meyer's brave façade
slowly fractured.

"Liliah, I—I can't think of that. I'm damned if I do, damned if I do not. I'm sure your father reminded you about my title—"

"And how Lord and Lady Grace wouldn't consider you without a title . . ."

"Exactly. I have to hold on to hope. But I, I do need to tell you . . . Liliah, if we are forced . . . nothing between us will change." He lowered his chin, meeting Liliah's gaze dead on, conveying words he couldn't speak out loud.

"Thank you," Liliah replied, feeling relieved. As much as she hated the idea of a platonic marriage, it hurt far worse to think of the betrayal that would haunt them all should Meyer take her to bed. It hurt to think she'd never know physical love, yet what choice did they all have? Should they take that step, Meyer would be thinking of Rebecca during the act, Liliah would know, and would not only be betraying her friend, but how could she not be resentful? Far better for them to simply bide their time till an arrangement could be made—she would simply step aside. Maybe take a lover of her own?

How she hated how complicated her life had become.

Liliah took a deep breath, mindlessly performing the waltz steps. A smile quirked her lips as she had a rather unhelpful—yet still amusing—thought.

"Ah, I know that smile. What is your devious mind thinking?" Meyer asked, raising a dark brow even as he grinned.

Liliah gave him a mock glare. "I'm not devious."

"You are utterly devious." Meyer chuckled. "Which makes you a very diverting friend indeed. Now share your thoughts."

Liliah rolled her eyes. "Such charm. Very well, I was simply thinking how it would be lovely if we could simply make the wedding a masquerade and have Rebecca switch places with me at the last moment! Then you'd marry her rather than me and it would be over and done before they could change it!" She hitched a shoulder at her silly thoughts.

Meyer chuckled. "Devious indeed! Too bad it will not work." He furrowed a brow and glanced away, as if thinking.

"What is *your* wicked mind concocting?"

"Nothing of import." His gaze shifted back to her. "Your mentioning of the masquerade reminded me of an earlier conversation with a chum."

Liliah grinned. "Is there a masquerade ball being planned?" she asked with barely restrained enthusiasm.

"Indeed, but it is one to which you will not be invited, thank heavens." He shook his head, grinning, yet his expression was one of relief.

"Why so?"

"It's not a masquerade for polite society, my dear. And I shouldn't have even mentioned it."

"A secret? Meyer, you simply must tell me!"

"Heavens no! This is not for your delicate—"

Liliah snorted softly, giving him an exasperated expression, before she slowly grinned.

"Aw hell. I know that smile. Liliah . . ." he warned.

"If you won't tell me, then I can always ask someone else—"

"You'll do nothing of the sort!"

"You know I will."

"You're a menace!" Meyer hissed, his expression narrowing as the waltz ended.

"So, you'll tell me?" Liliah asked, biting her lip with excitement.

Meyer was silent as he led them to a quiet corner of the ballroom, pausing beside a vacant alcove.

"This is a yes!" Liliah answered her question, squeezing his forearm as her hand rested upon it.

"I'm only telling you so that I can properly manage what you hear. Heaven only knows what you'd draw out of an unsuspecting swain. At least I'm immune to your charms and won't give in to your pleas."

Liliah almost reminded him that he was doing just that—but held her tongue.

"There is a . . . place." Meyer spoke in a hushed whisper, and Liliah moved in closer just to hear his words above the floating music. "It's secretive, selective, and not a place for a gently bred lady, if you gather my meaning."

Liliah nodded, hanging on every word.

"Only few are accepted as members and it's quite the thing to be invited. One of my acquaintances was far too drunk the other night and spoke too freely about this secretive club—mentioning a masquerade. That is all."

Liliah thought over his words, having several questions. "What's it called?"

Meyer paused, narrowing his eyes. "Temptations," he added reluctantly.

"And they are having a masquerade?" Liliah asked, a plan forming in her mind, spinning out of control.

"Yes. And that is all you need to know."

Meyer broke their gaze and looked over his shoulder at the swirling crowd.

"Go to her. We still have one waltz left and then I'll ask you all the questions you'll refuse to answer." She winked, playfully shoving her friend toward the dance floor.

"When you put it that way . . ." He rolled his eyes and walked off toward the crowd.

Liliah thought back over what Meyer had said, considering his words—and what they might mean. A masquerade—inappropriate for ladies.

It sounded like the perfect solution for a lady wishing to be utterly inappropriate. All she had to do was discover the location, steal away, and maybe, just maybe . . . she'd get to experience a bit of life before it was married away. Was that too much to ask? Certainly not, and as long as she knew the name, surely she could discover the location.

For the first time since this whole misbegotten disaster, she felt a shred of hope.

Utterly scandalous hope.

Connect with

Us

Visit us online at
KensingtonBooks.com
to read more from your favorite authors, see books
by series, view reading group guides, and more.

for sneak peeks, chances to win books and prize packs,
and to share your thoughts with other readers.

facebook.com/kensingtonpublishing
twitter.com/kensingtonbooks

Tell us what you think!

To share your thoughts, submit a review,
or sign up for our eNewsletters, please visit:
KensingtonBooks.com/TellUs.

Books by Bestselling Author
Fern Michaels

Available Wherever Books Are Sold!
Check out our website at www.kensingtonbooks.com

Romantic Suspense from
Lisa Jackson

Absolute Fear	0-8217-7936-2	$7.99US/$9.99CAN
Afraid to Die	1-4201-1850-1	$7.99US/$9.99CAN
Almost Dead	0-8217-7579-0	$7.99US/$10.99CAN
Born to Die	1-4201-0278-8	$7.99US/$9.99CAN
Chosen to Die	1-4201-0277-X	$7.99US/$10.99CAN
Cold Blooded	1-4201-2581-8	$7.99US/$8.99CAN
Deep Freeze	0-8217-7296-1	$7.99US/$10.99CAN
Devious	1-4201-0275-3	$7.99US/$9.99CAN
Fatal Burn	0-8217-7577-4	$7.99US/$10.99CAN
Final Scream	0-8217-7712-2	$7.99US/$10.99CAN
Hot Blooded	1-4201-0678-3	$7.99US/$9.49CAN
If She Only Knew	1-4201-3241-5	$7.99US/$9.99CAN
Left to Die	1-4201-0276-1	$7.99US/$10.99CAN
Lost Souls	0-8217-7938-9	$7.99US/$10.99CAN
Malice	0-8217-7940-0	$7.99US/$10.99CAN
The Morning After	1-4201-3370-5	$7.99US/$9.99CAN
The Night Before	1-4201-3371-3	$7.99US/$9.99CAN
Ready to Die	1-4201-1851-X	$7.99US/$9.99CAN
Running Scared	1-4201-0182-X	$7.99US/$10.99CAN
See How She Dies	1-4201-2584-2	$7.99US/$8.99CAN
Shiver	0-8217-7578-2	$7.99US/$10.99CAN
Tell Me	1-4201-1854-4	$7.99US/$9.99CAN
Twice Kissed	0-8217-7944-3	$7.99US/$9.99CAN
Unspoken	1-4201-0093-9	$7.99US/$9.99CAN
Whispers	1-4201-5158-4	$7.99US/$9.99CAN
Wicked Game	1-4201-0338-5	$7.99US/$9.99CAN
Wicked Lies	1-4201-0339-3	$7.99US/$9.99CAN
Without Mercy	1-4201-0274-5	$7.99US/$10.99CAN
You Don't Want to Know	1-4201-1853-6	$7.99US/$9.99CAN

Available Wherever Books Are Sold!
Visit our website at **www.kensingtonbooks.com**